Susanna inte...

She intended to right their relationship, to get back to something far more comfortable than this crazy intimacy.

A simple *thanks* would restore balance, distract her from the awareness making every nerve ending tingle, making her remember what she *wasn't* wearing beneath the soaking wet sweatshirt.

Then she met Jay's gaze, saw his face. The awareness she saw in his expression mirrored hers, and it was torture.

For one wild moment, time stopped.

Not a breath passed between them.

Not a sound.

Only the awareness of the pent-up restraint they'd both held in check and the certainty that restraint was about to end.

Dear Reader,

I'm delighted to announce exciting news: beginning in January 2013, Harlequin Superromance books will be longer! That means more romance with more of the characters you love and expect from Harlequin Superromance.

We'll also be unveiling a brand-new look for our covers. These fresh, beautiful covers will showcase the six wonderful contemporary stories we publish each month. Turn to the back of this book for a sneak peek.

So don't miss out on your favorite series—Harlequin Superromance. Look for longer stories and exciting new covers starting December 18, 2012, wherever you buy books.

In the meantime, check out this month's reads:

Happy reading!

Wanda Ottewell,

Senior Editor, Harlequin Superromance

The Time of Her Life

JEANIE LONDON

HARLEQUIN®

entertain, enrich, inspire™

Recycling programs
for this product may
not exist in your area.

ISBN-13: 978-0-373-71819-1

THE TIME OF HER LIFE

Copyright © 2012 by Jeanie LeGendre

www.Harlequin.com

Printed in U.S.A.

ABOUT THE AUTHOR

Jeanie London writes romance because she believes in happily-ever-afters. Not the "love conquers all" kind, but the "we love each other so we can conquer anything" kind. It's precisely why she loves Harlequin Superromance— stories about real women tackling life to find love. The kind of love she understands, because she's a real woman tackling life in sunny Florida with her own romance-hero husband, their two beautiful and talented daughters, a loving and slightly crazy extended family and a menagerie of sweet strays.

Books by Jeanie London

Other titles by this author available in ebook format.

To all the caregivers.
May you be blessed.

With appreciation to all the staff at University Village.
Your loving service and generosity of spirit
continually inspire me to set stories in the
caring world of senior living.
You touch more lives than you know ;-)

CHAPTER ONE

THE OLD PROVERB "change is the only constant" seemed to echo inside the empty house as Susanna Adams stood in the doorway of her home for the last time. And she kept standing there, somehow not ready to leave even though she'd done nothing for weeks but prepare. Apparently all the activity of packing and storing twenty years of memories in a portable storage container had been nothing but a diversion.

Once she left, she'd need to lock the door then drop off the key with the real estate agent. She wouldn't be able to get inside her home ever again. What if this move was a huge mistake? Suddenly, taking that one last step symbolized everything she was leaving behind.

Glancing into the quiet darkness, Susanna took a steadying breath and tried to capture the moment in memory. She knew every square inch of this house by heart. The wall separating this foyer from the living area, a wall she'd often bumped into with her arms full of groceries. How many bruises had she sported through the years because some brainy architect thought the wall should extend beyond a clear passage to the living room?

Susanna had no clue. She only knew that without the kids' photos marking their stepping stones through school years or Skip's stuffed fish showcased front and center, the wall looked foreign. Only a wall surrounded by unfamiliar shadows.

Without her family, this house was just a house, the way it had been when a real estate agent had unlocked the door for the first time twenty years ago. Before she and Skip had filled every room with expectations and dreams.

They had been such big dreamers.

The thought grabbed Susanna around the throat, made her swallow hard. They'd bought this house while still in college, ignoring every bit of advice from their parents and friends.

"You're too young to get married."

"Finish college and start careers before settling down."

"Live a little before saddling yourselves with a mortgage."

She and Skip had filled this house with dreams of a life together where anything could happen. And did.

They'd started careers while having their family, had paced floors in the wee hours through colic while still managing to make it to work on time the next morning.

They'd been T-ball coach and Brownie leader. They'd taken turns as chaperone for school field trips. They'd been homeroom mom who baked designer cupcakes en masse and homeroom dad who tended every classroom pet from mammal to reptile.

"What's the rush? You've got a lifetime to settle down."

No, they hadn't. They'd had only a limited number of years together, certainly not the lifetime everyone had promised. Thank God they'd ignored the advice and hadn't wasted a second. As Skip was losing his battle with non-Hodgkin's lymphoma, he'd said his only regret was not getting more time with her and the beautiful family they'd made.

That was *still* her only regret.

So, Susanna had forged on while he missed the teenage years, the championship games, the homecomings, the proms, the graduations. Survival helped her through grief, helped her focus on what was important—keeping life familiar for the kids. She'd been playing the roles of both mom and dad, keeping life moving in the direction she and Skip had intended for their family.

Now both kids were away at college. Bedtime stories and good-night kisses were a thing from the distant past as Brooke was three states away in Virginia and Brandon five states away in South Carolina. If she could ever take this last step and get on the road, she'd only be one state away from each.

Then selling the house wasn't a mistake, was it?

What else could Susanna do? She had an opportunity for job advancement that would get her family back on solid financial ground for the first time since Skip had died. True, there was risk, but she didn't like the alternative any better—continuing to knock around this empty house, losing her mind from loneliness.

The kids didn't know. She was the parent, the only one they had left. She'd reared them to be independent adults. They needed to go off and experience life, not tie themselves to home, worried about leaving their mother alone.

But was she being selfish by selling the only home they'd ever known? Once she locked this door, none of them could come back to the one place they would always have memories of Skip.

She hadn't realized how much those memories, and the tangible evidence of his presence in their lives, had kept him alive. But as she stared into the foyer, she realized how close he'd been in spirit, as if he'd only gone on a business trip and would be awaiting them at the airport to bring him home.

Now all visible reminders were packed away, their family scattered. Brooke and Brandon lived separate lives on separate campuses in separate states. Susanna was the only one left at home with the memories. Now she'd be forced to move on, too.

Was she ready?

Being a single parent was one thing. She'd had purpose to keep the family together, to help her kids deal with their father's death. Being a single woman with a life of her own was another thing entirely.

That was something she'd never really done. After leaving home, she'd tackled college dorm life with her best friend beside her. Then, as a young bride, she'd moved from the dorms to this house with Skip....

Susanna honestly didn't know what came next, what she could handle. She only knew that loneliness had grown all too familiar of late and something had to change.

Another deep breath.

She had to take this next step in life as an individual or else she'd remain here, feeling left behind, pining for everything she'd once had.

Life was change. Susanna knew that, and the kids could travel on school breaks far more easily to her new home in Charlotte, North Carolina, than they could return to New York where she was now. That was the reality of the situation. She'd figure out how to move on, even if she couldn't see beyond placing one foot in front of the other.

Memories would travel with them wherever they went.

One last glance into that shadowy interior... Susanna pulled the door shut quietly, slipped the key into the lock and turned the bolt for the last time.

JAY CANADY MOVED PAST doors in the administrative corridor, pausing only to glance into the financial office.

"Got a call from the gatehouse," he said. "The new administrator is on her way."

He didn't bother waiting for a reply but kept going until just shy of the front lobby, a spot where he could view the comings and goings around the reception desk, while remaining mostly hidden from view.

Mostly was the operative word. Jay wasn't fooling anyone around here. And certainly not the daytime receptionist. Amber routinely accused him of lurking behind potted palms to catch her tweeting on her iPhone during her shift.

He wasn't doing anything of the sort, but as owner and property administrator of The Arbors, A-list memory-care facility and family business, he was fond of hiding. Moments when he wasn't in popular demand were few and far between.

But hiding never worked for long. Especially with Amber. She didn't need X-ray vision to find him on any one of the sixty acres that made up the property. She wielded that iPhone like a lightsaber, texting him whenever he wasn't within earshot and getting miffed if he didn't reply immediately.

Jay should institute a new policy: no cell phones on shift. Radios only. But what was the point? In the very near future, none of his policies would mean squat.

The thought made him smile. As soon as the new property administrator walked through the door, everyone around here could start reprogramming their internal GPSs to take problems to someone else for solutions.

"Got your fingers crossed?" a voice crackly with age asked.

"You betcha." Jay raised a hand to display the good-luck gesture. He didn't bother turning around to see the man who'd shuffled up behind. Careful steps had announced Walter's approach long before he'd reached his destination.

Like Jay himself, Walter Higgins was a fixture around The Arbors. The longtime chief financial officer was another employee who could track down Jay no matter where he was. But Walter had the distinction of being an employee who also had a role in Jay's personal life.

Not that the entire staff couldn't him call 24/7. They could and did. Often. But Walter's calls weren't always work related. Not only had he been managing The Arbors' finances since before Jay had been born, but Walter had become an honorary grandfather since Jay's real granddad had passed away.

That connection had been cemented when Jay's late grandmother, after grieving the loss of her forty-year marriage, had gotten involved with Walter. Jay had never asked—never would, either—but he suspected Walter had loved Gran all along and stayed single until he got his chance to woo her into an honest relationship.

Jay would certainly miss Walter. But selling The Arbors didn't mean giving up the people in his life. He had some work to do proving that to Walter, though.

The electronic hiss of sliding doors dragged Jay's attention to the main lobby. His breath tightened in his chest as a dark-haired woman in a business suit strolled through with brisk steps.

"I thought you said they were sending a middle-aged widow with grown kids," Walter grumbled.

"*Widow* with *college* kids." The distinction obviously made a difference. "Northstar provided a bio. If memory serves—and it still does, which is always a good thing—the new administrator is around forty. Not middle-aged."

Not for Jay, who was pulling up the rear at thirty-two, or for Walter, who was pushing eighty-six. "I'm not even sure that's her. There wasn't a photo."

"She could be my granddaughter, Jay. My *great*-granddaughter."

"How's that? You never had any kids."

Walter grunted, narrowing his gaze at the reception desk. The woman currently greeting Amber wasn't Jay's idea of what a widow with college kids would look like, either. The suit emphasized her curves. She wasn't tall, but not short, either. Just really curvy.

Withdrawing a business card from her jacket, she handed it to Amber, who leaped from the chair on immediate hyperalert. Reaching across the desk, she extended a hand in welcome.

Walter scowled harder.

Judging by Amber's actions, this woman was the new administrator, whether she was what Jay expected or not. The woman flashed an easy smile that animated a heart-shaped face framed by a tumble of dark hair.

She was a very beautiful woman, which really shouldn't be the first thing Jay noticed. Not if he planned to retire from the memory-care business with some peace of mind.

Competent. Experienced. Professional. Compassionate. Those were the things he should be looking for.

He'd noticed one of four.

Dressing professionally was a start, he supposed. And what did competence, experience or compassion look like, anyway? Jay shook off the thought. Worry was getting the best of him, but he wouldn't admit that to Walter, who sought any reason to launch into The-Arbors-is-your-responsibility lecture again.

Jay had heard the arguments and the lectures. More than once, thank you.

"Okay. She's professional," he said. "Attractive. Stylish. A bit younger than I expected—"

"A bit?"

"Haven't had access to her personnel file," Jay reminded. "Technically she works for Northstar Management."

"Which is why I can't figure out why I'm adding her to our payroll. She doesn't come cheap, Jay. You'll be eating a fair sum if this deal falls through."

The deal wouldn't fall through. "We've got to assume some risk. It's only fair. Northstar would acquire this property tomorrow if it wasn't for me insisting on a transition period."

As much as Jay wanted out of here—and he did in a big way—he couldn't leave without witnessing Northstar's procedural changes and being reassured they would uphold The Arbors' standard of care. This new administrator had six months to actualize Northstar's promise to provide growth potential while maintaining the excellence of service established by Jay, and generations of his family before him.

That was the best he could do. He was leaving, although Walter still hadn't given up hope he might yet dissuade Jay. But the decision was made. He'd worked hard to put together a plan to insure the future for The Arbors, the staff and residents.

Walter could grouse all he wanted—the only thing left to do was get through the transition. Jay almost felt bad for the new administrator. Walter wouldn't be a pushover. He'd compare her to Gran, whose shoes were awfully big to fill, as he was so fond of saying. So big that not even Jay had filled them.

But Walter only wanted what was best for The Arbors. That much Jay knew. The rest of the staff, too. They were all competent and experienced professionals. Well versed in what it meant to be an employee at The Arbors.

The Compassion to Care.

That catchphrase had been around since the very beginning, when Gran had started the place to care for her mother during an era when not much had been known about Alzheimer's disease.

Gran had wanted to provide some quality of life, so she'd transformed a wing of the house on Granddad's farm into an ALF, an assisted-living facility. This was long before Jay's time, but he knew she'd added one bed at a time so her mother would have pleasant companions to fill her days.

Gran had learned all she could about Alzheimer's care and kept up with the research. Her tiny ALF had grown from one bed in the main house to one hundred and twenty beds in a new three-story facility with a nursing center on the ground floor. The Arbors had become an A-list memory-care community with a long waiting list for admission.

Would this around-forty widow with college kids have the compassion and ability to carry on Gran's legacy? Northstar Management had promised to send the perfect person to replace him so he could get on with living his life. Finally.

He'd given so much to this place that, if he didn't get out soon, there would be nothing left of him. This place was sucking him dry.

"And you really won't close the deal if you're unhappy with—what's her name again?" Walter asked.

"Ms. Adams. Ms. Susanna Adams."

"If you're unhappy with *Ms. Susanna Adams?*" Everything about Walter, from the creased white eyebrows to the hard stare in his eyes, which still read between the lines, broadcast his doubt.

"Really, Walter? You're questioning my integrity?"

He shook his head. "Just your ability to see clearly."

The same could be said about Walter and his stubborn refusal to even consider a future with Northstar. He'd seized any chance to talk some sense into Jay, had been rallying the troops to his side at every opportunity.

Fortunately, the troops knew who signed the paychecks and didn't have Walter's personal family ties to risk the potential consequences of a mutiny. Jay had shocked them all with his decision to sell. Now he was a wild card, and no one was sure how hard they could push him. Jay knew that as well as he knew everyone in The Arbors. If he hadn't hired an employee personally, his mom, dad, gran or granddad had.

"I've covered all the bases, Walter. You know how many hours I spent with the attorneys creating the contracts. I know you didn't forget because they billed *you*. And Alzheimer's isn't contagious. Not even with as many years as you've been here."

Walter folded his arms over his chest, rocked back on his saddle shoes with his mouth compressed into a tight line. He'd promised Gran to look after the place until his dying breath, and he meant to do exactly that. Did all this stubborn resistance stem from worry that the new owners might force him to retire because of his age?

Jay hadn't considered that before. "The very last thing I want is for the residents to sacrifice standard of care or my employees their jobs."

"*Former* employees."

"Not yet they're not. And not until I'm sure everything is moving in the right direction." The twenty-first century, to be exact. "I'll never expand The Arbors as a private company the way Northstar can with Fortune 500 financial backing. They're top-notch in senior care. The absolute best in the nation. We need to stay on the cutting edge with research so we can continue to provide the care Gran wanted."

"You're on the cutting edge. Your grandmother single-handedly got the Alzheimer's Association to fund the research at University of North Carolina at Chapel Hill. She'd have talked them into conducting it right here in Charlotte if UNC had been outfitted to handle the clinical trials."

"Seven years ago." Before everything had changed. Before his mom had wound up a resident in the facility she'd once help run. Before Gran had died. Before his dad had died. Before Mom had died. Before everything had become Jay's responsibility.

"Don't see why you can't do the same, Jay."

Jay was not going to defend himself, not standing in the hallway whispering. Walter was dead wrong on this, whether or not he admitted it. Gran had had Granddad to help, and income from the farm to foot the bills while she devoted herself to her Alzheimer's crusade. She'd had Mom to help before she'd had to care for Mom, and Dad to help after Mom couldn't. After Dad had died, Gran had Jay.

Jay didn't have anyone. Well, there was Drew, of course. *Major* Drew Canady, Jay's older brother who'd been smart enough to run off and join the Marines. He'd seen the handwriting on the wall and had made sure he wouldn't be around to get stuck running the family business.

Now Drew had a life when Jay couldn't even remember the last time he'd done anything but spend every waking moment dealing with the never-ending demands of this place. Dementia care frightened off most women fast, and he didn't have time for his friends anymore.

So when in hell was Jay supposed to make time to lobby the state legislature or Alzheimer's Association or pharmaceutical corporations or private medical research facilities *and* run The Arbors with its endless assessments, intakes, evaluations and treatment plans?

There were two hundred and fifty employees. There were one hundred and twenty residents, and most came with families who needed to be reassured, educated, informed and answered to about quality of care. There were volunteers and private companions and churches and all the outside resources that ministered to the residents to provide quality of life.

And quality of death. How many nights had Jay hoofed it here in the dark to meet funeral directors and deal with grieving families after a resident died?

Walter knew better than anyone what running this place entailed, and he'd heard all these arguments before. He might not want to retire until he was wheeled out of his office on a gurney, but he wouldn't live forever.

Neither would Jay, and he had no intention of spending the rest of his life without actually living. And life wouldn't start until he left The Arbors.

Susanna smiled at the young woman behind the reception desk, who didn't appear much older than Brooke.

"Good morning," the girl said, the lilt to her voice all Southern charm and novelty to a born-and-bred Yankee.

"Good morning." Susanna handed a business card to the young woman whose engraved badge identified her as Amber.

Susanna had already reviewed personnel files, so this young woman must be…

Amber Snelling, first-shift receptionist.

Currently working on her BSc in Operations Management.

Daughter of the Activity Director.

Amber glanced at the business card, eyes widening. "Ms. Adams!" She was on her feet instantly, extending a hand. "Welcome to The Arbors. We knew you were coming in today, but Mr. C. didn't tell us when."

Mr. C. would be Jay Canady, administrator and owner. The man hadn't told his staff when she would arrive, which meant he couldn't be too worried about them being on their best behavior. That said something about Mr. C.'s confidence in his employees.

"I came from Raleigh and wasn't exactly sure how long the drive would take."

"Raleigh. Wow." Amber said. "I hope Mr. C. brought you through Asheboro so you didn't deal with the traffic on 85."

Mr. C. hadn't brought her through Asheboro because Susanna had let her GPS lead the way. "I'm happy to report the traffic wasn't bad at all."

Of course, traffic was relative, and Susanna only had New York to compare.

"What time did you leave?" Amber asked.

"Around five."

She glanced at her computer display. "Hmm. Not too bad. Mr. C. told everyone you're from New York—as if I couldn't tell from your accent. Have you been to Charlotte before?"

Susanna shook her head.

"Well, make sure you ask about shortcuts while you're learning your way around. Of course, if you're anything like Mr. C., you probably won't get off the property all that much. But be aware that some shortcuts are better than others. Someone around here is bound to know which is which."

"Thanks, Amber. I'll remember that."

Amber glanced in the direction of the administrative offices then surprised Susanna by continuing the conversation. "When you do manage to get out of here, visit

Concord Mills. It's a huge shopping mall by the Charlotte Speedway, so when you go make sure you plan to spend the whole day."

"Then I'll have to bring my daughter when she comes to visit. Shopping is one of her favorite things to do." When Mom was swiping the plastic, anyway.

"Your daughter doesn't live with you?"

"Only in between semesters. She's in her third year at William and Mary."

"I'm in my third year, too. At UNC. But I'm probably older than your daughter. I work here full-time, so I never take more than three classes. My degree is taking forever."

Susanna wasn't sure how to reply and went the philosophical route. "I'm sure when all is said and done you'll look back and think school took exactly as long as it should have."

"I hope you're right."

Did The Arbors encourage staff to be so friendly, and chatty, or was Susanna sampling real Southern hospitality? She didn't want to cut off the conversation rudely, but she needed to let the owner know she was here, so she didn't appear late.

When she opened her mouth to prompt Amber, a man suddenly appeared with an older gentleman in step behind him.

"Mr. C., Mr. Higgins. Guess who's here?" Amber announced.

"I see." The younger of the two gentlemen inclined his head to acknowledge the receptionist. Then his gaze fixed on Susanna as he strode toward her, all broad shoulders and quick energy. His smile was wide and fast. "Jay Canady, Ms. Adams. Welcome to The Arbors. Walter Higgins, our CFO."

For a moment, Susanna stared. *That voice.* Deep-throated, like honey melted in whiskey, not a drawl, but soft, stretching vowels that made every syllable distinctive. It took another moment to realize he was waiting for a reply. She'd stopped breathing. Literally.

What on earth was wrong with her?

"A pleasure to meet you, gentlemen," she managed. Then she was shaking hands and making more chitchat while distracting herself with memory associations so she wouldn't forget names.

Walter Higgins, dapper elderly chap with a bow tie. CFO, my old job.

Jay Canady, aka Mr. C. The man who wants to sell off this gorgeous facility.

Not that she would need a memory prompt to remember him.

Susanna had reviewed the man's biographical data. Although she knew he was thirty-two years old and the third generation to run this facility, Jay Canady wasn't what she'd expected.

He was all chiseled lines and ruthless masculinity. Neatly trimmed blond hair contrasted sun-scorched skin that suggested he spent time outdoors, a fact reinforced by his toned physique. And his eyes were the greenest green she'd ever seen.

Susanna wasn't sure what she expected a man who ran a memory-care facility to look like, but she hadn't expected hints of David Beckham and Eomer from *The Lord of the Rings*.

"Northstar promised to send us the perfect property director, and here you are," Jay said.

"Perfect for The Arbors, anyway," she said quickly. "I can't imagine any place lovlier. The drive from the gate was breathtaking."

"You should see the arbors in spring bloom," Walter said.

"She will," Jay said. "But not until spring. Now let's get you settled before the parade begins. Everyone wants to meet you. I'll take you to your new office so you can settle in before I give you the dime tour."

The dime tour? How charming. With a polite hand on her elbow, Jay whisked her from the lobby and down a corridor of administrative offices.

"Welcome to The Arbors, Ms. Adams," Walter said about halfway down the hall. "Say the word when you're ready to tour the financial offices. We run a tight ship. You'll be pleased."

"I'm sure I will, Walter. It was a pleasure meeting you."

"The same." If Walter had been wearing a hat, he would have tipped it. He was such a dashing gentleman.

"I understand Walter's been an employee since the beginning," she said after he vanished into an office, leaving her alone with Jay.

"Before, actually. My grandmother hired him before she ever broke ground on this place."

"That continuity of staff says a lot about your facility. It's not common nowadays."

"Has plusses. Minuses, too. Our out-of-house tax attorney was around since the start, too, but he didn't trust computers, so he wrote everything by hand."

"That must have presented some challenges," she said diplomatically.

Jay pulled a face. "He finally retired. We hired a new firm that conducts twenty-first-century business. But I suspect Northstar will reassign those out-of-house duties."

She liked that he put business practices immediately on the table. "Once we start going through everything, I'll be able to tell you for certain. One of our partners is Rockport Investment Banking. I think you'll approve their caliber of service."

Jay didn't reply before they reached the office at the end of the hall labeled with a simple gold plate: Administrator.

Pushing the door wide, he allowed her to precede him.

The office must have cornered the building because two walls were nothing but floor-to-ceiling windows. The view beyond only proved The Arbors was heaven on earth. Beyond the manicured slope of lawn stretched a lake, calmly reflecting the arbors that circled the far end and the towering forest that hid most of the main house from sight.

She recognized pines and fir but there were other trees in glorious autumn bloom, bright splashes of color that hinted at how spectacular this view would be a little further into the season when the leaves really started to change.

"What are those red trees?" she asked. "I've never seen anything like them."

"Around here we call them flaming trees."

"They're gorgeous." She wanted to take cell phone photos to send to her family and friends. "Tell me I'll be able to work in here and not stare out these windows all day."

Jay smiled and seemed to like her response. Good. She needed to get off to a good start with this man.

"I'm sure the view will inspire you to do remarkable work," he said. "It's tradition. One that needs to continue."

There was a warning in that sweet whiskey voice. Cocking a hip against the desk, she met his gaze. "Concerns?"

"Just want to make sure we're on the same page. I've been dealing with the suits and attorneys. They're all quick to promise they can take The Arbors to the next level. I want that, but not at the expense of my residents or staff. The quality of care is what makes us unique. You'll be in charge of making sure everyone's taken care of. Thought I should put that up front so you know what I expect."

Hmm. Demanding, bossy even, but Susanna appreciated the honesty. Her own boss, Gerald Mayne, had warned her she'd have a tough job reassuring Jay that Northstar would continue the quality of service his family had established as a private facility. Jay took seriously his responsibility to those who relied upon him, which made her wonder why he was selling The Arbors at all. Gerald hadn't shared that information.

"That's what I want, too, Jay." Susanna meant it. "We've got six months together, and I intend to make this transition smooth and positive. That starts with understanding what you do around here. Then we can figure out how to implement policies and procedures to get The Arbors on board as a Northstar property. How does that sound?"

"Like we're on the same page."

Susanna certainly hoped so, because absolutely everything important in her life rode on these next six months.

On her success.

CHAPTER TWO

J AY HEADED TOWARD the maintenance and engineering building to retrieve another radio—he'd given his to Susanna—pondering their first meeting. Unfortunately, leaving the administrative offices forced him into the front lobby, where Amber lay in wait.

"Thank you so much, Mr. C." Her tone bore up her sour expression. "I guess you needed an engraved invitation to meet the new administrator. She must think I'm a total idiot."

"What are you talking about? You made her feel right at home. That's what I pay you to do."

"I was covering for you, and you left me hanging."

"Why didn't you page me, then?"

"You were standing twenty feet away in the bushes. Did you really want the radio to go off where she could—"

"Since when do you use the radio?"

"Oh, right. Like I'm supposed to send a text message in front of *my new boss*."

Jay chuckled. Amber had practically been reared at The Arbors because her mother had worked here for years. She was comfortable in a way even the longest hires weren't. She'd volunteered for school service hours, had been a part-time transportation aide during high school. Understandably, she was worried about all the changes.

He tried to soothe her ruffled feathers. "You bought

me a few minutes to get the lay of the land. I thank you for that."

She gave an exasperated huff and spun around in her chair, dismissing him. He smiled and continued on his way, hoping the new administrator had come prepared to deal with this crew.

Circling the building, he headed toward the north end of the property and the maintenance buildings tucked away there, concealed by the trees and the slope.

Jay found Chester in the garage. A middle-aged African-American man with more and more gray in his hair each passing year, the maintenance and engineering supervisor was the calm in the middle of any storm. Jay couldn't remember the man so much as raise his voice in his twelve years on the payroll.

"Need another radio, Chester."

"You got it, Mr. C." He disappeared through a doorway, where all electronics were locked in the climate-controlled office.

When he returned, Jay asked, "Everything okay? You get an ETA on the mower yet?"

Chester nodded. "The repair shop promised I can pick it up by Friday. Don't fret. Worst case is it rains, and I get the crew out with push mowers."

"The crew won't like that."

A slow smile spread over Chester's face. "You know it."

And that was that. Jay appreciated a supervisor who was a man of few words.

Arriving at the main building, he bypassed the front entrance and a second helping of Amber's verbal abuse and made for the employee exit at the north wing. As he rounded the corner, Jay realized he'd made a tactical error.

The *new* administrator's office.

He paraded in the middle of that view Susanna had been so excited about.

And there she was, showcased in the window. She'd removed her jacket, and the slip of a blouse she wore outlined her delicate curves with some silky fabric that looked soft to the touch.

Ironically, she stood in the same place he'd always stood, in a similar pose even. Hands wrapped around a coffee mug, trying to absorb the peace of the grounds when life inside The Arbors spun at tornado velocity.

He wondered what she was looking for and wondered why he wondered.

But he'd stepped right into it, so to speak, and there was nothing to do but keep moving. Susanna startled when she saw him—an unexpected intruder mere feet beyond the glass. Then her face lit with a surprised smile.

He waved.

She waved back.

God, he was such an idiot. This shortcut needed to be deleted from his repertoire. The walk past the window took forever, but he finally reached the north exit. Entering the code on the keypad with impatient thrusts, he tried to shake off annoyance at his stupidity.

What if Susanna felt rushed because he'd practically shown up in her office? And what had she been sipping in that mug? Had she ventured down to Dietary for some coffee?

Without knocking, Jay shoved open the door to Walter's office and plunked down in the chair in front of the desk.

"What's up?" Walter glanced away from the computer screen.

"She drove in from Raleigh this morning. I should have at least offered her coffee."

"Her, as in Ms. Adams?"

"Know anyone else who drove in from Raleigh today?"

Walter raked a tight gaze over Jay. "I can have Chester set up a card table for you. That can be your new work space."

"I won't need it, thank you. I'm not planning on working anymore. Just transitioning."

Walter arched a white eyebrow. "You think so?"

"That's the plan."

"Your mouth to God's ear, boy. And you might do well to ask for a little assistance from your mother, father and grandmother while you're at it. God rest their souls."

Jay should have known Walter would drag in divine intervention. And to his surprise the divine did intervene—when the radio crackled at his waist, saving him from continuing this stupid conversation.

"I'm ready for a tour whenever you are, Jay," Susanna said through the speaker.

"On my way." He headed out of Walter's office without a backward glance.

Susanna had barely opened his former office door before the apology poured out of his mouth.

"That shortcut won't be a problem. Employees only use that exit to the parking lot on the other side of the building."

He hoped she didn't think he was spying on her.

She chuckled good-naturedly. "No worries. Amber mentioned shortcuts this morning."

He wasn't sure if that was good or bad, but he did notice she'd covered up that silky blouse with her jacket again.

"Probably a good thing you showed up when you did. It's too easy to get distracted by that view. You did say you managed to get work done in here, right?"

"You will. When no one's distracting you." Like he had.

Glancing at the mug sitting on the shelf beside the watercooler, he said, "I'm glad someone thought to take care of you. I could have offered you a cup of coffee after your drive."

She waved him off with a graceful motion. "Thanks, Jay, but I take care of me."

There was *something* in that statement. Jay had no clue what, but he wondered. "You travel with coffee?"

Her soft laugh swallowed up the air between them. Or maybe it was the fluid display she made as she leaned over to reach inside her laptop case to produce a small foil package. "VIA. Instant Starbucks coffee for people on the go. Your water dispenser provides hot water. You can drink this cold, though, too."

"It's your water dispenser now. I'd like to say you can get a decent cup of coffee around here, but I'd be lying. I budget for the good stuff, but when it's brewed in big quantities… Keep a supply of those on hand."

She dropped the package back into her case. "Appreciate the heads-up."

"That's what I'm here for."

Her smile flashed wide and bright, and he noticed again how attractive she was. *Not* what he needed to be noticing.

"Let's get this show on the road." He grabbed the door for the lady and motioned her through, forcing himself *not* to notice how attractive she was from behind, too.

He kept his gaze leveled at the back of her head—where it belonged—not noticing the way her shiny dark hair caught the light, bouncing around her shoulders with her every step.

Excitement must be getting the better of him, because the plans he'd been making for eight months were coming together in the very feminine form of this new administrator.

SUSANNA'S TOUR BEGAN with the entry code to the secure doors off the front lobby—lockdown, as the wings of patient rooms were known—and hadn't slowed the whirlwind pace in the hours since. She tried to tamp down her nerves, which hummed at full volume, as she absorbed everything at once.

Gerald had led her to expect a top-notch facility, and The Arbors appeared to be that. At a glance, the staff seemed professional and friendly, residents well-groomed and active.

Jay was a charming host as he directed her through the facility and instructed her on a floor plan that served both utilitarian and aesthetic purposes. Four wings branched off from the lobby and two centrally located elevators.

The elevators were large enough to accommodate wheelchairs, walkers and gurneys, providing the only access to the upper floors besides locked emergency stairs at the end of each wing.

"We'll assign you codes to get through the outer exits, too," he said. "They can be handy when traffic backs up."

"Which happens quite a bit, I imagine."

He appeared to consider that, tipping his head to one side so that strands of blond hair slipped over his brow. "Actually, not too much unless we call 9-1-1. Then we reserve the south elevator until emergency arrives. The residents don't do a lot of traveling between floors unless they're going to the third floor for therapy, so that helps."

Pausing with his hand poised over the keypad, he glanced at her and added, "I provided Gerald with our policy and procedure manual. Have you had a chance to look at it yet?"

"Cover to cover."

His smile came fast, a smile that nearly blinded her with approval. "Good."

This man wanted the arrangement to work as much as she did, Susanna realized. She wasn't sure how she knew, but she did. And the awareness both surprised and reassured her. With Jay's assistance, this transition should go smoothly.

She hoped. The first step began with Susanna convincing Jay to go through with acquisition.

But he wanted to be convinced…and that realization made her feel much better. "Reviewing schedules and staffing budgets is different from seeing the result of a well-staffed facility in action," she said as they exited the elevator.

"It takes adequate staff to provide adequate care. It's criminal what some facilities get away with."

He came to a sharp stop outside the elevator and thrust the hair off his forehead with an absent gesture. "You do not want to get me started on my opinion of federal regulations."

"Noted." Obviously a hot spot.

"Here at The Arbors, we have a shift R.N. who manages the LPNs, the licensed practical nurses, on every floor and deals with the physician who makes rounds each day. Yes, I said *physician,* not nurse practitioner or physician's assistant."

He was clearly proud, and as Susanna's expertise was in the facility finances, she knew the budget and what that service could cost. One of the areas she would be looking at to bring the budget variances in line with Northstar's specifications.

She kept that to herself since they were off to such a promising start. There would be plenty of time to address the differences between corporate and private management.

Entering the first-floor nursing center, she paid careful attention to the designations of the staff who ran in and out of rooms. LPNs were responsible for dispensing medication. Certified nursing assistants, known as CNAs, helped with patient care while the patient care technicians, or PCTs, handled hygiene and grooming.

Dieticians worked in top-notch kitchen facilities and their assistants transported meals to restorative dining areas for residents who were unable to feed themselves. Housekeepers. Maintenance and engineering staff. Each nurses' station serviced two wings, not only as home base for the caregivers but a gathering area for many residents.

"No, no, Mrs. Highsmith, you can't go to your room right now," an LPN said as she stopped a tiny woman in a wheelchair and deftly brought her around to face the nurses' station. "Stay here and keep me company while I fill out these charts, all right?"

Susanna didn't catch Mrs. Highsmith's response before Jay whisked her along yet another hallway. The only downside to the facility setup was that with every wing laid out in the same way and decorated to convey a homey ambiance, she couldn't quite pinpoint where she was.

"I will eventually gain my sense of direction around here, won't I?" she asked Jay.

He laughed with his rich warm voice that managed to be the only sound she heard over the noise of a busy floor. "Just watch the room numbers until you get the hang of the place."

"Not that he's the best judge." The somber male voice came from behind them.

She and Jay stopped and turned to find Walter exiting a conference room.

"The boy's been working this property since he was gurgling and cooing to entertain the residents."

"Thank you, Walter," Jay said dryly.

Susanna bit back a laugh, not sure what amused her more, the thought of Jay as a *boy* or a green-eyed baby.

"The residents loved you then and they love you now." Walter held up a hand and whispered conspiratorially, "Everyone loves him around here. You've got big boots to fill."

Another warning, but before Susanna could respond, Jay said, "Everyone can't wait to see the last of me."

"You wish."

Jay scowled so hard Susanna refrained from comment. Judging from what she'd seen so far, she'd have to side with Walter. She made another mental note but didn't get a chance to worry about potential staff resistance as Jay hurried her away. She met everyone on shift until she practically vibrated from information overload.

When her phone rang, Susanna seized the opportunity. "My daughter," she told Jay. "I need to take this."

"Radio me when you're ready for the north wing," Jay said.

Susanna made her escape with a smile and the phone cradled against her ear. "Hang on, Brooke." She used her passcode for the first time to exit the secured area.

"Hey, pretty," she said, making her way toward her office. "Sorry to keep you waiting."

"I'm dying here, Mom." Brooke sounded peeved. "You never texted me to let you know you'd made it to Charlotte."

And Brooke wasn't the only one, Susanna realized. Everyone would want to know she'd arrived safely. One text and Brooke could have passed along the news, so no one would have had to worry. Said a lot about Susanna's anxiety level.

"I'm so, so sorry. The drive was fine, but I hit the ground running as soon as I got here and haven't stopped since. Touring the place and meeting everyone."

"Yeah, yeah. I'll use that excuse the next time you blast me for forgetting to let you know I made it back to school."

"I was so worked up about getting here I wasn't thinking. No excuses. I should have texted."

"You admit you were wrong." But she didn't give Susanna a chance to respond before asking, "Is everything going okay? Do you like North Carolina?"

Brooke was eager to know if *she* would like their new home base. Susanna launched into an excited account of The Arbors, from the view in her office to the whirlwind tour of the facility. "I haven't seen where I'll be living yet, but if it looks anything like everything else around here, the cottage will be amazing. It's another world."

Brooke laughed. "Must be. You sound like you're gonna hyperventilate."

"I can't believe I'm in North Carolina."

"This will be great, Mom. Just relax and give it a chance."

That made Susanna smile. Brooke would be mortified to realize she was already mimicking her mother. But Susanna did appreciate the reassurance. Brooke understood the enormity of this move. "You're right, pretty. You're absolutely right."

"Um, yeah."

Susanna laughed, welcomed the sound of her beautiful daughter's voice. With adrenaline pumping so hard and steadily through the morning, simply talking to Brooke felt like the first spec of normalcy. For this moment, Susanna was mom again, grounded, not a woman on her own in a strange new world.

"I couldn't wait any longer to know if you were still alive, so I had to call. But I've got to get into class. I sit in the front row, and guaranteed someone's lurking my seat now. I'd hate to break up the Rat Pack so early in the semester."

Susanna gripped the phone tightly, not ready to end the call, a lifeline to everything she loved. But as a mom with an empty nest, she got to catch up with her kids, not cling.

Brooke's Rat Pack was important. They were a group of students who'd started interdisciplinary studies together, women and men ranging in ages from Brooke at twenty to Annie, who was well into her seventies. Susanna liked that her daughter connected with people from varying levels of life experience rather than limiting herself to the party set.

"Go get your seat, pretty. All's well in Charlotte. I'll send a text to let everyone know, and we can talk more later."

"Sounds good. You won't forget?"

"I won't forget. Promise."

"Well, I'm glad you're alive. Love ya."

"Love you, too. Have a good day."

Susanna paused at a window, holding the phone and staring out at the sunlit lake, managing the sense of loss, so magnified by nerves. The life she loved wasn't over, just changing. She and Brooke were exploring new territory in their relationship, and this move only underscored that change.

Susanna needed to let go of the childhood mother/daughter relationship with all the parenting and rebellious overtones. Brooke didn't need much parenting anymore. Just some guidance and advice when she asked. A sounding board when she needed to talk and sort things out in her head.

Instead of longing for what had passed, Susanna needed to be excited about their new relationship. Her daughter was growing into an amazing young woman.

Could Susanna possibly be any more blessed?

That answer was no, and she shouldn't let fear of change or anxiety about all the things riding on this job overshadow her appreciation of the moment. Those moments shouldn't ever be taken for granted.

Finances had been unbelievably tight since Skip had died. She'd managed to keep the family going on one salary by putting his life insurance policy to good use with the house and some mutual funds. But the expenses had grown along with the kids.

Between Brandon's ball tournaments and training camps and Brooke's art history internships both in and out of the country, travel expenses alone were breathtaking. Then there were the cars. Insuring two under-twenty-one drivers—especially when one was male—*still* was challenging.

But college had worked out better than Susanna could ever have hoped. Both kids were high achievers. Without their scholarships, they would have had to rely on the prepaid educations she and Skip had purchased years before. There would have been no selling the house because the kids wouldn't have been able to afford housing even if they'd stayed in New York.

No, Susanna had absolutely nothing to complain about, and maybe the tide was finally turning. She'd been in survival mode since Skip had died, grasping every single second with her kids and continually putting one foot in front of the other.

For the first time in so long, Susanna could almost see a glimmer of light at the end of what had been an endless tunnel. They were alive and healthy, and they were within driving distance again. This promotion to property administrator gave her a chance to improve the quality of life for all of them.

If everything went as planned.

CHAPTER THREE

JAY SPUN AROUND WHEN he heard shuffling footsteps. Sure enough, Walter bore down on him with a curious expression.

"What are you doing in the bushes— Oh, I see," he said in his deaf-old-man voice that carried halfway down the hall.

There was no missing the view from this prime spot behind a majestic palm in the dayroom entrance. Susanna stood beside the CareTracker, a touch-screen computer that protruded from the wall. Kimberly, the shift R.N., appeared to be explaining how to work the charting system.

"One might think you don't trust the new administrator," Walter said.

"I don't know her, so how can I trust her?"

"Think spying is the way to go, do you?"

"You sound like Amber. I am not spying." Jay spent his every waking moment with Walter and everyone else around here. How could they possibly think he was doing anything but hiding from them? Jay grabbed precious seconds alone with both hands and would continue to do so for six more months. Then he wouldn't have to hide again.

"Have some faith, Walter. Why would I need to spy on Susanna? Look at her handling Kimberly. Professional. Friendly. Pleasant smile. Great legs."

Great legs?

Jay tried again. "At least she won't scare the residents. I think we should at least give her a chance, don't you?"

"You want me to lurk in the bushes, too?"

"Just taking a minute to catch my breath."

"And enjoy the view." An accusation.

Jay couldn't exactly deny it now, could he? "Don't give away all my good hiding places."

That got a reaction. Walter rolled his gaze heavenward, no doubt sending up a prayer to Gran for divine intervention. "You need to get a life, boy."

"Um, yeah. That's kind of the point of selling this place." Jay stepped from behind the palm and headed down the hallway, dodging the lecture he sensed forthcoming.

Walter would not piss in Jay's cereal today. Not when his plan was getting underway. He'd gotten Susanna settled in the cottage last night, and had arrived to find that she'd preceded him onto the property this morning. Imagine that. There was hope this plan might actually work, and he didn't want to jinx anything by listening to Walter's negativity.

Susanna's second day was all about understanding routines at The Arbors. She got to work before the third shift ended, before the morning routines got into full swing when the residents awoke. Touring the first-floor halls, where residents required hospital-type care in the nursing center, she chatted with staff who were closing out the shift with quiet efficiency.

Her day was off to a more relaxed, albeit earlier, start today, for which she was grateful. She needed to get her feet under her as an administrator, and starting the day on her own, without Jay running interference, did much to soothe her nerves.

She discussed individual cases with the LPNs, tried to

commit resident names to memory and found that someone very generously put scrapbooking skills to good use.
Personalized collages of biographical data, hobbies and
a photo hung beside each door. She'd noticed them yesterday, but took the time today to appreciate the effective
genius of the collages. Putting faces to names made the
learning curve so much simpler.

Mrs. Donaire had been a professor in France.

Mrs. Highsmith had eight children, eighteen grandchildren and four great-grandchildren.

Mrs. Munsell had an obsession with Elvis.

The collages would provide easy topics to chat with
the residents about to help Susanna get to know everyone.

"Kimberly, who's responsible for those biographical
collages?" Susanna asked the head R.N. during a pause
in the explanation how to chart patient information on the
computerized system.

The Arbors used cutting-edge medical charting tech-
nology, which meant all resident contact was documented
so all caregivers accessed only current information.

"Tessa, the activity director," Kimberly said. "Did you
meet her yesterday?"

Susanna nodded. "Amber looks a lot like her."

"Except for that pretty dark hair. Amber gets that from
her daddy." Kimberly smiled. "The residents make those
collages with Tessa's help. It's one of the ongoing activities around here—getting to know me."

"I noticed that on the activities calendar and assumed
it was some sort of meet and greet," Susanna said. "So,
so clever."

"Tessa would appreciate knowing you think so. Mr. C.
gave her all kinds of grief for putting nail holes in the walls
when she hung up those frames."

Susanna glanced at the frame beside Mr. Butterfield's

door. The man was a retired career naval officer. His work appeared to have had something to do with submarines. "I suppose we have to make sacrifices for a greater good."

"Better not let Chester hear you say that," a familiar voice said from a distance.

The sound of that voice brought Susanna up quickly, a flutter of breath in her throat as she found Jay looking morning fresh, cheeks pink from a recent shave and hair damp.

"Good morning," he said with a throaty edge to his voice, a rough-silk sound, as if he wasn't fully awake yet.

"Good morning." All her predawn calm evaporated beneath a rush of adrenaline, so intense it surprised her.

"Only one person around here cared about those holes, Mr. C." Kimberly rolled her eyes. "You know those collages are excellent memory prompts."

"Only for the folks who can remember their names."

Susanna stared. Joking about memory problems in a memory-care facility? That was about the last thing she expected.

Kimberly waved him off with a laughing "Pshaw."

Susanna listened curiously, knowing Gerald, or any VIP from Northstar, would likely faint on the spot if they'd overheard this particular exchange. Corporate professionalism being what it was, anything that wasn't politically correct was taboo.

"I didn't realize the collages were memory prompts," she said mildly.

Jay nodded. "To be fair, every effort to build memory helps, and the volunteers find them especially useful while they're getting to know their way around."

"New administrators, too," she admitted.

"Guess they're worth all the holes, then."

He didn't look convinced, but politely acquiesced for

her benefit. Susanna wasn't sure how to respond to that. She felt somehow robbed of her words, as if she couldn't think clearly.

"No holes for the birthdays and death notices posted in the front lobby." She filled the sudden awkward silence with a completely irrelevant observation.

"True," Jay agreed, leveling a gaze her way, somehow the green of his eyes all the more vibrant for his freshly scrubbed appearance. "That information is handy. Not only to engage the residents who can remember those sorts of details but to remind the staff and volunteers."

"Tessa briefs everyone in the mornings on special events," Kimberly explained. "We provide balloons, and Liz serves cake at lunch so it's a big party."

"What a wonderful way to help the residents celebrate and feel special." Susanna knew that keeping the residents engaged was a full-time job and an essential part of healthy senior living. "Tessa's also responsible for decorating around here?"

Jay nodded.

"I have to admit I couldn't imagine anyone outdoing the activity director at my last facility. But I'm impressed."

Every foyer leading to a separate wing had been decked out with decorations to recreate Hawaiian beach scenes— palm trees and bright umbrellas and lawn chairs. A section near the first-floor activities area had been cordoned off and filled with sand while the wall was covered in a floor-to-ceiling digital image of a Pacific coastline.

"This is such a tough time of year to make exciting," Susanna said. "Summer's over. Labor Day is over. In New York, we can play up autumn, but here in Charlotte it seems a bit early."

Kimberly brushed her fingers across the touch-screen

display. "We won't be in full leaf change for another month. It's something to see if you haven't already."

"I think I'm in for quite a treat," she agreed, then thanked Kimberly for taking the time to walk her through the CareCharter program and found herself alone with Jay.

"You got off to an early start today," he said.

"Lots to accomplish."

He nodded. "If you don't mind, I need coffee. Walk with me to Dietary and tell me how your first night went."

"Phone calls to let everyone know that I made it to Charlotte safely." Phone calls to Brooke and Brandon before she'd passed out face-first on the big four-poster bed in the guest cottage. "Then I spent some time with the personnel files, refreshing myself on the staff. I've been through them before, but it was nice to put faces with the names."

Jay beelined for the industrial coffee brewer in the kitchen and offered her a cup, which she accepted gratefully.

"Doesn't sound as if you did much settling in." He dispensed a cup for himself.

"I'll have time to get organized this weekend."

He took a long swallow and grimaced. "See what I mean?"

She met his gaze over the rim of the mug. "Not quite VIA, but not too bad."

"That's kind." He swallowed another sip. "But it's leaded, and that's what's important."

Susanna chuckled. "Oh, I remember what I wanted to ask you, Jay. You have a lot of family members on staff. I'm curious. Is this a Southern thing or a private-facility thing?"

It certainly wasn't a corporate thing when the legal department had clear-cut guidelines about what constituted conflict of interest.

Jay paused with the cup to his mouth. "I'll go with the private facility. We've established The Arbors as a great place to work. Our five family members span three generations and four departments. Different last names."

"Wow. And no conflict of interest?"

"None. In fact, it's exactly the opposite. Lots of loyalty with the families." He raised his cup in a salute. "But Northstar can conduct new hires how they see fit. My staff will be grandfathered in."

No, Jay definitely wasn't pulling any punches. Susanna inclined her head and sipped to avoid a reply, not wanting to engage in controversy so early on her second day.

Gerald had explained how rigid Jay had been regarding The Arbors' employees. After the acquisition, there would have to be substantial cause and a fair bit of documentation to terminate any of the staff. She hoped he was right about the loyalty.

"The fact you have employees on staff for decades says a lot about the facility you run."

"Something good, I hope."

"Yes." That was entirely honest. Northstar very much appreciated hardworking employees and worked equally hard to keep them. Susanna was a perfect example. She'd been with the company almost twenty years.

Jay seemed to appreciate the praise and smiled, which melted the hard lines of his face. Susanna was struck by how accessible he was. She'd only known him two days and it was so easy to talk with him. Personable. That's exactly what he was, which was probably why everyone around here liked him so much.

She did have big shoes to fill. Jay's leadership was what set the tone for the staff, and here she was a first-time property administrator—a world of difference from a man who'd grown up learning to meet the needs of The Arbors.

Northstar had placed their trust in her abilities by offering her this position, but she also knew that their faith had been encouraged by her boss, Gerald, who was also a friend. Still, everyone seemed to be interested in making a good first impression, and as the day progressed, Susanna found herself far too busy to do anything but learn her way around.

It wasn't until the sun had set and second shift had served dinner that Susanna was ready to call it a day.

"I thought of something I wanted to ask you before I leave, Jay," Susanna said, after retrieving her laptop case from her office and bidding Walter goodbye. "Do you park in the employee lot? I haven't noticed an assigned administrator space, and I don't want to inadvertently commandeer anyone's spot in the employee lot."

Jay had dispensed with his jacket sometime between lunch in the second-floor dining hall and the intake meeting in the conference room. Now he loosened his tie with a few quick tugs, lending him a more casual appearance.

"I don't drive my car. I usually walk or take a golf cart."

"Oh, that makes sense. Gerald mentioned that you lived in the main house. I didn't realize it was so close."

"Just over the rise from the guest cottage."

A new neighbor for her new home, which was charming, although she hadn't actually seen it in the light of day yet. But by moonlight and the paling sky of predawn, her new home couldn't have been more perfect.

Susanna had only seen one photo of the main house in the property portfolio, and it appeared to be from another era. Even the sliver of roofline she could see peeking above the trees from her office brought to mind *Gone with the Wind*.

"You take the road?" she asked.

"There's a path through the arbors. It's a hike on foot but not bad with a golf cart. We should probably get you fixed up with one, too. They're handy for getting around here even if you drive in. Just park nearest the employee entrance you use. It's first come, first served around here."

"Okay, thanks." They left the administrative corridor and headed to the lobby, and silence fell between them. Suddenly Susanna was all too aware of how Jay unbuttoned his collar and breathed as if this were his first unconstrained breath all day.

"We had a par course at my last property, and it was my favorite way to spend lunch breaks when I could get them," she said to fill the quiet.

"It's good to get outside every once in a while."

"Especially during the months when it wasn't buried under six feet of snow."

He laughed, such a rich sound. Was it possible even his laughter had a hint of the South, too?

They emerged in the front lobby, walking side by side. Security served as nighttime reception and Jay told the man at the desk, "Pete's on tonight, if you need anything."

Then they passed through the open doorway, where two furry golden beasts bounded at her, tails wagging, yelping and barking a friendly greeting.

"Hello, guys," Susanna said in her dog-friendly squeaky voice as they circled her legs, clearly wanting attention. She extended a hand, waited to see how it was received.

The dogs shuffled nearer, half sitting, half standing, vying to get closer to her like two almost-identical twins elbowing each other out of the way. With a laugh, she knelt and gave each a hand, ruffling their chests in a place most dogs loved to be petted, laughing as they preened beneath the attention. "That feels good, guys, doesn't it? So who are you? You're so friendly."

One sharp whistle answered her question. The barking stopped and the dogs bounded toward Jay. But only for an instant before they shot past him toward the facility entrance.

Susanna watched with amusement as Jay rolled his eyes and whistled again, bringing the dogs to a halt in the entrance and the sliding doors that opened drunkenly.

"Come on, you two," Jay commanded "We're not going in tonight. It's too late. You can visit your buddies another day."

Susanna hadn't come across any other dogs in the facility and assumed Jay referred to the staff or the residents. Greywacke Lodge had been affiliated with an organization that trained dogs specifically for senior visits, and most residents loved the friendly canines. Judging by the way these two dogs kept glancing at the entrance, looking disappointed if possible, Susanna suspected they enjoyed visits, too.

"Boys, sit," Jay instructed. "Try to make a good first impression for once."

Susanna couldn't imagine these two making any other. They were obviously well trained. "Golden retrievers?"

"Yep. Their names are Butters and Gatsby."

"Oh, that's sweet. Butters is younger?"

Jay narrowed a disapproving gaze at the dog that could barely sit still. "How can you tell? His lack of manners?"

True, Butters's hind end kept popping up, tail thumping wildly before he'd remember he was supposed to be sitting.

"My fault entirely," Susanna admitted. "How is he supposed to behave when I'm doing the squeaky voice?"

"Yeah, well, he should." Jay scowled at the dog who'd sidled up against her to be petted again. "They like you."

She ruffled the soft fur around Butters's neck. "They're so friendly, I'm guessing they like everyone."

"Okay, *you* like them."

"I do. My kids had Hershel while they were growing up. He was a golden and Akita mix."

"Had?"

"Wonderful quality of life until he was fifteen. We still miss him."

Jay nodded, but she could tell he approved. Something in the twinkle of his deep-green eyes. There didn't seem to be any artifice with this man, Susanna realized. Professionalism didn't distance him from saying how he felt or force him to only express the politically correct response.

Yet somehow he was very professional. She'd witnessed that firsthand. A natural leader.

Susanna found that very different, very refreshing from the often tentative diplomacy of corporate-speak.

Jay tossed his jacket over his shoulder. "You ready to head home, boys?"

Both dogs were on their feet instantly, glancing at her as if excited for the company.

"Enjoy your walk. I hope you all have a good night." Somehow in the artificial light of the lamp, Jay no longer looked like the administrator and owner of The Arbors, but simply a man who'd worked a long day.

"It was a good second day, Susanna. Enjoy your night." Then he herded the dogs away and headed toward the slope.

Susanna was still watching as they passed beyond the glow of the parking lot lights and vanished into the darkness, warmth growing inside her because of his approval.

"Two days, Suze?" Karan Steinberg said incredulously over the phone. "I can't believe you didn't call me last night."

"I'm so sorry. We didn't leave work until late, and by the time Jay helped me get my bags to the house and I got everything organized, I passed out."

"Well, forgiven, then. But only if you slept all night. Did you? Don't lie to me."

"I would never lie. I can't believe you'd suggest—"

"I'll take that to mean no, you didn't." Karan's sigh filtered over the phone. "Suze, what am I going to do with you?"

Susanna leaned back in the chair, a caned oak rocker that was one of a set gracing the gallery in front of her new home, the most picturesque cottage she had ever seen. Though it was dark, the moon illuminated the surrounding forest, and the quiet night sounds reminded her of the sunroom in the home she'd left in New York.

The evenings had once been a special time for her and Skip. After long, busy days. After bedtime stories and tucking in the kids, Susanna would brew a pot of coffee and she and Skip would sit in the sunroom and share the events of their day. For a blissful few moments, they reconnected as a couple to the peaceful night sounds of the conservation lot that bordered their backyard.

"Don't worry, Karan," Susanna said, knowing her friend would continue to do precisely that. "I'll settle down once I get comfortable here. There's been a lot of travel and a lot of change. Nerves are completely normal."

"You're holding up?" Karan asked. "All's well?"

"So far, so good. I've been going nonstop all day at the facility. And I'm here, if not unpacked. I'll get there when I get there."

"But you're happy with the arrangement?"

"I was so relieved when I saw this place I got weepy. Jay must think I'm the biggest idiot."

"Who's Jay?" Karan asked.

Karan zeroed in on what she considered most important. Men would always top that list. That had been the way it was in middle school. That was the way it was in middle age.

Not that *almost* forty was exactly middle age. Not if Susanna planned to live to be a hundred, anyway.

"Jay Canady, owner and property administrator of The Arbors."

"The man you've got to convince to sell the property."

"One and the same." A man with a charming smile and melodic voice.

"What's he like? Helpful, I hope."

"Very, I'm happy to report. Not really what I expected."

"How so?"

Susanna paused before answering. "He wants the acquisition to happen, but on his terms. I haven't figured out much more than that yet. I'm too busy getting acclimated."

"Do you think you're going to like the job? It's a lot different than what you'd been doing."

A lot more responsibility. Karan was probably right to worry especially because she knew everything involved in making this move—all the worries, all the uncertainty, all the indecision.

She also understood how much of Susanna's peace of mind rode on things falling into place to reassure her that relocating her family had been the right choice. Karan knew everything because they were BFFs, as Brooke always called them.

Best friends forever.

This would be the first time since middle school they'd lived so far apart. Of course, Karan traveled a lot, not to

mention splitting home base between residences in the
Catskills, Manhattan and on the Connecticut shore, but not
even college or marriage—*marriages* in Karan's case—
had placed as much distance between them as this job.

"I think this place is what I need right now. The learning curve will distract me, so I won't miss the kids so
much."

"As long as it doesn't keep you too distracted. You
need to get a life, Suze. It's time. Past time, to be honest."

"I know. I know." But knowing and doing were two different things, Susanna had discovered. Between her kids
growing up and moving away and leaving New York behind herself, she felt as if the grieving process had started
all over again. Maybe not as overwhelming as it had been
in the months after Skip's death, but she felt just as isolated, alone.

Rising, she headed inside, nudged the door shut behind
her, suddenly needing light and walls around her. "I took
a big step by taking this job."

"You did," Karan acknowledged.

Setting the cup on the coffee table, Susanna glanced at
a photo she'd placed in the living room. The only unpacking she'd done aside from hanging up her suits had been
to place a photo in every room, so wherever she turned
she'd see the face of someone she loved.

Karan and her husband Charles's wedding photo was
in the dining room. Brooke's and Brandon's smiling faces
graced several rooms. In this photo they sat in front of last
year's Christmas tree. Their last Christmas in their home.

Ugh. "It's another world around here." Susanna
switched gears to bridge the distance she suddenly felt
from her old life. "You will not believe my new place. Totally *Gone with the Wind,* I swear."

"Tara or the slave quarters? You keep saying *guest cottage*. It sounds small."

"Don't start." She sank onto the sofa, into soft cushions. Definitely down-filled. Something she'd never have been able to indulge in when the kids had been young. A sofa like this might have lasted two hours during the pillow fights or fort-makings at one of Brandon's slumber parties.

"There are flowers everywhere. The place is called The Arbors for good reason. Walter said it'll be even more beautiful when everything's in spring bloom. I can't even imagine. The place is already heaven everywhere I look."

"I know you love that, Ms. Green Thumb. And here you were worried about leaving your conservation lot. Who's Walter?"

"The property CFO."

"He'll be staying with you after the transition?"

"Walter and everyone else on the payroll. Jay has negotiated provisions for all the personnel. I won't be making any changes without putting up a fight."

"Then let's hope you like everyone. Particularly Walter, since he's doing your old job. You're a tough act to follow."

Susanna envisioned the white-haired gentleman with the deep drawl. "He's been on the payroll for longer than I've been alive. He's got things under control."

"Sounds like your first few days are going well."

"Thank God. At first glance, everyone appears capable and efficient. They've definitely been friendly. Lots of real Southern charm around here."

"Everyone is probably as worried about keeping their jobs as you are, Suze. Remember that. Once Northstar starts cutting the checks, those loyalties will make the transition, too."

"Fingers crossed. But I am encouraged. With the facility and the people."

"And the living arrangements."

"Thankfully." Not that decor and design mattered all that much. Unless the place had been a trailer on cinder blocks, Susanna was moving in because the price was right.

Free housing was part of her package. Gerald had convinced Northstar she should be on the property to accommodate a staff used to constant access to Jay. And Jay had needed to assume some financial responsibility to offset expenses in the event he chose not to sign in the end. This was one of the perks that didn't cost him.

But Susanna never shared financial worries with Karan if she could help it. Her BFF had grown up in a much loftier tax bracket. As a result she was casual with money in a way that only came from never having to worry about whether or not there'd be enough.

"Explain to me how you're going to be homeless when I own all these houses?" Karan had said in some variation more than once. *"Take the kids and live in the lake house or the beach house or go to Manhattan. Brooke loves it there."*

For Karan the move would be that simple. She had such a giving heart. Ironically, she also had no clue how generous she was, which was one of the very reasons Susanna adored her.

"Define *encouraged*," Karan said. "Does that translate to mean you'll get used to living in the guest cottage?"

"This place is perfect for me. I'm one person."

"Not if you want me to visit. Or your kids."

"Brooke can sleep with me and Brandon can bunk in the office. You know we're big on slumber parties. For you and Charles, there's a Hilton on the other side of the UNC campus. I already checked."

"Good. How big is Jay's place?"

"Think Tara in *Gone with the Wind*."

Silence.

"What?" Susanna asked.

"Well, I'm not sure how I feel about a man who lives in a plantation and leaves you in the slave quarters. He couldn't clear out a wing? He is selling the place and moving, right?"

"Jay didn't put me anywhere. Northstar made the arrangements."

"What are they doing with the plantation?"

"One of my objectives is to make recommendations. Northstar is looking at the potential for a rehab facility or maybe adding a facility that's not specifically Alzheimer's related. I haven't seen the place in person yet, but it's old, so renovating to code could be expensive. I'll have to see."

A task for another day. She could tackle only one thing at a time without feeling overwhelmed. She was already bolting upright in bed hours before the alarm rang.

"Well, you've got time," Karan said generously. "Brooke won't graduate until next year. I'd be surprised if she didn't decide to settle near you."

"If the acquisition goes as planned, I'll know whether or not I want to buy something. If Brooke likes it in Charlotte, we'll set up a new home base."

"And you can get a life again. You don't want to spend the rest of your life alone, do you?"

"No, please." She exhaled a long breath. "Not the dating speech. I'm too fragile for that right now."

"No mercy. You're too young to wait around until Brooke or Brandon make you a grandmother. You need to get out and have some fun. I realize it's been a while for you, but there's more to life than just working and taking care of everyone. I know you had all your plans laid out, but things have changed. You need a new plan."

Susanna had always been the focused one, the one who'd known what she wanted. Karan was worried. And right. Susanna did need to figure out how to move on with her life.

And she would. But until the kids were on their own, finances took precedence. Meeting her family's needs was top priority, which meant she had to do everything in her power to insure that Northstar acquired The Arbors. And that meant when she wasn't in the facility learning how to be a property administrator, she was at home boning up on Alzheimer's care.

Was she hiding from moving on with life? Probably. Did Karan know she was hiding? Probably.

But there were only so many hours in the day. "I'll figure things out, Karan. One step at a time, and you'll help me. Just like you always do."

CHAPTER FOUR

JAY HAD VISITED THE COTTAGE every night since Susanna had arrived a week ago. First night he'd helped her unpack her suitcases and shown her around. Second night had been a blown electrical breaker. Third night was a problem with the washing machine, which hadn't been used since Walter's niece had needed a place to stay during a divorce.

Repairs were the nature of old houses, and old houses were Jay's life. While the facility and guest cottage didn't come close to touching the age of the main house, they weren't new by anyone's estimation. In fact, when he figured out where he wanted to put down roots, he'd build a brand-new place so he wouldn't have to worry about anything going wrong for a while. And when something eventually needed repairing, he could to run to any Home Depot to pick up standard-size parts. Better yet, he'd call a repairman.

But that sweet plan was still months away. With any luck he'd fix everything that needed fixing before signing the final papers, so Susanna could get a few repair-free months. Then the grief would belong to Northstar.

The dogs had accompanied Jay on each of his visits, and tonight was no different. They ran beside the golf cart as he steered into the yard then they bolted for the door.

Jay whistled, but the dogs ignored him, nails clattering on the wood as they clambered up the porch steps. Following, he found the door ajar and hoped Susanna had left it open; otherwise, he'd be back again tomorrow night to replace the lock.

"Butters, Gatsby," he called through the doorway, hoping the beasts hadn't trashed the place.

That familiar high-pitched greeting from the back of the house sparked another round of barking. Jay stood in the threshold, undecided about whether to wait for an invitation. He didn't want to be as rude as his dogs, so he remained outside, listening to the commotion within.

Butters and Gatsby liked Susanna. Jay wouldn't admit this aloud, but he could tell everything he needed to know about a person from his dogs. They were the best yardstick. Might sound crazy but he'd learned the trick while trailing his great-grandfather to the barns when this place had still incorporated a farm.

"Animals will tell you what's going on in a person's heart," Great-Granddad had said. He'd been gesturing to the goats and herd dogs, but he'd meant all the animals on the farm. *"If they shy away, you'll do well to shy away, too."*

Wisdom or wives' tale, Jay couldn't say, but the advice had stuck and hadn't yet failed in all these years.

"Lose anyone?" Susanna's voice brimmed with laughter as she appeared with the dogs flanking her, their shaggy tails wagging close to lamps and knickknacks.

She'd already changed from her work clothes into jeans and a pullover sweater that outlined her trim curves.

"Boys," Jay said, and both dogs finally decided to show some manners by obeying the command. "Sorry about that."

"Not a problem. They're such sweethearts. I invited them to visit any time they like. And I promised some treats as soon as I shop." Reaching down to ruffle Gatsby's chest, she displayed a wedge of creamy skin when her sweater rode up on her waist. "Sorry, boys. I've got grocery shopping on my to-do list, but I can't seem to get there." She glanced at Jay. "What do they like if and when I do actually make it to a store?"

It was such an innocent glance to accompany an innocent question. She was being nice, he knew, but when he met her gaze, her eyes so blue they looked almost purple, her one nice gesture drove home how closely their lives had become entwined in the short time since her arrival.

He wondered what she'd been eating if she hadn't shopped. Liz, the dietary manager, had been sending lunches to Susanna's office, but that couldn't be all Susanna was eating, could it?

"Dog bones if they're eating like dogs. Chicken and steak when they're not."

She smiled in that quick way of hers, as if she was just looking for reasons to smile. "They're in luck, then. Dog bones will go on the grocery list, and I cook chicken and steak."

"If you spoil them, you'll never get rid of them. Consider yourself warned."

"They're welcome here anytime."

The greedy beggars could spot a sucker a mile away. They crowded around her legs until she felt obligated to pet them and make those squeaky cooing sounds again. Jay took the opportunity to shoot off a text to Pete, who was duty manager tonight.

"So how are you settling in?" Jay asked when she finally realized the dogs would vie for her undivided attention all day if she let them. "Place working out? It's small."

"It is," she agreed, "but it couldn't be more perfect."

That smile still tugged at the corners of her mouth as she surveyed the room, looking pleased. "Just me here."

"Saw the pictures of your kids all over the place. Will they be coming to visit?"

She nodded, her features softening with a mother's expression, all fond memories and love. "Hopefully Thanksgiving. My son plays baseball, so his schedule can be tricky with practice and ball camps."

There was a lot of longing in that statement, which said something about how much she cared. Something reassuring, which calmed a bit of the guilt that still crept up when he least expected it. And when he did.

Was he being selfish to want the kind of life that made him sound like Susanna did, a life where he had something more to look forward to than home repairs, the never-ending needs of the facility and dementia? Was that really too much to ask? He still lived in the house he'd been born in. He'd put in his time.

"I know you haven't asked for my advice, Susanna, but I'm going to give it, anyway. Make a point to get off the property. There's a lot going on in town, and it's good to get away. The Arbors has a way of commandeering time. We call it Standard Arbor Time and it's nonstop, around the clock."

"I think I've seen a glimpse of that this week." She sounded charmed by the idea.

Jay supposed he shouldn't be surprised, with the way she worked from sunup to sundown. But something told him busy was exactly the way she wanted to be right now. Funny how life had them in exactly the opposite places. She'd reared her family and wanted to be busy. He wanted to get busy rearing a family and filling his days with something other than dementia care.

He wondered how long ago her husband had died. Had his death been unexpected? Jay didn't ask. Her personal life was none of his business even if there had been some tactful way to ask about a dead spouse. There wasn't.

Leaning against the arch separating living room from dining room, she folded her arms over her chest. "Amber mentioned a mall by the racetrack. And I read about a historic plantation I'd like to visit that's not far from here."

"That's a start." And then they were staring at each other across the expanse of newly polished floors and overly friendly dogs. He might have kept standing and staring except Butters sidled toward the wall shelves, knocking some sense into Jay.

"The golf cart?" he prompted, forcing himself to stop enjoying the view. "It's easy to operate, but you need to know about the battery. Chester will keep his eye on it. You let him know when it needs to be fueled."

"I can park it near the maintenance and engineering shed where you keep yours?"

He nodded.

"Please show me whatever you think I need to know. I didn't mean to keep you. You were kind to offer your help."

Pushing away from the wall, she breezed past him with that same breathless energy and graceful motion he noticed every time he looked at her. She headed outside and he moved to follow, but the dogs cut him off, nearly knocking him over in their haste to trail her. Sorry beasts.

Jay headed after them, making sure he didn't pay attention to the gentle sway of Susanna's hips as she took the stairs with light steps or to the dark curls bouncing on her shoulders. She chatted the whole way as if she didn't want to hear any more silence between them, either.

"I understand from Gerald that your grandmother is responsible for building the main facility. What about this cottage? There are so many antiques."

"This place was my mother's." Her hideaway from the world.

"She collected antiques?"

"Sort of. Stuff she picked up here and there. My place is filled to the brim. She has a collection of mantels. You'll have to see them one day."

Had he just invited Susanna to his place?

There was a hitch in her step as she slanted a curious gaze his way. "Mantels? As in fireplaces?"

"You got it. I've got mantels without fireplaces attached to them. She turned one into a bed frame. She was crazy for them. Doors and windows, too. Used to drag the family to pick through old buildings while most folks were doing yardwork or watching Saturday morning cartoons."

"The mantel in my living room?"

"From a pre-Civil War cypress cottage near the coast. Took her a while to bring that one back to its original finish. It had taken a beating from being so close to the salt water."

Susanna stepped up her pace again. "Humph. How imaginative. I would never have thought of anything so creative."

"She was that." Before Alzheimer's claimed her, and all he had left of his loving, laughing and infinitely creative mother was a bunch of mantels, doorknobs and windowsills.

"I for one am very grateful," Susanna said graciously. "Did she use this as the guest cottage?"

"Sometimes. When we had guests who didn't want to stay in the house with us. She had some cousins who used to visit from Ireland. They were older and with my brother and I tearing around like wild boys… Well, let's say they enjoyed a place where they could go for some quiet. My mother, too. She used the cottage for work. She liked to leave the house and have a place where she could concentrate without too many distractions."

"Work?" Susanna's interest piqued visibly. "Your mother didn't work at The Arbors?"

"Everyone in my family worked at The Arbors." Past tense. Wasn't anyone left but him. Except for Drew, who didn't count, but Jay wouldn't dwell on something he couldn't change. And he couldn't change his brother. "My mother was a writer, too. Whenever she was on deadline, she liked to wrap her head around her work. Used to tell my brother and me not to show up unless we were bleeding."

Susanna went to the passenger side of the golf cart. "I've said the same to my kids."

Jay would take her word for it, since he hadn't gotten to that part of his life *yet*. "Ever drive one of these before?"

Susanna shook her head, more glossy waves tumbling around her neck and shoulders in a display that was so feminine, so at odds with her ultra-businesslike appearance.

But not right now. Not when she was casually dressed, all tiny and curvy and tucking her waves behind her ears as she leaned eagerly toward the controls for instruction.

Circling the golf cart, he hopped in and explained the basics. He showed her how to disconnect the battery when she parked the vehicle then took her for a spin to the access road, with the dogs trotting beside him as they always did.

Then they swapped seats and she took him for a spin, starting off tentatively but increasing speed as she gained confidence.

"Not so close, Butters," she shrieked while making a turn. "They won't get too close and get hurt?"

"Not a chance. They keep up with me all the time. Have

since they were pups. And if they don't get out of the way of a moving vehicle they deserve what they get."

He had to work to keep a straight face as he enjoyed her horrified expression. "They'll move if you get too close."

"Keep your distance, Butters. I'm serious."

"That your mom voice?"

She scowled at him, and he lost the battle with a smile.

"So what did your mother write?" she asked after another lap around the cottage.

"Fiction. Literary stuff for magazines. Short stories mostly. Had a few anthology collections published."

Slowing as she cornered the house yet again, she paid close attention to the dogs as she parked. "How interesting. I bet she got lots of inspiration from around here. From what I've seen so far, this place is another world."

"Oh, it's that. No question."

She chuckled, taking the opportunity to ruffle Butters's neck when he nuzzled up to her. "Keep out from under the tires. Promise me."

The dog was so greedy for attention he would have promised to live forever. Jay escorted Susanna back to the porch before heading out with his dogs again, but she stopped short and said, "Where on earth did that come from?"

Taking the stairs with light steps, she made an attractive display as she leaned over the big basket propped in a rocking chair. Even in profile, he could see her expression soften as she inspected the gifts.

Perfect timing, Pete.

"Guess I should have had it waiting when you got here a week ago," he admitted. "But I didn't think about it until you said you hadn't made it to the grocery. Welcome to The Arbors."

"Oh, Jay, how kind. Thank you so much. This couldn't

be more perfect." She looked as if she was going to pick up the basket, so Jay skipped up a few steps and took it from her.

"Tell me where."

She held the door as he stepped through, or tried to, since the dogs bullied their way in first. "Kitchen, please."

He scowled at Gatsby, who headed straight for the sofa. "Don't even think about it."

For once the dog obeyed.

"I'm so excited," she said. "I won't even have to fight my kids for the chocolate. That'll be something new."

The new director of The Arbors had a sweet tooth from the looks of it. She was rooting through the basket. "These pears are gorgeous. And caramel popcorn. Oh, I'm in for a good time."

"Hope you enjoy it."

She glanced up and met his gaze with pleasure deep in her blue eyes. "This was really sweet. Thank you. I couldn't have asked for a better first week—work or home."

She was making too big a deal out of his effort. All he'd done was text Pete to bring the same welcome basket they gave to all The Arbors' new ALF residents.

But he was glad she liked everything.

Herding Butters and Gatsby outside, he let the dogs scamper down the steps and said to Susanna, "Enjoy your night."

Then he headed in the direction of the shed to pick up the path to his house, resisting the urge to glance back to see if she was still there.

ANOTHER WEEK PASSED before Susanna managed to get the golf cart out of her shed. A frenzied week spent learning names and procedures and routines. A week spent observing medical assessments, intake meetings and care plan evaluations.

A week spent conducting performance appraisals of the various departments and orientation meetings to explain how she and Jay would work together during the transition. She let the staff know what to expect and coached them on how to address her with problems and questions. She reassured them all would be well and hoped they believed her.

Vanity had been the biggest deterrent to driving the golf cart. She was all about inspiring confidence with the staff and fitting in and couldn't gauge the effect of the drive on her appearance. Frizzy hair? Melting makeup? Sweat stains?

But she'd begun to feel ridiculous and wasteful for taking the car on the short drive, when Jay arrived at the facility every morning with every hair in place. Except for the hair he was always pushing back off his forehead, but Susanna guessed that was a result of a cowlick rather than the morning ride.

She waited until dawn began to fade the sky before heading outside. She hadn't wanted to tackle the unfamiliar path in the dark even though she'd been raring to go for an hour already.

Two weeks into her new life and the nerves still hadn't worn off. She crashed at night, bone weary from the long days of information overload. Unfortunately, she was still bolting upright as quickly as she had upon first arriving at The Arbors, and usually long before the alarm, thoughts racing with the upcoming day's agenda.

With any luck, the ride in the brisk predawn air would start her day off right. God knows she could use some fresh air.

Then there was the fact that she didn't want to miss anything on this journey. Especially not Jay's house.

Her phone vibrated as she clambered into the golf cart, and she hoped her plans wouldn't be derailed by an emergency at the facility that would force her back into the car.

But the name on the display surprised her. "Good morning, Karan. What are you doing up at this ungodly hour?"

"Your guess," Karan replied. "Saw Charles off to surgery and was wide-awake. Figured I'd give you a call since you're the only one I know awake at this hour besides my doctor husband."

Susanna held the phone to her ear and backed out of the shed slowly. "You're in time for a journey through the arbors to The Arbors."

"Maybe I'm not as awake as I thought—"

"Remember those acres and acres of flowers I mentioned? I'm taking the golf cart to work so I can see them."

"I hope you don't wilt like a flower. Isn't that what you Southern belles do?"

"I don't think I've been here long enough to qualify as a girl raised in the South."

"Pshaw. You've been a G.R.I.T. from the minute you crossed the Mason-Dixon Line. A Girl *Relocated* to the South."

"Tee-hee."

"You sound awfully chipper this morning," Karan said. "May I assume work's going well and you're getting some sleep?"

One out of two wasn't bad, and *some sleep* was relative. "Can't complain. I'm finally going to see Jay's house. It should be right off this path."

"I thought you were supposed to assess the place."

"Not on the top of my to-do list. That report won't be due until the acquisition."

"You sound confident. Things must be going well."

Susanna held on tight as the cart bucked over a protruding tree root. "We've hit a few bumps, but nothing we haven't been able to work through."

Yet. They hadn't tackled the profit-and-loss statements, either. Jay insisted on full disclosure so he could gauge the corporate effects on The Arbors, and she was using every ounce of her financial expertise to figure out how wide the disconnect was between his services and payroll and Northstar's parameters. Juggling was the key, which put sleepless hours to good use.

"We're still in the honeymoon phase," Susanna admitted. "Jay's walking me through the way things work at The Arbors so we haven't done a lot of procedural projections. There's time."

"You think that's the best way to handle—"

"Ohmigosh, Karan. I think this is it," Susanna blurted when a low brick wall appeared through a sudden break in the trees, a vision of manicured civilization in the forest.

"The plantation?"

"Yes. This has to be it. We've got formal landscaping. Tiered bushes and ornamental grasses and flowering vines. It is. Here's the entry."

There was no gate, only an opening marked by stone urns, both stained by rust from the irrigation water. The flagstone walk bore similar stains and wound into another world.

Jay's world.

"Ohmigosh." Susanna whispered reverently into the quiet morning. "This must be the backyard. There's a huge lawn with those big oak trees you see in movies. Generations old like the arbors. Jay told me his great-grandmother planted them."

"See the house yet?"

"House doesn't even begin to describe it, Karan. Seriously. Can you say 'antebellum plantation'?"

"Tara?"

"Actually, no." Susanna laughed. "Except for the ambience of another era. The house isn't even white. Just the eaves."

Those eaves towered above two floors with massive white columns that outlined a wraparound gallery. The house had been constructed of blond brick, and the walls contrasted with the black shutters that framed every floor-to-ceiling window. And there were a lot more windows than the three that graced the porch of her cottage.

She couldn't even begin to fathom what might drive someone away from The Arbors, and she knew the curiosity might kill her.

"You know, Karan, my cottage is very similar in design. I'll bet that was intentional. A miniplantation."

"Brooke should like that. She's always loved dollhouses."

As Karan would know since she'd indulged that particular fancy since Brooke was old enough to be trusted not to gnaw on the tiny furnishings of the ridiculously expensive dollhouses Karan gifted her with.

"Fingers crossed. I really want the kids to consider wherever I live as home base. At least until they settle down."

"As long as you're there it will be home base."

Susanna appreciated the reassurance. The most important thing was being together. "I think I can see the driveway. I'll bet if I took a left at the fork instead of the right that brings me to the cottage, I'd wind up here."

"I can't believe this is the first time you're seeing the house. With as much as you say 'Jay this' and 'Jay that,' I can't believe he hasn't invited you over for a Bundt cake or pecan divinity or whatever Southerners do to welcome neighbors."

"It's not like that, Karan. I told you. But I'm really dying to know what could possibly possess him to sell this place. It's a total mystery."

"Ask him."

"I can't ask him something personal like that."

"Why not? Seems a logical question to me given the fact you're taking over his job."

"Because I can't."

There was a beat of silence on the other end before Karan said, "You're working awfully hard to delineate boundaries between professional and personal. What's up with that?"

"I don't know what you mean." Susanna only knew she'd better get a move on. She didn't want to get caught gawking at Jay's house like a tourist.

"I'm talking about how many times you've mentioned getting personal with this man. I hear it every time we talk. You're curious about him, Suze."

"Of course I'm curious. Why doesn't he simply parcel off the land, sell The Arbors and keep his family home?"

"Why don't you ask him? Oh, wait. That's personal. Are you interested in Jay? I mean *interested,* interested."

"Stop it. That isn't funny." Neither was the heat rushing into her cheeks at the mere mention of being interested in Jay. "I'll have a hand in deciding the fate of the man's house." And wherever Jay was headed must be incredible considering what he'd be leaving behind. "That's all, Karan."

"Mmm-hmm."

"I can't even believe you. Some best friend."

"What can't you believe—that I know you so well? What kind of best friend would I be if I let you lie to yourself?"

Susanna slowed the golf cart to a stop, pulled the phone

away from her ear and scowled at it, a thrill of annoyance overshadowing the excitement of a moment ago. "That's unfair."

"Are you sure?"

Susanna didn't answer because that simple question had a complicated answer. Karan wasn't entirely wrong. Susanna couldn't think about being interested in another man, not Jay or anyone. The very thought made her uncomfortable deep inside, not so much guilty as...unable.

She hadn't realized until this very moment.

"I'm broken," she admitted.

"No, my dear sweet friend," Karan said in a thoughtful tone. "You're just making peace with the hand life dealt you. You and Skip had big plans, and things didn't turn out as you expected. You need a new plan."

"Is that what's happening?"

"I think so. You were with Skip for your entire adult life. Now he's gone. It's got to be easier to shut down a part of yourself than it is to open up and take chances on living a life you didn't imagine."

Susanna let the idea filter through her, stared down the path beneath the arbors in the paling dawn, vines winding through trellises and archways so twisted it would be difficult to follow any one to the root. Impossible to separate.

She and Skip had been like that. Their lives entwined into one, so now she couldn't find her own roots, didn't think she'd ever bloom again.

"I'm broken. If I wasn't, I'd be able to figure out how to move on, because I know better than to waste a second when none of us have any idea what the future holds."

"True, true," Karan said. "But you're not wrong to feel the way you do, Suze. You know, but you're human."

"I have everything in the world to be grateful for. I shouldn't be stuck—"

"You are grateful. You're the most grateful person I know. You don't waste a second with your kids or me or anyone you love. I'm just saying that you need to branch out. Before you're old and gray and no man would ever want you."

"Karan." But Susanna found herself smiling.

"There's nothing wrong with being interested in Jay."

"This isn't about Jay. It's about me."

But Karan laughed a knowing laugh. And kept laughing until Susanna hit the gas and took off, obligated to drown out the laughter with some very rational arguments.

"He's helping me learn the ropes around here. And even if that wasn't the case, even if I was stupid enough to jeopardize the acquisition by mixing business with pleasure, Jay couldn't possibly be in the running."

"Why's that?"

"The man is younger than I am. *Seven years* younger. That's another lifetime. And, oh, did I mention he's *leaving?* As in selling this place?"

"I hear what you're saying. Now hear what I'm saying. I know you. Listing all the reasons you can't be interested in a man isn't going to change the fact if you are."

"I'm not. I just met him, for heaven's sake."

"I'll reserve opinion if you don't mind. I'm the one you used to drag through Ashokan High so you could *accidentally* run into Skip, remember? 'He has second lunch so let's walk all the way around the freaking school to get to our lockers so we have to go through the cafeteria.' This ringing a bell?"

Susanna crushed the phone against her ear as if that might block out the sound of Karan's voice. Her heart suddenly pounded too hard. "You're ridiculous, Karan. I'm not in ninth grade. I'm forty years old—"

"You're not forty yet, thank you very much."

Of course she wasn't, because then Karan would be forty, as her birthday was nearly a full month before Susanna's. "Whatever. I outgrew crushes a long time ago."

"So long ago you might not remember what one was?"

"Puh-leeze." She sounded alarmingly like Brooke. Daughters grew up to be like their mothers but Susanna had had no idea the reverse was true. "I'd remember a crush. Trust me."

"You sure about that, Suze? The last time you had a crush on anyone you were a virgin. That makes the sum total of your experience, one man, a really long time ago."

And he'd been the right man.

"I had a lot of sex in my fifteen years of marriage, thank you." Likely even more than Karan, who'd had three marriages to two men plus one long-term relationship and a lot of time off in between. Susanna kept that observation to herself.

"It matters. You were comfortable with your husband. You both grew together. That's different than dating."

"My kids are dating."

"Sounds like their mother might want to be, too."

"I have not had enough caffeine for this yet."

The path wound around the west side of the lake. Zipping past her own office window, too dark to see inside except for the tiny red glow of the emergency exit sign above the door, she headed toward the maintenance and engineering building, relieved to see empty space where she knew Jay normally parked.

She didn't want to see him, not with all these thoughts Karan had planted in her head.

"I have to go." She needed to recover from their topic of conversation.

"Susanna, seven years does not make you a cougar if

he's an adult and not a man-child. Biological age doesn't make that distinction. Maturity does."

Susanna mentally twitched. *Cougar.* Just the thought was enough to conjure visions of Jerry Springer and celebrities older than herself who dressed like Brooke.

"You are killing me here."

"Don't be silly, and don't shut me down. You've been alone a long time."

"Like I've had time to even think about *that.*"

"I know you haven't had time. But I don't want to see you blow right past something good if the time is right."

"Are you not listening to me? The time isn't right. Even if I was interested, we're in two entirely places in our lives. I've raised my family. He doesn't even have one."

"Does he want one?"

"How should I know?"

"You could ask… Oh, wait. That's personal." There was a smile in Karan's voice. "I'm compelled to mention that you can enjoy yourself without mating for life."

Susanna came to a sudden stop and stared into the mist over the lake, unsure she'd heard correctly.

"You know what I'm talking about, Susanna. Kissing frogs, remember? Every date doesn't have to be a potential bridegroom."

Susanna couldn't even dignify this conversation with a reply. Maybe if they were discussing another man, *any* other man. But not Jay with the bright green eyes and charming laughter. Not the man she had to coax past the honeymoon phase and into Northstar's business model with a smile on his face.

CHAPTER FIVE

DAYS PASSED BEFORE Susanna could look at Jay without recalling that disturbing phone conversation with Karan. Days when every smile was suspect. Days when every laugh felt indicative of whether she needed to kiss a frog. Or wanted to.

No.

Karan was wrong there. But the rest…transitioning into a woman who, while still a mother, could live a fulfilled life of her own. Karan wasn't wrong about that. Something was in Susanna's way, had been since Skip had died. Until she'd sold the house, and her two biggest reasons to get up in the morning had gone off to college, Susanna hadn't been forced to analyze the situation too closely, too honestly. She'd been in her familiar home working her familiar job, which had helped to balance the *un*familiar.

Skip's death. Financial struggles. Grown kids.

She no longer had the luxury of familiar. Add to that pressure from every angle. The kids were counting on her to create a new home base, to continue providing. They looked to her to be an emotional anchor as they branched into adulthood. They looked to her to financially provide all that their scholarships and summer jobs couldn't.

Add Northstar, who believed she'd persuade Jay to close the deal. And The Arbors' staff, who expected an administrator on par with the one who was leaving. And Jay, who looked to her to transition his private facility into a corporate one without losing the private.

Pressure, pressure, *pressure* wherever she turned.

She found herself asking: How could she transition The Arbors when she wasn't successfully transitioning in her life?

And Karan thought she should be worried about dating? *Only* Karan.

Susanna couldn't do a thing but tackle the learning curve of a property administrator. She couldn't do anything but continue to educate herself about Alzheimer's care. She certainly couldn't afford asking questions that undermined her confidence. She needed to keep moving forward and not complicate life any more than it was already.

Susanna found a bit of a break from her worries in the comfort zone of quarterly reports as she prepared for the financial review with Walter.

On the morning of the first of their formal review meetings, Susanna arrived on the property earlier than usual. After checking in with the duty manager, she conducted her own walk-through of lockdown. As she emerged from the stairs on the third floor, she nearly ran into a resident on a crack-of-dawn stroll from the dining room with plastic bags of bread stacked high in the basket of her walker.

Mrs. Harper apparently didn't notice Susanna, who stopped short to avoid a collision then watched curiously as the small but agile woman with the head full of steely curls tooled down the hall toward her apartment. Travis and Goldie, caged parakeets who made their home in a hallway alcove, tittered excitedly as she passed. Travis wolf-whistled, but the object of his attention kept a slow and steady pace, not acknowledging the compliment in any way.

While the ALF portions of the facility weren't as closely monitored as the first floor, all three floors were on lockdown, which meant someone knew Mrs. Harper was running around when most residents were still in their apartments.

"That one does gets around, Ms. Adams," the floor nurse explained after she emerged from an apartment. "Keeps us on our toes. Wish more residents would take advantage of the freedoms they have up here. The exercise is so good for them."

Susanna agreed and was about to ask about the bread but the radio crackled and the duty manager announced, "Got the shift report done. Will you sign off, or is Mr. C. around?"

Encouraged the management had approached her rather than wait for Jay, Susanna hurried to the first floor and forgot to ask about the bread.

JAY HAD HEARD THROUGH the grapevine that Susanna had long been on the property today, but he hadn't seen her yet. She'd been spending a lot of time in her office these past few days while he'd been busy babysitting Walter, who wanted to go over the budget variances for "one last look" for the fiftieth time before the formal financial review, where his work would be held against a corporate yardstick.

After Jay had finally escaped Walter at noon, he was quickly cornered in the north wing common area on the third floor by Winnie, a private aide.

"Did you tell Mrs. Harper she can't have the bread?"

Jay stared stupidly for a moment, mentally translating. Thanks to Winnie's heavy Spanish accent, her question came out sounding something like:

"Did-a you tell-a Meesus Harper she canna have zee bread?"

"Why would I tell Mrs. Harper that?"

"I do not know. That's why I asked."

Fair enough. "No. I did not tell Mrs. Harper she couldn't have the bread. What's the problem?"

Winnie launched into an animated tale, and Jay caught about every fourth or fifth word. Unfortunately, when Winnie got going, her hands started flying and she spoke so fast a native Spanish speaker would struggle to get the message.

Jay eventually got the gist. "No, I did not tell the new administrator to cut off Mrs. Harper," he assured Winnie.

A woman in the mid stages of Alzheimer's plus an administrator who hadn't yet familiarized herself with all the residents' routines made for an interesting encounter.

"There's some sort of misunderstanding, Winnie. Tell Mrs. Harper I'll sort things out and not to worry. She can pick up her bread as usual on—" today was Monday "—Thursday. I'll make sure Dietary isn't throwing any away."

"Gracias, Mr. C. *Gracias,"* Winnie said breathlessly. "I tell her right now. Right this very minute."

"You do that, Winnie, and thanks for letting me know."

Jay escaped, heading straight for Dietary, where he let Liz know that the long-standing order for bread still stood. Then he found Winnie again, who explained that while she'd managed to calm Mrs. Harper down, she'd only managed after the woman had called her son to report the grave injustice. "I tried, Mr. C. Too late. You may geet a call from Mr. George."

"No problem, Winnie. I'll explain what happened." Once he figured that out.

After a brief appearance in physical therapy, he headed

to Susanna's office. She sat behind her desk, squinting at the computer monitor with a pensive expression.

He got right to business and explained the situation.

"I don't understand, Jay," she said. "Mrs. Harper thought I said she couldn't have leftover bread anymore?"

He nodded.

"Oh." Her mouth did the most distracting things when she was thinking. Lips parted around a breathy sound then tucked tight. She was perplexed. So was he. This woman was his ticket out of The Arbors. Nothing more. So why did he notice her sheer blouse stretched across her bosom as she sank back in her chair?

"I must not have done a very good job of expressing myself," Susanna finally said. "I saw Mrs. Harper with all that bread and was curious. Little lady. Lots of bread. I thought it was a good opportunity to introduce myself, so I tracked her down in the dayroom."

"She says her rosary there every morning. In the afternoon she goes to the south wing. Did she tell you her son brought those rosary beads from the Vatican? Blessed by the Pope."

Susanna smiled. "She did. We chatted and I asked about the bread. She never actually told me what she did with it, so I'm not sure what I said to give her the impression she couldn't have any more. I'm sorry there was confusion. Do you think I should address the issue with her?"

Susanna's offer surprised him. Admirable, but Mrs. Harper probably wouldn't remember by now. Susanna must not be familiar with the extent of Mrs. Harper's dementia. There were a hundred and twenty residents here, each with a unique set of circumstances and a debilitating disease that progressed differently in each and every person. It would take time for Susanna to learn the nuances of each resident.

"Winnie calmed her down," he said. "If her son calls, you could explain to him. Might be a good opportunity to introduce yourself. I'd be surprised if he called, though. He knows if there's a real problem, I'll let him know."

Susanna's big, blue eyes softened, and Jay thought she looked a bit relieved.

"So what does she do with all that bread?"

"Feeds the ducks. That's where she goes every morning after breakfast before she says her rosary. Down to the lake."

"By herself?"

While confusion was a standard state of affairs around here, Jay only expected to encounter it in the residents.

"I don't think she has her own passcode, but if I find out differently we'll reprogram the system," he said lightly.

She made a face, clearly not amused. "Who goes with her?"

"One of the staff takes her. Usually Tessa or Shirley while everyone is at breakfast, but if they're not available, then Amber takes her. Or Walter. I've gone with her, too. We send whoever can be spared."

"Have you ever approached Mrs. Harper's son about providing the services of a personal aide like Winnie? Winnie herself might even be available a few extra hours a week since she's already here."

For a suspended moment, Jay simply looked at her. Then it clicked. Susanna was worried about the payroll.

He cut her off at the pass. "Mrs. Harper is ninety-three years old. Half the time she can't remember her own name let alone her son and daughter-in-law's. But she remembers to bring bread to those ducks every morning because she knows they expect her. Not only is the exercise good for her, but Liz doesn't have to waste bread that doesn't get eaten. From start to finish the event takes thirty minutes at the most."

She frowned, but Jay wouldn't back down on this one. Mrs. Harper was more independent than most of the residents, and her family didn't need the added expense of an aide for one daily trip outdoors.

Northstar was supposed to be in the business of upscale senior living. The property administrator they'd sent should know The Arbors wasn't in the business of nickel and diming the residents. And a woman who ran a memory-care facility shouldn't need a lecture about what Alzheimer's cost its victims. Mrs. Harper had lost her family and friends, had lost *herself* on most days. Feeding the ducks was a big deal to her, one that put a smile on her face and made her feel good.

"I need a classification for the reports, Jay."

He detected a hint of annoyance in her tone. "Classify it as physical therapy, then, but it's really quality of life, Susanna. That's what we provide at The Arbors."

Period.

BY THE TIME SUSANNA had completed the financial review with Walter, she was not only impressed by that dear gentleman's skill at integrating financial and operational measures, but at her own progress managing stress. To be fair, her progress likely had to do with long hours spent analyzing Walter's performance measurement system and discussing how the acquisition would impact the financial structuring of The Arbors.

Walter possessed a lovely blend of modern and traditional financial leadership skills, balancing complex tasks of management and investment analysis while still acting as a conventional guardian and advocate of good planning.

Walter understood that certain things would change

after the acquisition by necessity. He also corroborated her own suspicion about Jay's concern about losing control.

"Boy's between a rock and a hard place," Walter had told her. "He's alone running this place since his parents died, and inheriting the job is different than choosing the job."

Yet he didn't want to abandon the people in his care. That said so much about the man Jay was. Walter's comments hadn't left Susanna any polite way to ask how Jay's parents had died without conducting an interrogation, and Susanna didn't want Walter to think she was gunning for inside information. But understanding his sense of obligation to The Arbors certainly explained his rigid and sometimes unrealistic expectations.

Trying to understand Jay was becoming a full-time preoccupation. She could never quite tell how he would react to some procedural suggestion she might make to bring operations more in line with what Northstar would require. He seemed to bounce between cooperation and stubbornness without any consistency. At least any that she could pinpoint yet.

There was still time. And the more she managed her stress, the clearer she could think. A positive step that suggested she was finally settling into her new position.

Sleep helped, too, and she'd *almost* managed to sleep through the nights with some help from melatonin, a natural mineral Karan's husband, Charles, had recommended.

Feeling rested would definitely come in handy, because she faced a demanding day. Today's meetings would implement a transfer of information into Northstar's systems for daily, weekly and monthly reports from all departments.

She wanted to check in with the duty manager first before sequestering herself in her office to go over her notes for the meetings. Reaching for the radio, she flipped the switch and said, "Good morning, Pete. This is Susanna. Where are you?"

The radio crackled and his voice shot back, "Outside Kimberly's office. Mr. Jankowski had a rough night."

"On my way."

Susanna found Pete outside the office at the CareCharter, previewing the display. "So what's up with Mr. Jankowski?"

Pete had a boyish face that made him appear younger than his mid-forties until one got close enough to realize what appeared to be blond hair was gray. "Trouble breathing."

"He started a new medication." Kimberly turned to the display where Mr. Jankowski's medical chart was visible. "He had his second dose after dinner then rang for the PCT around two o'clock this morning. I took a baseline and have been monitoring him since."

"A lot of trouble?" Susanna asked.

"I'm administering oxygen."

"What did Jay say?"

"Haven't called him," Pete said.

Susanna naturally assumed they'd notified Jay since they hadn't contacted her. There were specific procedures in place to handle emergency situations with the residents.

She was missing something. "Then where are we on this?"

"Debating whether or not to wait for the doctor to make rounds." Pete met her gaze.

Susanna saw the indecision in his expression, which offered only one solution. "Mr. Jankowski should go to the emergency room."

Pete frowned. "Actually, we were thinking of calling the doctor to advise us."

Following Kimberly's gaze, Susanna scanned the display to assess the extent of Mr. Jankowski's respiratory distress. "You think waiting for the doctor to make rounds is adequate?"

"Dr. Smith is usually in before nine, so it won't be much longer."

She glanced at the time on the display: 6:15 a.m. "When do you think you'll see a change in his condition if the problem is the medication? When the effects of the last dose wear off?"

"The side effects might linger," Kimberly explained. "He might need another medication to counter those effects. This also might be an episode relating to his heart condition if the new medication the doctor prescribed isn't working. Only the doctor can make that determination."

"Mr. Jankowski really hasn't been here long enough to evaluate with any certainty," Pete added. "He arrived a little before you did. We're still in the process of getting to know him and becoming familiar with his needs."

All of which took time, as Susanna well knew. She also knew the policy regarding the handling of medical situations was in place for a reason and didn't understand why there was so much hesitation about taking Mr. Jankowski to the emergency room. Especially since they didn't know him well.

As much as she didn't want to second-guess the staff or give the impression she didn't trust them to do their jobs, she was a firm believer in erring on the side of caution.

She respected liability, and explaining to a resident's family that every measure had been taken to care for a loved one was often the only consolation the family would get.

"Do you think the doctor will order tests?" she asked.

"If this is an episode, he'll likely order an EKG and an echo," Kimberly said.

"Which means the emergency room will be the most comprehensive place to administer those tests."

Kimberly frowned. "We administer those tests here."

"There's lead time involved with getting the mobile units. You believe that's in Mr. Jankowski's best interest?"

"I'm reassessing every half hour, Ms. Adams. Ryan's on the second floor, and I've got him peeking in, too. Mr. Jankowski is fairly comfortable at the moment. He needs to be evaluated, but he'll be so much more at ease here. And less compromised with all the airborne viruses this time of year."

Fairly comfortable?

Susanna wasn't particularly reassured. Mr. Jankowski's original heart condition remained untreated if he wasn't responding to the new medication. She wanted the man comfortable, too, but not at the expense of his health. Which brought her right back to erring on the side of caution.

"I'm not sure I understand what the problem is," Susanna said honestly. "Is there a reason you're both reluctant to take him off the property? If so, what is it?"

Kimberly didn't get a chance to explain anything because Pete said, "Jay's here. Let's hear what he has to say."

There was no missing the relief in his voice, and Susanna tried not to take it personally. She was still working to earn the staff's respect. That process would take time, as the caregivers acquainting themselves with Mr. Jankowski's needs took time.

Pete didn't wait for Jay to enter the passcode, but took a few quick steps ahead and pressed the door release.

Jay strode through the opening doors, a man with a purpose, and Susanna was surprised by how relieved she was to see him.

One look at them, and the smile faded from Jay's face.

"What's wrong?" he asked in his throaty morning voice, joining their huddle and overtaking it with his broad-shouldered presence. Suddenly, he was all Susanna could see.

Pete explained the problem, and Kimberly beat a hasty retreat. "Time to check on Mr. Jankowski."

Jay nodded then tapped his radio. "Let me know how he's doing. We'll go from there."

Kimberly nodded then took off.

"Can't do a thing until Kimberly gets back, so I'm going to get started on the end-of-shift reports," Pete said.

Having been a duty manager herself, Susanna knew Pete wasn't going to get much done. She'd been abandoned.

Jay didn't need a crystal ball to realize that he'd walked in on some tension. "Anything I need to know?"

Susanna backed against the wall as a dietary aide approached, maneuvering a tiered meal cart through the doors.

"Good morning," she greeted the woman, dressed neatly in the standard black slacks and white button-up shirt.

"Good morning, Ms. Adams." She smiled at Jay while passing.

"I didn't think we had policy discrepancies with emergency procedures," Susanna admitted. "But Pete and Kimberly were reluctant to consider the emergency room as a viable option."

Jay arched an eyebrow curiously. "Since when is the emergency room the first course of action with Northstar? I don't remember reading that anywhere. Did I miss the fine print?"

"Not first course. But Mr. Jankowski started having

difficulty breathing at two this morning. I know Kimberly has been monitoring him, but that's quite a while."

"The determination to send a resident to the emergency room is made purely by the duty staff, as it should be," Jay said.

"I agree. They were reassessing when I showed up. I appreciated the chance to appraise their performance firsthand."

"Then you're questioning Kimberly's assessment?"

"Only the reluctance. I was surprised they didn't notify either one of us that Mr. Jankowski was in distress."

"They must not have thought he was in *that much* distress or we'd have heard about it. Trust me. I don't have minimum wage workers. Everyone is well compensated for their certifications and all the ongoing education. Kimberly is extremely qualified to assess medical situations."

"I understand, Jay. I'm conservative. Given the situation, I thought the emergency room should have at least been considered."

"Susanna, I'm not sure I understand the problem."

That made two of them.

"Maybe we just had difficulty communicating. Maybe they thought I was overly cautious and weren't sure how to tell me."

Jay folded his arms over his chest and considered her. "Do you think so? No one ever has any problem telling me what they think."

That almost made her smile. "As long as we take care of Mr. Jankowski I don't have a problem. I haven't had any problems communicating with anyone before now, so if I run into a problem again then I'll have to look at the issue."

Jay inclined his head, trying to be as diplomatic as she was. "That sounds like a good plan, but tell me something.

How long would you typically monitor a resident at your last facility? Was there a guideline?"

"Not really," she admitted. "Each situation is so individual. But we always erred on the side of caution, so we had more flexibility in the nursing center, where we were outfitted to handle more demands than we did in the ALF or independent living."

Jay blinked. "Independent living? Really?"

One *really* and the world shifted.

Suddenly Jay was drilling her with a stare as hard as emeralds. "Independent living in a separate facility?"

Susanna suddenly felt as if she were standing under an interrogator's lamp. "Twelve hundred units. We also had an active senior community. Two-bedroom, two-bath villas."

"Sounds like quite a place." His gaze didn't budge. "I know Northstar manages several memory-care communities, but that place you came from—what was the name?"

"Greywacke Lodge," she provided automatically.

"Greywacke Lodge wasn't one of them, was it?"

That's when it hit her. She wasn't sure why it had taken so long for her to put two and two together.

Northstar hadn't provided Jay with her detailed and specific work experience. He hadn't a clue that her experience was in senior living and not exclusively in memory care.

But he'd figured it out. Had Pete and Kimberly? Is that why they'd vanished?

Susanna jumped in with evasive maneuvers and tried not to sound defensive. "Greywacke Lodge consists of several facilities that cover all areas of senior living, including memory care. We had Harmony House within the ALF."

"How many beds does Harmony House have?"

"Thirty-five." Which sounded so vastly different from the one hundred and twenty beds that made up The Arbors.

"Exclusively Alzheimer's?"

"Dementia care." Which included, but was not limited to, Alzheimer's care.

Jay didn't say another word. He didn't move. He didn't take his eyes off her, but Susanna knew he wasn't happy. It was all over him, the sudden stillness, the way he contained his response in such a noticeably physical way.

"Nothing personal, Susanna, but that wasn't what I was expecting," he admitted. "Northstar led me to believe they were sending someone with memory-care experience."

"I've been training since Northstar proposed the move and am now certified in all areas of Alzheimer's care."

Certification wasn't the same as hands-on experience.

He didn't say it aloud. He didn't have to. Skepticism was in every hard line on his face.

And stupid, stupid woman that she was felt as if she'd disappointed him with her inexperience. "I also bring a long career in health care that makes me uniquely qualified to transition The Arbors from private to corporate while retaining your standard of care."

That sounded suspiciously like business administration and not patient care. Jay had the patient care experience as well as the graduate degree in business administration *and* a lifetime of learning the ropes. She knew because she'd researched him. But Northstar hadn't extended him the same courtesy.

What had Gerald been thinking?

Especially since her lack of Alzheimer's care wasn't the only hole in her experience.

Susanna inhaled deeply. She wanted to point out that they'd been working side by side for over a month and he hadn't had any concerns about her performance until this minute.

But Jay kept staring, clearly reformulating his opinion.

Then another thought occurred to him. Susanna could see it as if a lightbulb went on over his head.

God, don't let him ask. Please don't let him ask!

His gaze narrowed. "You *were* the property administrator of Greywacke Lodge, weren't you?"

CHAPTER SIX

JAY STARED INTO SUSANNA'S face, her eyes so blue they managed to distract him from the hollow feeling in his stomach. Because he knew, before she ever opened her mouth, a mouth that should be put to far better uses than this conversation. Kissing came to mind. Moist lips parted around soft, excited breaths. *Definitely* better than telling him what he didn't want to hear.

And that's what she was going to do. He could see reluctance in the vivid depths of those too-blue eyes. He could feel her hesitation in the pit of his stomach.

He couldn't say why he felt so in tune with this woman that he sensed what was coming, but when she opened that attractive mouth and said, "I was the CFO," he wasn't the least bit surprised. Not at all.

Except maybe by the way her words filtered through him, a matter-of-fact declaration delivered in a hush of a whisper, a silken sound so at odds with her hard admission.

Chief financial officer?

He needed a clone of his late grandmother and Northstar had sent him a replacement for *Walter?*

No, Jay wasn't surprised. He hadn't been able to break free of this place for his entire adult life. Why should he think now would be any different?

There was never quiet in The Arbors. Even on third shift when most folks were sleeping, there was always background noise—the chirping of heart monitors, the huff and hiss of respirators, the blare of call buttons.

There were people sounds, too.

Caregivers whispering greetings or assessments as they moved in and out of rooms during rounds.

Dietary staff, whose first shift started in the middle of everyone else's third, chatting as they prepped meals.

Mrs. Carlson mumbling to her long-dead husband while she slept, voice carrying through her room's open door.

Mr. Vincenzo in the north wing, growling whenever he clunked a knee or elbow against the bed rails. They'd ordered an oversize bed and padded the rails to make him comfortable, but he still slept as if he were trying to break out of prison.

Right now all Jay could hear was the silence between him and Susanna, so thick it dominated the hallway.

She finally said, "Please accept my apology. I had no idea Northstar wouldn't provide my history. I'm surprised."

That made two of them. He'd figured Northstar had known its business. He wouldn't say that, either. "They provided your bio. You've been with them a long time."

"Over eighteen years. Started off in health care then moved into senior living."

"And you've been running the financial department."

She nodded. "I was also a duty manager. All directors worked in shift management, including the property administrator. She felt it was important to stay engaged with our residents and staff, and the only way we could do that was by working with them."

Jay approved of that much. Administration that worked in an ivory tower, or *administrative corridor* as it were, certainly couldn't understand the day-to-day needs of a facility from a working perspective. No one benefited much then.

Okay, so she'd researched and prepared and gotten certified. Bully for her. Jay didn't feel he should congratulate her for that. Preparation and experience were two different things and he'd insisted on both. The simple fact was: Susanna wasn't what he'd asked for.

He'd been so blinded by her pretty smile and so grateful to have her here that he hadn't interrogated as he should have. He'd trusted Northstar to send him what he'd asked for. True, the situation had seemed very promising...or had he only been determined to believe she'd fit right in at The Arbors because he wanted out that badly?

Badly enough to leave folks who counted on him with an inexperienced director? "Northstar told me they'd send the perfect person."

Raising her hand, she smiled tentatively, testing the past month of companionable working relations. "That would be me."

"I acknowledge you've done excellent work since your arrival, but I was specific about the job description. Experience in Alzheimer's care was the first item on the list. It was my only nonnegotiable requirement."

So why had Northstar sent someone he wouldn't consider leaving in charge?

Jay had no answers. Only questions. And two CFOs, one of whom wasn't interested in retiring. And a qualified property administrator who was more than ready.

Susanna didn't say a word, only faced him stoically. He couldn't read anything behind the expression on her face. Which made the situation that much worse. He'd wiped the smile from her face and made her feel bad, and himself, for that matter. He wasn't prone to tantrums because he didn't get what he wanted.

Fortunately for both of them, he had to cut short his re-action when Kimberly reappeared, and said, "I'm back."

Susanna stepped lightly in front of him and, if he were to guess, he'd say she was even more relieved for the distraction than he was.

"How's he doing?" he asked Kimberly.

She didn't glance away from the display as she inputted data. "No change."

"Do we need to get him to the E.R.?" Might as well get that out of the way.

Kimberly cast a sidelong glance at Susanna, whose expression might have been carved from marble. "Not unless his condition deteriorates. Otherwise, he's stable. I can continue to monitor him until Dr. Smith arrives."

Good enough for Jay. She didn't bother asking Susanna's opinion. Looked as if he was back on duty. "Do you want to move him to the first floor?"

"Unnecessary. He's comfortable in his apartment, and Ryan offered to stay until the doctor gets here." She smiled. "Ryan will enjoying sitting and reading tabloids with no interruptions."

"And racking up overtime to pay off that new bike."

Kimberly chuckled. "That, too."

"Okay, then. I'll call Dr. Smith's service and leave a message so he doesn't make any detours on his way in."

"Let us know if anything changes," Susanna said.

Kimberly nodded before turning back to the display.

Then Jay slipped the cell phone from the carrier at his waist and scrolled through his contact list. He retreated into Kimberly's office. While he was leaving the message with the doctor's service, Pete returned to get an update. Susanna explained the plan of action in a voice as neutral as her expression.

Pete acknowledged Jay with a wave then took off again,

leaving Jay with the woman who'd not only thrown a wrench into his day but his entire life plan.

"So where do we go from here, Jay?" The past month of companionable working relationship might never have been. She was by the book right now with her brisk Yankee voice.

"I won't make excuses for my company's decisions, Jay. Not without having all the information. What I can tell you is they offered me this position because they felt I was the best qualified for the job. They could have moved an administrator from another property, someone who had memory-care experience."

Leaning back against the desk, he folded his arms over his chest and considered her. "You're better than everyone else?"

Fifteen minutes ago, she would have smiled, but not now. "For The Arbors. Yes, I am. You've got a unique set of circumstances here that call for a unique skill set. Transitioning from private to corporate requires a competent but delicate hand. You're fiscally successful and well-known for your quality of care. You'd like to see The Arbors remain successful and expand. There are lots of factors involved. You know that."

He couldn't argue her point. He didn't need to, not when there were other things to argue. Northstar's definition of *perfect* and his were two different things.

"Northstar felt whatever I lacked in direct supervisory experience didn't outweigh what I brought to the table," she continued. "I'm fresh off a hundred-and-twenty-hour training program to certify me in memory care. They knew I'd learn the ropes, particularly as you'd be here through the transition period. I'm sorry they didn't present me in that fashion. I feel as if they've undermined my credibility in the process."

Inclining his head in acknowledgment, he was unsure what bothered him most—she didn't have experience or that he hadn't been told. Both. He honestly couldn't say he was surprised by the corporate mentality, though. Checks and balances. Pros and cons. Six of one, half dozen of another as the saying went.

"I hear you," he said, "and don't disagree with any of it. But I asked for an administrator with memory-care experience for a reason."

"To make sure The Arbors will be cared for?" she asked.

"Yes." He couldn't leave without a clear conscience.

Jay squelched that thought. He was done with feeling obligated. He'd lived his entire life obligated to this place, and the time had come to let go.

So how did he politely explain to her that he didn't feel corporate know-how and her transitioning skill set could make up for years of experience with Alzheimer's patients?

How did he explain to Susanna that he didn't want her pretty blue eyes distracting him from doing what he had to do?

CLUTCHING THE PHONE, Susanna let her eyes flutter shut and reined in her emotions before making the phone call. She needed to steel herself for the conversation ahead because she refused to present as anything but a professional. But emotion rode so close to the surface, waiting to overstep the boundaries of business and demand answers from a man she considered a friend.

She'd given up her job, her home, her *life* to make this career move. Everything important depended on her performance, from her family's finances to Northstar's acquisition. Yet Gerald had sent her into a new work environment, knowing she didn't meet the basic job description. Northstar had sent her in to do a job then undermined her credibility.

Why would they set her up this way? There was no real chance her inexperience would go unnoticed, particularly as Jay had been involved in every area of the acquisition. The omission of her work experience had been deliberate, of that Susanna had no doubt.

Northstar was a management company, for heaven's sake. They staffed businesses, not just senior living facilities, but health care operations, industrial properties, hotels…businesses across the board. If they were going to staff a property administrator who didn't meet the fundamental criteria for the position, they should have told her *before* she'd arrived on the property. Cleared the way for her to do her job before she sacrificed her life in New York.

So why had Gerald sent her in unprepared to tackle this job with a control freak? How could anyone think Jay wouldn't notice her inexperience? The only surprise was how long it took him to notice. She supposed that spoke highly of her job performance.

And worst of all was how much she felt as if she'd disappointed him. God, even the memory of today's exchange made her wince.

Jay's expression dominated her memory, his surprise, his displeasure, the way he'd finally reined in his reaction. And he had. She knew him well enough to know how much. He'd been angry, but he'd expressed his displeasure during that horribly awkward exchange in a way that was forthright but not hurtful. In a way that wouldn't corner her into a defense.

Not that she could have defended herself. There would

be a learning curve. She'd known it. Her bosses had known it. The only person who hadn't known was Jay.

Opening her eyes, Susanna leaned back in the caned rocking chair and gazed into the clear night sky, the rising moon casting the silhouette of her new yard in silver.

Her new home. For how long?

Susanna didn't want to make this call, disliked confronting Gerald as much as she disliked admitting her inexperience had been exposed to Jay and he might call Northstar and insist they send someone he considered qualified. And she was hurt Gerald would position her this way without any warning…. She never would have concealed her inexperience.

Just the thought rubbed Susanna the wrong way. Was that why Gerald hadn't told her?

Inhaling deeply, a breath filled with the sweet scent of night-blooming jasmine, she tried to calm the tension that had her nerves on end.

Then she depressed the speed dial and waited for the call to connect. Unless he had a nighttime engagement, Gerald should be settling in to relax after a long day.

He picked up on the second ring. "Susanna," he said in his hearty voice. "Good to hear from you. How are things going?"

"We've hit a snag, Gerald," she said simply.

"What kind of snag?"

"Jay asked Northstar to provide a property administrator with a specific level of experience, which I don't come close to having. I assume there's a reason you sent me here without sharing my credentials with Jay. Or preparing me."

To her astonishment, Gerald chuckled. "You're such a diplomat. Your credentials are need to know. You work for Northstar. Not Jay Canady."

Maybe it was the laughter. Or maybe she was just upset

enough to throw caution to the wind, but Susanna didn't mince any words when she said, "I don't agree. You sent me here to reassure the man, not upset him. But how am I supposed to do that when I don't have all the information? I can't reassure anyone when the rug gets pulled out from under me."

No more laughter. "What happened?"

Susanna gave him a bare-bones overview of the day's events. To her credit, she kept her voice steady, kept to the facts. She didn't hint at how mortified she'd been that her work history had been concealed from Jay, how helpless she'd felt because he'd felt as though he'd been lied to by Northstar.

And *she* was Northstar.

"This is business, Susanna. You know that. Jay's in a tough position. No question. He's used to calling the shots at The Arbors and he wants to make sure he covers everything. But his micromanaging isn't going to work during this transition. That's why you're there—to build a bridge between the old administration and the new. You'll help him understand why things are changing so he can make peace and move on. You're the best person for the job. We've decided that, and you work for us. Don't second-guess yourself."

Susanna stared into the night, wrapping her brain around the fact that she was being used to manipulate Jay. She understood Northstar wasn't going to answer to him. She understood they wanted to flex their corporate muscles in an area that would drive home that subtle point and shift the balance of power to their side.

She understood the corporate mentality. But they should have known they were asking for trouble given Jay's involvement in hammering out this deal. If they weren't going to honor Jay's specific request, they should have at least owned responsibility for the choice.

He might have insisted on having things his way or he might have allowed himself to be persuaded to try things Northstar's way. No matter which way he'd chosen, the situation would not have blown up in *her* face.

But Susanna knew that corporate operations were corporate operations, and she was down on the food chain. Gerald's explanation told her everything she needed to know. Her opinion would not reinvent the way Northstar operated.

But she was hurt by his disregard for her personally, and quite honestly, for Jay, too. Maybe he was micromanaging, but only because he cared. So much. He'd gone above and beyond to handle Northstar with integrity, but Northstar hadn't returned the favor. Why? Because they knew how much Jay wanted to leave The Arbors? Or because they didn't take his demands seriously?

Susanna didn't know.

"Let's see what Jay does next," Gerald suggested. "He'll either push the issue or back off. The ball's in his court now. Let's leave it there. You proceed exactly as you've been unless I tell you otherwise. If it's taken Jay this long to realize you're not an old hand at memory care and property administration, then you're doing everything right. There's still plenty of time to reassure Jay The Arbors is in good hands. You'll do that without trying too hard. Do you hear me?"

"I hear you." The words were all she could manage past the sick feeling in the pit of her stomach.

"Okay, then enjoy the night and I'll let you know if I hear from Jay. Otherwise, just keep doing what you're doing. Everyone at corporate is content with the progress you're making down there. That's all that matters."

No, Susanna wanted to say. That wasn't all that mattered. Instead, she said, "I hope you're right."

After disconnecting the call, she rocked back in her chair and willed the night breeze to cool her clammy skin and the unfamiliar sounds of the forest to soothe her anxiety.

She'd considered Gerald a friend, but apparently when friendship and business collided, business took precedence. No matter how Susanna viewed the situation, she still came back to feeling as if Gerald had used her to manipulate Jay.

A property administrator with experience in memory care.

Was that really unreasonable? Susanna didn't think so. Jay was the best person to make that determination about The Arbors. Not only was he the person who knew the place best, but he was the person who cared the most.

Susanna couldn't help but remember the way Jay had sat beside Mr. Jankowski's bed during the examination. He'd explained what was happening in his calm voice, why it was okay. And now that Susanna viewed the situation through the filter of Jay's insights about memory care, she understood what he'd been doing—bridging the distance between Mr. Jankowski and an unusually busy room with lots of unfamiliar activity.

In many regards, his care of Mr. Jankowski—and that of Kimberly, Pete and Dr. Smith—hadn't been any different than the level of care at Greywacke Lodge. All employees brought something different to the table, but the bottom line was about meeting the residents' needs. The caring environment was one of the things she enjoyed about working in senior living.

Dealing with Alzheimer's meant the care went one step further. Would she learn to gauge a resident's needs with the sort of instinct Jay had demonstrated today? Or was instinct inherent to a man who'd been reared in this environment? If that was the case, then Jay had every right to worry about who succeeded him, because no one could replace him.

Not her. Not anyone.

And that was the real tragedy, because so many people relied upon him. Why was he determined to leave?

Susanna didn't know, but she wanted to.

JAY AND THE DOGS CLAMBERED up the gallery steps to the house. If he'd have known he would be coming home this late, he'd have left on a porch light.

His home had never felt quieter than it did in the dark, such a striking contrast to a long day in the busy facility, always noisy but for the rare occasions of illness quarantine.

The instant the door opened, the dogs rushed past him, making a beeline for the kitchen and dinner.

"Like I'm starving you," he said to no one in particular as Butters and Gatsby were long gone, their nails tapping over wooden floors in the distance.

Flipping on lights, he strode through the foyer, glancing at the mantel inside the drawing room as he passed.

He remembered telling Susanna about his mother's obsession, but wasn't sure where that impulse had come from because he honestly couldn't remember how long it had been since he'd noticed the mantels. Since before his mother had died, at least. Three years. Where had all that time gone?

Jay knew the answer—The Arbors.

He hadn't lived one minute, just kept waking up every day, doing what everyone needed him to do, meeting everyone's needs but his own, walking by his mother's mantels without even seeing them or any of the memories inside this house. He couldn't reclaim a second of that lost time, but he could stop losing more. He went through his nighttime routine.

Feed the dogs.

Change out of his work clothes.

Grab dinner if he was hungry, a beer if he wasn't, and get started on his chores.

Something always needed to be done around here, which answered the question about why he hadn't thought about those long-ago excursions hunting for treasures. If he had, he'd have moved on long ago. These old houses were nonstop work. No wonder so many were torn down when there was no longer family willing to deal with the constant upkeep. He wasn't willing anymore, either.

Tonight was definitely a beer night. Maybe even a two-beer night after Susanna's surprises.

Independent living.

He still couldn't figure out what to do. She had seemed so promising. The perfect property administrator. Or had he only seen what he wanted to see because he was so damn desperate to get out of here?

To be fair, she had seemed perfect on the surface. She learned quickly, was organized and worked well with the staff. A good administrator from all appearances. He'd meant what he'd said about her work. She was good.

Good wasn't enough.

The new administrator needed the compassion to care and the experience to handle the unexpected situations that arose with the residents, their families, the staff.

The new administrator needed a strong foundation in facility administration and memory care. With those pieces firmly in place, he or she could then learn all about the things that made The Arbors unique and steer the facility into the future in step with evolving Alzheimer's care.

The Arbors couldn't be allowed to simply become a care facility for its residents, a place for them to mark forgotten time, cared for in a safe environment so family members didn't have to worry.

That was never his grandmother's intention. She wanted to provide quality of life and that meant staying on the cutting edge of research and making a difference in the fight against the disease.

Jay had been barely living up to the family legacy. Barely. The new administrator would come in, backed by corporate muscle that would provide the resources to continue the fight. He wasn't deluding himself into thinking this would be an easy role to fill, which was why he'd gone to Northstar in the first place. They were unparalleled in management staffing and had experience in top-notch senior care.

If any company could produce a person capable of replacing Jay, Northstar could. But instead of the perfect administrator, they'd sent Susanna, who needed on-the-job training. Jay wasn't opposed to providing that training, either, but six months couldn't possibly replace years of experience and familiarity with Alzheimer's. What happened after Jay left? What happened when something unexpected came up and he wasn't around?

Why did everything have to be so damned complicated, anyway? All Jay wanted was to move on. A new career. A new home. A new life with people in it who could remember his name or didn't always need something from him.

He wanted to be out from under the nonstop work, the never-ending obligation. He wanted to do something other than slave over this place night and day. He wanted to wake up one morning, blow off work and take the dogs to the coast.

He wanted to reconnect with friends and kick back with a beer in the middle of the afternoon to watch a game. He wanted to go to bed one night without the seven thousand things he *hadn't* accomplished during the day cluttering his brain.

Was that really so much to ask?

Butters and Gatsby abandoned him to sleep off their turkey dinner on the sofa in the family room. Had his grandmother been alive, she'd have shooed them off the furniture. They'd have shooed, too—until she turned her back and they hopped on again.

Jay didn't bother. "You two rest after your tough day."

Opening the beer bottle, he headed upstairs to remove the baseboards in his grandmother's bathroom. If he got them off tonight, he could wipe them down with bleach to kill any mold growing on the plaster after the flood last weekend, compliments of a broken ball cock.

Not a big deal, just one more pain-in-the-butt problem that dictated every minute of every day when he wasn't in the facility. Jay supposed he should be grateful to do anything that didn't involve scheduling 250 employees or reviewing budget reports or selling The Arbors' services to potential residents' families. But he'd inherited home improvement as a hobby. He'd rather be kayaking.

What difference did moldy baseboards make, anyway? For all Jay knew, Northstar could level the house and all this effort would be wasted. But could he pursue the acquisition when Northstar was yanking his chain?

The baseboard snapped in his hands.

"Damn it." Now he'd have to replace it. Or try to, because like everything else around this antiquated house, replacements were always a problem. The standard size of everything from 1888 didn't translate into the twenty-first century. Not a baseboard. Not a breaker. Not a nut. Not a bolt.

Not even a property administrator.

"Damn it," he said again because it made him feel better.

Dropping the baseboard on the floor, Jay leaned against the tub and took a deep swig of beer.

Was it really too much to ask for Northstar to send an administrator with more than thirty-five beds worth of memory-care experience?

With some actual *administrator* experience?

Sinking his fingers in his hair, he pushed it back and tipped the bottle to his lips again. If Northstar got someone else in here, someone *experienced* this time, Jay would have to start the transition period over again. Five weeks wasted.

He'd lived his entire life in this house and now he honestly didn't know if he could survive another six months.

God, he was tired. Too tired to even try to sift through his options. He didn't see any.

Fight with Northstar then trust them to provide what Jay had originally asked for?

Look for another management company? Northstar was supposed to be the best. They were definitely the largest that staffed senior living facilities, some even exclusively memory care.

Except for Greywacke Lodge.

But finding a replacement for Northstar—if one existed—would take the one thing Jay didn't have to give—more time.

"So you're saying you won't close the deal if you're unhappy with Ms. Susanna Adams?"

Walter's words seemed so prophetic now. How could Jay not have noticed her inexperience?

That was the one answer that came easily tonight. He hadn't been looking closely enough at her skill set because he was too busy looking at her. Her delicate curves and her sweet smiles and listening to her silvery laughter. She was one very beautiful distraction.

And he was so desperate to feel some spark of life that he'd been rushing into work every morning, suddenly not minding all the sameness and the demands. He'd told himself the burden of this place had felt lighter because the transition period was finally underway. He could see the end in sight.

But he realized now he'd been seeing Susanna.

He was so damned starved to feel something other than the crushing sense of obligation that he'd only seen what he'd wanted to see and ignored the rest.

What a pathetic commentary about his life.

His *pseudo* life. He needed a real one. A life that involved more than residents and employees as his constant companions. How long had it been since he'd accepted an invitation to a game, to a party, to a wedding?

So long everyone he'd known had stopped asking.

Jay set the bottle on the floor with a loud clink of glass against tile. Pushing to his feet, he left the bathroom and went into his room to grab his iPod. He had to get out of his head before he drove himself crazy. Or broke more baseboards.

While passing through the sitting room of his suite, he spotted a flicker of a light in his periphery and turned to gaze out the window in that direction.

His house sat on a rise, so he could make out the dark silhouette of the cottage through the trees. It had been a long time since anyone had used the guesthouse, and the sight startled him.

Susanna.

One light went on. Another went off.

He knew what she was doing—moving from the living room to the kitchen. Turning on one light before shutting off the other.

Was she just now getting around to dinner? Seemed kind of late, but for all he knew she liked late meals. Widowed working woman raising kids. Couldn't have been early by the time she got home and made dinner. Or maybe her kids had prepared dinner. Mom had taught him and Drew to cook. Drew hadn't been that fond doing anything but eating, but Jay liked cooking.

Well, once he had. Nowadays, Liz sent meals to his office and he ate at the facility. He couldn't actually remember the last time he'd cooked a real meal. Back in the days when Jay had brought dates home, he would break out Mom's cookbooks. He always impressed women with his cooking skills. Usually he impressed them right into bed.

One more sad commentary on how his life had melted into work until they'd become one. No wonder he was crawling to get out of here. Work was sucking the life out of him.

Another light shone from the back of the cottage. The bedroom. Then, sure enough, the kitchen light went off.

Jay had no clue what she might be doing. He only knew that he didn't want to be wondering, standing here on the outside looking in. He wanted a real life with a real woman he could be involved with, not a woman attached to work who was only distracting him from how miserable he was.

He was calling Northstar in the morning.

CHAPTER SEVEN

SUSANNA INHALED DEEPLY, *a breath filled with wet air and fragrance. Scents overlapped each other. Gardenia. Magnolia. Clematis. Hyacinth.*

Today was the perfect spring day. The sort of day where the very idea of work was sacrilege. She pushed the thought away with barely an effort because today was about appreciation and wonder and reminders about what was important in life.

Life itself.

Every aromatic breath was a gift, a reminder that the people in her life were the only thing that mattered. These perfect days were about renewing her spirit the way the world renewed, springing to life after a healing winter sleep.

Healing. She saw renewal everywhere. In the electric colors of the landscape. Hues so alive they tempted her to reach for silken petals, to run reverent fingertips along the weathered wood of the arbor. Even the whites distinguished themselves in the blooms of the magnolia, the clematis, strikingly different from the towering piles of clouds in the sky.

The sun shone through the spring foliage, cast an intricate dappling of light and shadow on the grass as she stood beneath the arbors. She belonged here. Every step she had ever taken in her life led to this place.

Now.

The only moment that mattered. The only moment that was hers to savor. A moment filled with magnolias unfurling to catch the sun in petal-palms, wisteria dripping in swollen bunches, so impossibly heavy that a gentle spring rain might snap their fragile stems and send them tumbling to the grass.

The mere thought of rain brought the realization of thirst, how parched she was in the heat of this partial sun, no different than this lush landscape, which craved moisture to nourish and refresh.

The realization of thirst brought sudden rain, only the sound at first, the gentle tap, tap, tapping against the shelter of overhanging branches and leaves. A shower of warm droplets that rooted out tiny cracks and niggled in, through leaves and lattice in a delicate descent.

Her skin thirsted for the rain as her spirit craved the simple joy of life, this reminder that routine made the days blur together, the effort she focused on work, only the means to an end. The end is all about the people who populate her world.

Helping them through their days.

Providing for herself and her kids.

Challenging herself to learn, to discover, to accomplish, to fail, to rest, to reach.

To love.

The only thing that made any difference at all. A discovery that nourished spirit the way rain nourished earth.

And trailed over her, awakening senses until she felt each warm droplet dance over bare skin, down the contours of her face, her neck, each fat droplet drawn to the next, uniting in silken ribbons that gained momentum, streamed around the bow of her shoulders, down her arms. Followed the curve of breasts in tiny cascades, making her nipples tingle with awareness.

With the knowledge of a presence.

Skip.

He was there, belonging to this moment as the rain poured from a sunny sky.

His gaze drank her in all at once, a gaze so potent she felt his appreciation as alive as the rain.

He enjoyed her nakedness, the sight of her.

She felt his appreciation deep within, felt beautiful beneath his gaze.

She wanted to entice, to bring him pleasure. Letting her eyes flutter shut, she parted her lips to catch raindrops on her tongue, her hair tumbling down her back, wet strands heavy.

Rising up on tiptoe, she lifted her hands to the skies. Warm droplets splashed between outstretched fingers, and her body stretched taut with the motion. Muscles shifted to redirect the rivulets of rain over new terrain, into the V of her waist, the slight roundness of her belly, the length of her thighs.

A show, designed purely to heighten the physicality of this moment, his awareness.

An invitation.

To satisfy the ache deep within, a yearning.

For him.

And he knew.

Because he yearned, too.

Reaching out, he grazed his fingertips over the curve of her cheek, a testing touch, his skin mildly rough, creating friction along soft skin.

All this exposed skin, and he touched her cheek.

But somehow his touch didn't surprise her. He was a gentleman always, thinking of others, making her desire as important as his own.

And his teasing touch was all about desire. His touch

felt as natural as the wisteria hanging from the arbors and the rain falling from the sky and the wet grass beneath her toes.

Trailing his fingers along the curve of her jaw, he explored her face with a featherlight touch, a touch that filled the moment with breathtaking promise. One innocent touch that made her skin exquisitely sensitive everywhere, as if one small caress trailed over her body.

An intimate caress that caused heat to gather low in her belly, awakening a response that had slumbered so long she'd forgotten how potent it might be should it ever awaken....

Susanna jolted awake.

For one blind moment, she only stared into the night, not a shadow or a sound striking any familiar chord through the fog of her sleep. Not the pale sheers that fell the length of the floor-to-ceiling windows, almost ghostly in the dark. Not the spindle-legged furniture. Not the fragile golden glow from some room beyond a door.

A night-light?

She stared into the room, eyes adjusting to the dark, too aware of her heart pounding with slow, throbbing beats. Her skin flushed until her pajamas clung uncomfortably.

Awareness came only in slow degrees but along with it came more awareness.

Of the nature of her dream. And her body's reaction.

Her breasts felt heavy in a way that only accompanied arousal. The fire low in her belly still smoldered.

She knew this feeling, though her body hadn't awakened in this way for so long. Rolling onto her back, Susanna flipped away the comforter, allowed the cool night air to clear the remnants of sleep and dispel the effects of *that* dream.

The memory of her oh, so handsome husband made her

smile. She had been many things at that time of her life—wife, mother, CFO—but Skip had never let her forget she was a woman, first and foremost, the woman he loved.

How long had it been since she'd felt anything but fear, anxiety, worry?

Since long before Skip died. The worry had started when he hadn't been able to shake what they'd thought was a flu, the low-grade fever, the swollen glands. He'd gotten listless, lethargic, unable to eat or sleep normally, and he'd started losing weight. By the time he'd finally admitted that she was probably right and he should see the doctor, even he'd been worried.

But neither had been prepared for the diagnosis.

No, it had been a very long time since she'd paid attention to anything but survival, and savoring each and every second with everyone she loved.

Funny, how her body would suddenly remind her she was still a woman. Was the melatonin having some weird effect?

Fanning herself with the comforter, Susanna frowned. Hot flashes made her think of menopause, but she hadn't even reached her milestone fortieth birthday—*yet*.

But something about that didn't feel right, either, and her drifting thoughts chased around and around, trailed over the fading images in her head. The flowers. The sun. The rain.

The arbors in spring.

Walter's rich Southern drawl suddenly made an appearance, too, sharing a promise of how beautiful the arbors would be when they bloomed again. She'd only seen internet photos, yet her mind had been filled with detailed images, the blossoms in living color and amazing detail.

The man who'd watched her.

As Susanna stared into the quiet darkness, she could

still see the eyes of that man in her dreams, eyes as green as the arbor leaves in spring....

All vestiges of drowsiness evaporated as she realized she hadn't been dreaming about her oh, so handsome husband at all.

SUSANA WAS A WRECK THIS morning. A complete wreck. Inspiring Jay's confidence had been her main objective. Instead, she'd convinced him Northstar had sent an idiot to run this property. Northstar had rolled her under the bus, leaving a bad taste in her mouth, and the divide between corporate and private wider than ever before.

And then there was *that dream*.

The very thought sent her scurrying for cover in her office. She'd likely beaten Jay onto the property, but she had no idea what to expect from him. She could be packing her bags before lunch for all she knew, and professionalism would be her only defense.

She didn't have the energy to deal with stupidity today. Not when her future hung in the balance. If she failed miserably, she held Northstar partially responsible for mishandling Jay. She couldn't be something she wasn't, no matter how hard she worked. She wasn't an experienced property administrator with exclusive memory-care knowledge.

Anxiety must be responsible for the madness happening in her brain. For *that* dream.

Susanna tried to find some calm in the activity of her morning routine. Hot water in a mug. VIA. A glimpse out the windows. But she was very early this morning and dawn wasn't ready to make an appearance.

She sat down at the computer, considered working on transferring data from The Arbors into Northstar's software, but the reality that Jay might put the brakes on this transition period made the effort feel like a waste. She couldn't concentrate, anyway. Not after that dream.

Time to take action. She went online and typed into a search engine:

What does being naked in a dream mean?

A full page of potential explanations popped up, and Susanna clicked on the first link.

To dream of being naked means to be free. There is nothing restraining you, you're free to do whatever you'd like.

No. No. No. Too personal. Susanna wasn't free to do what she liked. And certainly not with a business partner, a *younger* business partner, a younger business partner *who would be leaving town soon.*

If he didn't show her the door first.

She tried again: *What does dreaming of rain mean?*

More links.

To be out in a shower of rain denotes pleasure will be enjoyed with the zest of youth, and prosperity will come to you.

That was better. Pleasure and prosperity sounded good right now. That meant she might still have a job near her kids.

And if she didn't…Susanna could only control what she could control. If Jay decided to replace her because he didn't like her résumé even after five weeks of working together, then she'd attempt to reason with him. That was all she could do.

Susanna's phone vibrated. Crack-of-dawn phone calls always made her heart miss a beat. Scrambling to withdraw the phone from her pocket, she glanced at the display, holding her breath to face yet another potential crisis.

Karan.

"You're making a habit of waking up before dawn,"

Susanna said, suddenly so relieved for a lifeline to someone familiar in her anxiety-riddled world. "Should I be
worried?"

"Good morning to you, too." Karan sounded cheery and
unexpectedly awake for a woman who didn't have much
use for conventional business hours. "Nothing at all is
wrong with the world today. How about you?"

"You're up awfully early, or haven't you gone to bed
yet?" Susanna cradled the phone against her ear as another thought occurred to her. "Charles is okay? Everything good there?"

This was the second time around for Karan and her husband. Five years of marriage, a divorce then remarriage.

Only polite to ask. Maybe she wasn't the only one in
the world whose life was crumbling around her.

"I saw him off to surgery."

"Making a habit of that. Admirable." As a cardiotho-
racic surgeon, Charles's life was dictated by his patients'
needs. Karan's life, too, by default. "Give him a hug for
me."

"Will do. Won't see him until later, though. He hasn't
even pulled out of the driveway yet."

"And you called me instead of crawling back into
bed? Really, Karan. What's up? Can't sleep? Maybe you
should try some melatonin." Side effects like erotic dreams
wouldn't be any problem for a woman with a handsome
husband.

A beat of silence. "Is all well? You sound…*off*."

Of course, Karan would hear past what Susanna was
saying to what she wasn't. But there was no way on this
planet she could put into words *that dream.* Not even to
her best friend. Especially the best friend who thought
Susanna had a crush.

The memory of their conversation came rushing back,

and Susanna squeezed her eyes shut tight, as if she could block it out. No such luck, so she launched into a blow-by-blow of what had happened yesterday and Northstar's betrayal.

"Well, I'm not at all happy with your boss," Karan finally said. "Nothing like leaving you vulnerable. Not okay. But an idiot, Suze? That doesn't sound like you at all. You're far too practical to get so flustered. Jay wasn't rude, was he?"

"No. Nothing like that. He was shocked, and unhappy."

"Then he's the idiot. You're a gem."

"I'm not what he asked for. He's trying to make sure the level of care here doesn't change for the residents or staff."

"If he doesn't want things to change then why is he selling the facility?"

"The question of the day for which I have no answer. Personally, I think he's nuts. I can't imagine leaving here."

There was a thoughtful silence on the other end of the line. Karan said, "Jay isn't happy yet, Suze. *Yet.* He hasn't had time to discover how lucky he is to get you. Your bosses sent you there because you're perfect for the job. They should have informed Jay. You'll just have to convince him yourself."

"*If* Jay doesn't call off the acquisition or demand another property administrator. Northstar chose a poor time to flex its muscle, and now I'm in the middle. There's so much riding on this acquisition, not the least of which is my career, my income, my children's educations, my proximity to my kids and the roof above my head."

"Calm down, Suze," Karan said. "Breathe."

"I was taken off guard, I suppose."

Well, that was true, even if it wasn't the whole truth. The real truth was just bubbling up inside her, begging to burst free. She knew Karan would help make sense of what Susanna was feeling the way she always did. But the very memory of crushes and dreams made her stomach swim nauseously.

She couldn't give life to that feeling. Not now. She couldn't handle one more thing.

Not one.

"Maybe I thought I was more ready for a change than I really am," she admitted. "All I know is that if the acquisition doesn't go through, I'll be out of a job and a home."

"*That* job and *that* home," Karan pointed out. "Northstar will move you if things don't work out. The legal department won't let them do anything else. Trust me on this."

"Northstar has properties on the West Coast. I could wind up in Seattle."

"Suze, that's not—"

"And will they give me another chance as a property administrator? Or would they make me a CFO again?"

Without the property administrator salary, she'd be right back to struggling to keep up with dorm costs and meal plans and car repairs and auto insurance.

For all she knew Northstar might be annoyed Jay had recognized her lack of experience. They might demote her into accounting. How would she refuse until she found another job? In the current economy, that thought was downright frightening.

"I can't tackle unemployment right now, Karan, not unless I'm planning to live off the equity from the house."

That equity was everything she and Skip had worked and planned for. Her *only* asset besides her retirement anymore. There'd be penalties for early withdrawal from her mutual funds, not to mention supporting the kids and herself would blow through her assets before Brandon was even a junior.

No, if The Arbors didn't work out and Northstar offered her a job in Timbuktu, she'd take it.

And regret leaving Charlotte, because Susanna couldn't imagine any place as perfect as The Arbors. The hotellike luxury of other senior-living facilities was no comparison to the sunrise beyond these windows, the sky streaked in deep pinks and blues, the paling horizon of the rising sun.

She could always start up a side business, Susanna reminded herself. She was certified and could bring in good money freelancing accounting jobs, particularly around tax season, to supplement any loss of income. Karan would graciously assist with capital if Susanna would let her, and what else did she have to do besides work, anyway? Kids were gone. Dog was gone. House was gone. Husband was gone.

"You know, Karan. I can't figure out why this move never felt like such a gamble when I accepted it."

"Suze, you need to—"

"Maybe it simply never occurred to me I might fail. Not very practical for a practical person, don't you—"

"Susanna!" Karan interrupted in a tone Susanna had never heard before. "You stop right now. I know exactly what you're doing—you're *catastrophizing,* and it's unproductive. You're psyching yourself out and making things feel bigger than they are. Knock it off. *Now.*"

It took Susanna a moment to react. "Did you say *catastrophizing?*"

"Yes, catastrophizing. I shouldn't have to explain the concept. It's self-explanatory."

Susanna wasn't even sure *catastrophizing* was a real word, but the concept was indeed obvious.

Along with Karan's concern.

Okay, not only was such practical advice a departure, but a bit of a role reversal for their relationship, which had endured for so many years. Years of Susanna's practicality contrasting Karan's no-holds-barred whimsy. The reality of need contrasting the idealism of possibility. Survival honed endurance while privilege fostered restlessness.

Neither had been a road easily traveled; both ways had been pitted with potholes. But she and Karan had supported each other through marriage, divorce, remarriage, birth, life, death. Their friendship was still going strong, weighted now with maturity and life lessons.

"Seattle, Suze?" Karan laughed. "You better hope not because I won't visit. That weather destroys my hair. But, I'll tell you what. If you wind up jobless and homeless, I'll pick up a place on the outer banks so you can be near the kids. Charles keeps mentioning getting something further south so we can travel more easily to his family in Tampa. You like the beach, and so does my goddaughter."

Okay, the world was right again. Real estate as the solution to all life's problems. Classic Karan.

"You want me to call the real estate agent?" she asked.

"No. But you're right. I'm catastrophizing. Thank you for pointing it out."

"No thanks necessary. Just *stop*."

"I will. Promise." A promise she intended to keep.

The sun chose that moment to emerge over the horizon, shafts of gold shimmering across the lake's surface, penetrating the mist rising from the water.

The start of a brand-new day.

A fresh start on a day where anything was possible.

Even Karan calling at the most unexpected but perfect moment and dispensing uncharacteristically practical advice.

That's when it hit Susanna—there was something here, something particularly unique to The Arbors.

Hope.

That's what Jay fought hard to protect, was afraid to let slip away. Maybe that's what she needed to prove to him—she understood what The Arbors was all about. Not paperwork or procedures or federal regulations.

The Arbors brought hope to people and their loved ones who'd lost hope with the diagnosis of Alzheimer's. That's what The Arbors provided, and it was far more valuable than the caregiving.

"You're the best, best friend, Karan. Have I told you that lately?"

"Just returning the favor," she said.

"Well, enough about me. Why did you call again at this ungodly hour? I'm sure it wasn't to listen to me come unglued. Did we get to that part yet?"

Bubbly laughter filtered through the line. "We did, Suze."

"Did we?" Funny, Susanna couldn't remember.

"I just missed my best, best friend, that's all."

There was something more in that admission, Susanna was sure. She had no idea what. But she totally appreciated the sentiment and said, "Ditto."

CHAPTER EIGHT

JAY COULD HAVE CALLED Gerald Mayne from home had he programmed the man's direct line into his cell phone. Hadn't ever occurred to Jay he might need to. He was so used to operating out of his office—*former* office—he didn't carry a laptop or briefcase. Wasn't like he ever left.

But that was his first mistake: he'd given his office away to the wrong person, and now all the information he needed to work was locked behind Susanna's door, where he would need her permission to get at it.

His second mistake was that he'd taken Northstar at their word. Gerald Mayne had talked up Susanna as the perfect new administrator. He'd told Jay everything about her qualities and strengths, the respect she commanded from her coworkers, how valued she was as a corporate employee.

Jay could see how all of that was true. But Gerald had left out a few important details, and Jay, after meeting Susanna, had allowed himself to be distracted by her, amused by her, impressed by her, and had never questioned any further.

He wasn't sure whom he was angrier with—Northstar for ignoring his wishes or himself for never questioning their word, which completely smacked of desperation.

Desperation meant what was going on in his head wasn't lining up with the way he felt. He blamed Northstar for getting everyone's hopes up, which was another bone to pick with Mayne.

Northstar had set everyone up for disappointment. Susanna. The staff. And after a night of brooding, Jay was still angry as hell, but he knew he couldn't live with himself if he didn't make the call. He'd promised Walter to do what was right. The staff expected no less from him, either. He'd have to figure out some way to deal with the extension. A few more months wouldn't make any difference.

Except to him, because he had a future waiting for him at the end of the six-month transition. He would travel. See some of the places he'd missed while slaving away in Charlotte. He'd take that beach trip he'd missed when he was a high-school senior, after Drew had gone, when Jay hadn't had the heart to leave Gran alone because she refused to put Mom in the facility one second before she had to.

Only he wasn't heading to Bermuda but Tahiti with tiki torches and beautiful women in grass skirts.

Then when he got bored of the beach, he'd finally make the trip to Ireland to see his mom's cousin, who had invited him to visit when Jay had been younger.

He wasn't sure where he'd go after that. He'd always wanted to see the rain forest and ski somewhere with awesome slopes. Just depended on how he felt. The dogs would be bunking with Walter until Jay figured out where he wanted to settle down, and once he got the travel bug out of his system, he'd decide where he wanted to call home— anywhere but North Carolina.

The thought of his plan inflamed his anger all over again. Damn Northstar for their nonsense. This entire situation was inexcusable. Jay booted Walter's desktop and located the number. He placed the call, which rolled straight to voice mail since most offices wouldn't open until the start of the business day. He requested an ASAP return call.

He hadn't even disconnected when a familiar voice said, "Good morning, Jay."

Turning, he found Susanna showcased in the open doorway, as beautiful and fresh faced as the brisk air and sunrise that had accompanied him on his walk to work this morning.

"Oh, I'm sorry." Her gaze fixed on the phone he held against his ear.

She quickly stepped into the hall.

For an instant, he felt as if a kid caught with his hand in the cookie jar. "No, no, don't go. I'm done."

That distracting blue gaze darted past him to Walter's desk. She was jumpy. It was all over her from the way she'd ejected from the office to her tight smile.

Another heaping helping of guilt, anyone?

"Mr. Jankowski seems to be on the mend," she said. "Wasn't sure if you knew."

He shook his head. "Haven't touched base with anyone yet, but I'm glad to hear it."

"So where are we today, Jay?" Her tone was nononsense ultraprofessional, a perfect match with her business suit. "I'd like to address what happened yesterday, and if we're still moving ahead as scheduled. I didn't want to tackle data transfer if we're changing the plan."

Oh, he was changing the plan, all right, which would eliminate the need for her to do anything. Add *a lot* of guilt to the list of things he shouldn't be feeling for this woman. Not for making a choice best for the people who depended on him.

But not best for him, unfortunately.

Handing Susanna the key, signing the papers, packing his bags and getting the hell out would be best for him.

"So, how are we going to handle this situation?" she asked, which actually meant: *Are we still going through with this?*

Jay had the wild thought that he should call this off right now, before they got in any deeper. He'd waltz in tell his staff, *Just kidding, folks! False alarm.*

They'd all be relieved. Change never came easily. Management would be thrilled. Walter would say, *About time you came to your senses, boy.*

But that would mean *he* had to stay here running this place until he dropped dead or lost his mind, whichever came first. He refused to waste any more time. He'd given the first thirty-two years of his life to The Arbors, the next thirty-two were his.

The honorable thing to do was tell her. He would be diplomatic and make sure she understood his decision wasn't personal. But when Jay opened his mouth to explain, only a very dishonorable "I'm still weighing the situation" came out.

Weighing the situation?

By the time *that* registered in his rebellious brain, he was staring into her beautiful face, saw the desperate relief all over her exquisite features as she asked, "My office?"

He could practically feel her relief across the room. He wasn't sure why. Maybe he was delusional, cracking under the pressure of more obligations.

The residents. The staff. Walter. His unavailable brother. His dead grandmother. His dead mother.

Susanna.

He nodded, afraid to open his mouth and say something else to get him in any deeper.

Returning the phone to his belt, he followed her, rationalizing his actions. A discussion with Susanna's boss wasn't cowardice but the appropriate place to begin the proceedings. His deal was with Northstar Management. They'd chosen to change the plan, so they would have to inform their employee. That wasn't Jay's place.

He didn't feel any better.

A quick procession through the administrative corridor emphasized the change between them, impossible not to notice, a huge change from the easy camaraderie of the past five weeks.

"Why don't you sit there? It'll be easier to work." She motioned him toward his former chair behind his former desk.

There was no mention of coffee, although he could see her mug sitting in a place of honor atop the water dispenser, a cylinder of the instant coffee she liked perched against it.

He did as suggested and fixed his attention on the system, squelching his conscience and ignoring the way she shimmied around the desk with a few sure-footed moves, a contained grace unique to her.

She was making a difficult situation even more difficult. Especially when she dragged a chair around the desk.

He stood to offer assistance with the bulky chair. "Let me—"

"Got it, thanks."

She wasn't accepting his help today. He remembered what she'd said when they'd first met.

"I take care of me."

He should be grateful, he supposed. Distance was for the best since he'd already placed the call, and this situation would be awkward enough. But he felt anything but distant with her beside him, so close he inhaled the fresh scent of her hair as she leaned across the desk. Was there anything about her that *wasn't* distracting?

"Excuse me," she said. "Just let me grab my notebook.

I need to take notes to figure out what you have compared to what I need."

She wouldn't need anything, and he guessed she would handle that knowledge with the same ultraprofessional demeanor she was using to handle him right now.

Why she was so determined to be independent? Because she'd had to be since losing her husband?

Jay was back to wondering about her again.

Why didn't make any difference. His future was far away from The Arbors. Susanna Adams wasn't a part of it.

So he sat there maneuvering through screen after screen, explaining the data, trying not to feel guilty or cowardly and failing miserably, the same way he was failing to ignore the way wisps of her hair trailed his cheek when she leaned close to type in a password on the keyboard.

Oh, he was aware of her, all right. Straight down to the pit of his stomach.

"Want to go through the management reports now?" he asked, determined to focus on the computer if it killed him. "You've already seen most of them."

"I know everything I need is in your system. I need to identify what you're calling it versus what Northstar calls it. Then we can figure out the best way to instruct the staff to make this as simple as possible."

But nothing about the situation was simple. Not the decision to let her go. Not his awareness of her. Not his own urgency to turn over The Arbors to someone qualified to run it.

He glanced at the computer display—*9:02 a.m.*

Why hadn't Mayne called yet?

"You're making this harder than it needs to be," he said more sharply than he intended. Anger was getting the better of him. "Every function leads back to the hub, which makes your job easier. Trust me. Northstar's system design is prehistoric. Looks to me like they keep building onto an archaic program. They should ditch this entire system and design one that streamlines the process instead of wasting valuable management hours compiling all this unnecessary data."

Susanna blinked those big blue eyes at him but couldn't seem to think of anything to say.

He sighed inwardly and tempered his tone as he scrolled through the system map. "Personnel. Med data. CareCharter. Accounting. Administrative. Maintenance. You can access everything that goes on here. Press one button to download."

She jotted instructions on her notebook, but her only reply was a quiet, "Got it."

The system prompted for her password again. She depressed the Enter key as he steadied the keyboard, and their fingers accidentally brushed, warm skin against warm skin.

He could feel her touch straight down to his crotch.

She pulled back as if she felt the awareness, too.

Great. What a mess.

When his cell phone beeped, he couldn't decide who was more grateful, him or Susanna.

"I have to take this." He maneuvered around her as she slid back her chair to make room, giving him a choice shot of those shapely legs in the process.

"Canady," he growled into the receiver while making his way through the door.

"Gerald here, Jay. Returning your call."

Pulling Susanna's door shut behind him, Jay got straight to the point. "We've got a problem."

There was a beat of silence on the other end, then, "Sorry to hear that. What's up?"

Jay headed for the emergency exit at the end of the corridor. Inputting his passcode, he shoved the door wide, dragging in a deep gulp of the morning air, suddenly able to breathe again.

"I remember being specific about my needs when we hammered out the preliminary arrangement." He made a supreme attempt to sound professional when every breath seared his larynx.

"This is about Susanna's experience, isn't it?"

"It is."

"Jay, before we go any further, be reassured I heard everything you said about the sort of administrator you felt would be best suited to run The Arbors."

"If that's the case, then maybe you'll explain why you sent someone with no memory-care experience. She hasn't even run a facility before."

"I considered everything you said, Jay. So did the board and the attorneys and the execs with Rockport and University. We all want this deal to pull through as much as you do."

Not even close.

"We're achievement oriented at Northstar," Gerald continued. "We want to meet your needs and reach our goal at the same time. Our goal is your goal, Jay. You came to us because we're a corporation you can trust to move The Arbors into the future. A corporation you felt would do the job right."

"You don't have to tell me." *Or sell me.*

Clearly, Jay had been wrong. God knows it happened.

"You've got the experience for sure," Gerald said. "But as the administrator of a private facility. We're looking to expand the definition of service at The Arbors. That's why you came to us. You trusted we'd be your best bet to accomplish that goal. That's my point, Jay. You *can* trust us."

Gerald was on the offense, ready to run the ball. Jay should have known Susanna would have already spoken to her boss.

"How's that? I asked for one thing and you sent me something else entirely and didn't bother to mention it."

"Is that the issue here? That we didn't inform you?"

Gerald's question trivialized Jay's concern and made him sound petty, which spiked his anger big. But while Jay ran a private facility, he ran an efficient business. Top-notch care. Consistently balanced budgets. If Northstar didn't want to chuck this acquisition out the window, they'd better reevaluate their approach right here and now.

"I'm not happy you didn't do me the courtesy of explaining why you sent Susanna," he said. "We've got a transition period in place to establish a relationship. Any relationship that isn't based on trust isn't one I'm interested in. I get that you need to flex your corporate muscle. You don't answer to me. You made your point, but you undermined Susanna in the process, and that's not how I operate. If you'll roll your own employees under the bus then what's in store for mine?"

The silence over the cell connection was complete. Whether Gerald needed to regroup or was simply taken aback by Jay's bluntness, he couldn't say. He headed across the dewy grass, where cuttings from yesterday's mowing clung to his shoes. The morning sounds of wildlife chirped and rustled in the trees, indicating a day off to a much better start than his.

"No one's trying to flex anything," Gerald finally said. "I'm sorry you feel that's what's happening."

That's exactly what was happening, whether Gerald owned it or not. Add snake-oil salesman to his list of sins.

"Jay, you came to Northstar because you believed we could reach a mutual goal. That's precisely why we sent

Susanna. The Arbors needs a supervisor to bridge the distance between private and corporate and create a new level of service. She's a change agent, Jay. Smart. Professional. People oriented. She's experienced enough to do a top-notch job, but she also has a learning curve, which means she's open to the way you do things. We send in some die-hard with a few decades of experience under his belt, and he's going to be set in his ways."

The way Jay was set in his? Gerald didn't say that aloud, but the implication was there. Or was Jay only defensive?

"You insisted on this transitional period," Gerald pointed out. "One of the benefits of hanging around for six months is training your replacement. Susanna's open to what you're doing there. She's also at a time of her life where she can give you her undivided attention."

That much was true at least. Jay had been witnessing her work ethic since the day she arrived on the property. And he thought he was the only one with no life.

"I'm sorry I undermined your confidence in us by not explaining our reasoning for sending Susanna. There were a couple of things at play there, but it wasn't personal."

"What things?" Where he came from, making excuses for one's lack of integrity was bad business.

"There's a logistical difference in the way we conduct business, Jay. You're calling the shots down there. Up here, well, every decision makes its way up a chain of command then through the execs and the board before it even leaves Northstar to make rounds through the execs and boards of our partners. That's corporate. Explaining the decision-making process each step of the way isn't always practical or even possible."

"That still doesn't explain why you sidestepped an issue I was crystal clear about. I don't care how long the decision took you to make, Susanna's been here five weeks."

Four months and three weeks until Jay was finally out of here until the stopwatch reset.

"Either you thought you could slip this one by me or all that *making the rounds* lets details slip through the cracks, which means Northstar isn't as top-notch as I thought."

A heavy sigh on the other end. "No and no. I could have informed you, Jay, and I chose not to because I didn't want to make Susanna's job experience too big a deal. I knew once she got on the property, you'd recognize her merit. I wanted to give you that chance."

"You didn't think I'd give her a chance?"

"No, I don't. And—" he hesitated "—to be honest, I didn't think Susanna would take the chance if she knew she wasn't what you were looking for. I knew she'd love The Arbors, and I knew she was exactly what you needed. It seemed a good time for you to start trusting us to do our part. You want what we have to offer The Arbors, which means you need to ease up on the reins."

Now it was Jay's turn to be surprised by Gerald's frankness. Had snake-oil salesman been harsh or accurate? *Corporate* didn't seem much better. Gerald Mayne was the kind of executive who raked in a six-figure salary and worked up Liberals in the House. But the man sounded so damned rational. He obviously didn't get that Jay's entire life hung in the balance of this deal. He couldn't know. Jay knew that.

And still resented it.

Just as he reached the gate of Maintenance and Engineering, he changed trajectory, headed back the way he'd come.

He also didn't like how high-handed Northstar had been with Susanna. She'd left her job and New York to take a chance she hadn't been told she was taking. That told him everything he needed to know about Northstar.

Jay wanted to call off this deal completely. But he couldn't think clearly. His feelings were too involved. He didn't want to reset the clock. He didn't want to leave The Arbors in the care of a corporation he didn't trust. He didn't want to thank Susanna for the past five weeks and watch that ultraprofessional distance creep into her lovely face.

What did Jay want?

He wanted *out,* but he didn't want the consequences of getting out. Not when he had to deal with people lying to him.

"Let me tell you something," Gerald said. "Susanna isn't only my employee. She's someone I care about."

That admission came at Jay sideways.

"You care about The Arbors because of your family ties, Jay. Most administrators won't have that connection. They'll think of The Arbors as a job. Nothing more. But Susanna isn't a nine-to-fiver. She's a nurturer. When she cares about something, she cares big. You're not going to get what she can give from anyone else. She cares about her employees. About our company. About her patients in health care. About the seniors she served.

"She's a natural leader. People unify under her. We've seen that over and over again in her departments—"

"Then why haven't you made her an administrator before now?"

"Timing wasn't right. Considered her for a couple of properties, but she had a lot going on with her personal life. Susanna will take whatever training you give her and turn it into solid gold. That's who she is. She's young enough to meet the demands of The Arbors yet at a time of her life where her priorities are changing."

"I'm still listening." That was about all he had in him.

"She's been through a real rough patch, Jay. Her husband was diagnosed with cancer about seven years ago. They fought a tough fight before he died. Then she balanced family and work and single parenthood. She got her kids off to college, and now she's staring at a future that's a lot different than what she and her husband had intended. She's at a crossroads and needs a new direction to challenge her. She and The Arbors were made for each other. It's that simple."

Jay heard what Gerald said. He didn't want anyone else's well-being heaped on his plate, but he'd seen Susanna's excitement about the cottage, her new home. But take this man at his word?

"Give her a chance, Jay. You won't be sorry."

But Jay was already sorry. Sorry that a woman he was attracted to had shown up here just as he was leaving. Sorry he had to send her away.

The silence stretched as Jay's whole life unfolded before him. One decision to a man who made hundreds of decisions a day, and had for his whole life, shouldn't feel as if he was hanging from the edge of a cliff, and the only thing to do was let go.

Only it was a man who considered deception an acceptable tool who was telling Jay to dig his nails in a little deeper, to hang on.

The defiance that gripped him was at odds with the cool rationality in his brain. Jay could think, recognize the urgency for what it was, but knowing didn't temper the feeling one bit, the need to hit the ground running and not look back.

Jay could almost hear his mom in memory: *"Struggling that hard is your first clue that something isn't right, Jay."*

Instead of feeling burdened by the idea, Jay felt as if a piece had fallen into place, just one maybe, but a piece nevertheless. And another thought occurred to him, another of those pieces snapping into place.

"I take care of me," Susanna had told him.

Jay sure knew what it felt like to have only himself to rely on. To be all alone in the world, even when surrounded by people practically every minute of every day, people always looking to him to answer their questions and solve their problems, when no one offered to solve any of his.

It shouldn't matter, but it did. Jay couldn't say why. He only knew that he understood the feeling and how alone it felt.

That urgency in the pit of his gut still warred with the understanding in his head, but the words were out of Jay's mouth before he had a chance to think, to question, to regret.

"Gerald, all I can promise is that I'll give some thought to what you've said and get back with you."

"You won't be sorry, Jay."

But Jay was already sorry. He'd done everything within his power to insure The Arbors would be cared for. He was sorry a lifetime of doing the honorable thing didn't count when he finally wanted something in return.

Circling the corner of the building, Jay stepped out in front of Susanna's office windows almost defiantly, knowing she'd be there and not caring. He'd saved himself steps with this shortcut all his life, and he was *still* here....

But Susanna wasn't behind her desk. The office was empty.

CHAPTER NINE

SUSANNA WAITED FOR JAY to return, was stupidly glad for every second of his absence that gave her a chance to inhale deeply, easing up the tightness in her chest.

She couldn't sit still and went to her door, where the daily calendar would have been delivered into the mailbox when Tessa came on shift.

The daily calendar was a simple breakdown of times and activities in an easy-to-read font delivered to each resident with their breakfast.

A reminder that life went on and everyone was encouraged to participate. Activities dictated the residents' days and provided framework for the staff to schedule ongoing care and medical attention. A busy activity calendar provided quality of life that kept residents interested in living.

She glanced at today's calendar... *Memory Service.*

The concept was familiar. Greywacke Lodge conducted a biannual service to remember residents who'd passed away, a memorial by friends who'd been left behind and caregivers that—in many cases—had become fond of the residents. Glancing at the clock, she realized the service would start shortly. Unwilling to miss an opportunity to witness a special program, she left her office, running into Walter on the way.

"Good morning." She fell into step beside him. "We're still on for our budget variance review this afternoon?"

"We are." His face split into a wide grin. "Got you penciled in for one."

"Perfect." At least someone around here was happy to see her. Walter might not want Jay to leave The Arbors—he'd been upfront with her about that—but he had come to respect her work, and that had done much toward establishing a good working relationship between them. "I'm heading to the memory service. Does administration usually attend?"

"Always. The service is a big deal. More for the staff and families, of course, but the residents enjoy it, too."

Susanna understood what Walter wasn't saying. Many of the residents might not remember the friends they'd lost. She'd read somewhere during her research that memory loss was actually a protection for its victims, but made the reality all the more difficult for loved ones and caregivers.

The Arbors excelled at bridging the two. A lifeline to those with loved ones they didn't know how to help. That's what she'd seen since she'd arrived here, had been a part of.

She expected to find Jay in the lobby where the service would begin, but found only Tessa, Shirley and Amber wrestling dozens of huge white balloons.

A balloon Amber held popped with an explosive *blat,* and she jumped back with a yelp.

"I said *gently,* Amber," Tessa admonished. "You're pressing too hard."

Amber dropped a marker onto the table that held an assortment of balloons and ribbons. "That's the third one for me. I don't think I'm going to get this." Flouncing away, she circled the desk and sat with a noticeable huff.

Tessa scowled. "Robbie said folks are on their way. I'd like to start the service on time."

"Not in my job description." Amber spun her chair

around and grabbed a binder from the shelves behind the desk.

Tessa was distracted when several balloons attempted to break away and Shirley let out a loud "Oh, no you don't" as she lunged for them.

"What may we do to help?" Susanna headed into the fray with Walter keeping pace, glancing at her with an approving smile.

Amber winced and stared at them over the desk, her widening gaze suggesting she hadn't realized the new administrator had witnessed her rebellion.

Susanna smiled cordially. She knew the drill very well as she had a daughter of similar age. But how lovely that mother and daughter got to share their work.

"Thank you," Tessa said as Walter reached above her head and caught the escaping balloons. "I need all the help I can get. Got off to a late start this morning."

"Just tell us what we can do," Susanna said.

"Dietary is setting up the reception in the dining room as they break down breakfast, so we're good to go there. Residents will start arriving soon. Family members of all the residents we're memorializing will be here. The Llewellyns are already inside."

Almost as if on cue, a PCT accompanying several residents using walkers appeared behind the locked doors. Breaking from the group, Susanna handled the security panel then stepped back as the doors swung wide.

"Thanks," the male PCT said while maneuvering his charges into the lobby.

"Welcome, welcome," Tessa called out. "Pablo, how about getting everyone settled over there." She motioned to one of the huddles of furniture that created a conversation pit. "We'll keep everyone inside until we're all here."

"You got it, Tessa." Pablo steered a tall woman who

wore a bright floral-print dress toward the newly desig-
nated waiting area. "Over here, Mrs. Ramsey."

Susanna gave the door a nudge, which triggered the
mechanism into automatic motion. The door shut, and she
headed back to where Tessa was parceling out balloons to
Walter and her assistant.

There were names printed on many of the balloons.

"You release these?" Susanna asked.

Tessa nodded. "Send them straight up to heaven. Our
way of saying *we miss you.*"

Susanna was charmed. "What a lovely idea."

"Did you have memory services at your last facility?
I'd heard they were pretty common."

"I'm from Upstate New York," Susanna explained.
"Weather constraints kept us indoors. Our services ran
more along the lines of planting annuals in the atrium
in spring or hanging Christmas ornaments on the trees
in winter."

"Just two services a year?"

Susanna nodded. Memory care hadn't been the priority at Greywacke Lodge.

"Let's remember to keep everyone tight this time,"
Tessa cautioned, passing off balloons to Walter. "Last time
we had balloons in the oaks. I almost broke my neck getting them down."

"Wouldn't have been any problem if you'd have let
someone steady the ladder." Shirley chuckled.

Tessa frowned then leveled a harried gaze at Susanna.
"Is Jay coming? He usually says a few words to start the
service and introduces the preacher." She spun on her heel
and scanned the lobby. "Who isn't here yet, either, by the
way. Or will you be handling things today?"

"Jay had to take an important call. If he's not back, I'll

step in. Just introduce me to the preacher and give me a list of the residents we're remembering."

Tessa nodded gratefully. "Amber, where's the list?"

Amber pointed helpfully. "On the table."

Susanna thanked her and went to grab it, mentally preparing what she would say if Jay didn't show.

Introduce the service, the preacher...

Thank him for coming, the guests...

Whatever Jay was doing must be really important. She genuinely hoped she didn't have anything to do with derailing the man from his work today.

Cars pulled into the circle driveway. A four-door sedan moved ahead enough to allow the SUV behind it to have access to the door, as well, both drivers clearly familiar with the drill.

"Okay, we've got the Booleys and the Sagetts." Tessa thrust the rest of the balloons at Walter. "These, too, please. I need to greet the guests. Amber," she called over her shoulder as the front doors whisked open. "Radio one-west nurses' station and get someone to send the Llewellyns this way."

"Got it," Amber shot back.

Susanna saw another group of people—wheelchairs this time—approaching. She grabbed the door again as Amber hissed to Walter, "No one's answering."

Susanna noticed how Walter, that dear gentleman who wrestled with a massive balloon bouquet, was completely unruffled. "Try Pete. He's on the floor."

"And find out where everyone else is, while you're at it," Shirley suggested. "We're still missing quite a few."

Susanna held the door, smiling and greeting residents as they filed through, some propelling themselves forward ably, others steered by the accompanying PCTs.

"Pete's not answering, either." Amber shrugged. She'd done all she could do.

Tessa was already escorting the guests back toward the lobby, chatting and laughing as the front doors shot wide again.

"I'll go see what's holding them up." Susanna slipped past the wheelchair brigade and headed into lockdown.

She moved with purpose through the hallways, noting the number plates beside doors to direct her. A member of the housekeeping staff was maneuvering a cleaning cart out of a resident's room.

"Mr. Llewellyn's room?" Susanna wasn't familiar enough to remember offhand. Might never get a chance to be.

The housekeeper nodded to the left of the nurses' station and said, "One twenty-six. Bed by the window."

"Thanks." Susanna didn't even slow her stride, taking the corner at full tilt in her practical pumps.

She found the room, glanced at the biographical photo of a hearty man in a photo dancing with a bright-smiling woman wearing a country line dancer outfit.

Joseph Llewellyn, married sixty-four years to Elizabeth.

Father of two.

Grandfather of five.

Great-grandfather of one.

Occupation: Mechanical Engineer.

Originally from Cleveland, Ohio.

The bed by the door was unoccupied and neatly made, and the visiting couple stood at the far end of the room. Susanna strode in, introduced herself and greeted the man in a recliner wedged in an unusual position between the beds. To be close to the flat-screen television, presumably.

"Time for the memory service, Mr. Llewellyn," Susanna said.

"Come on, Dad. We don't want to miss this," the younger Llewellyn said before glancing at her. "We'll bring Dad."

"I'll see you there, then." Susanna left the room.

The mobile medical cart was parked only a few doors down, and Kimberly typed into a laptop opened on top of it. She glanced up from the laptop. "G'morning, Ms. Adams."

"Good morning, Kimberly. Collecting Mr. Llewellyn for the service. Are we missing anyone else, do you know? Last call."

"I think we've sent everyone who's going. Ryan just took the last group. Oh, wait, Ms. Adams. You might check Mrs. Donaire. I don't remember seeing her head out yet."

"Will do," she said with a smile, and headed past the nurses' station to Mrs. Donaire's room, where Susanna found a CNA applying makeup to Mrs. Donaire's roommate, Mrs. Previn.

"Is Mrs. Donaire attending the memory service?" Susanna asked.

The CNA shook her head. "She's waiting for a shower." Then she turned to Mrs. Donaire. "Hold up, honey. I'll be right there. I can't put Mrs. Previn out on the floor half-dressed."

The woman looked dressed from where Susanna stood, but perhaps makeup and hair had been important to her once. Mrs. Previn was in the advanced stages of Alzheimer's and hadn't interacted in a number of years, according to the staff. But she did look lovely with her peaceful smile and neatly coiffed hair.

"I know your shower will be worth the wait," Susanna

told Mrs. Donaire before slipping out of the room with a smile, knowing that sort of caring concern was priceless.

Moving down the hall toward the security doors and lobby, she wondered if Jay had returned or if she'd need to step in.

"He's not here," a raised voice said from inside a room as Susanna passed. "You don't belong here, either."

The distressed tone brought Susanna to an automatic stop. After a quick glance at the biographies, she stepped closer to the opened doorway to find a small woman with tight gray curls. She was contained within a strolling walker, a transportation device made from a PVC frame on castors for mobile residents who required more support than a standard walker.

"Millie doesn't belong here." Mrs. Munsell's voice escalated as she yelled from her bed by the window. "This isn't her room."

The gray-haired woman was wedged inside the doorway, the frame of her transportation device not allowing for easy access past the abundance of furnishings that transformed Mrs. Munsell's side of the room into a cozy Victorian parlor.

Millie turned a frantic gaze on Susanna. "Have you seen my husband? Is he with you?"

"He's not in here." Mrs. Munsell was well on her way to anxiety for all appearances. "I told you. Go look for him in your room. You don't belong here."

"Isn't this my room, honey?"

"No!"

"Oh, forgive me. I'm so sorry," Millie said, expression crumbling. She turned to Susanna. "He's going to go without me. You won't let him go without me, will you?"

"He's not here," Mrs. Munsell insisted.

"Millie," Susanna said, unclear where Millie thought

her husband had gone. "Is your husband going to the memory service?"

The woman turned a worried gaze to Susanna and shook her head emphatically. "No, no, honey. He's going to see Jesus, and he's waiting for me. Have you seen him? I don't want him to go without me. I have to find him."

Oh. Susanna motioned Millie from the room. "I'll help you. No worries. Why don't we go look together?"

"You'll help me, honey? You promise? Oh, sweet Jesus, help me find him or there's going to be real trouble."

"I'm sure he'll wait, Millie."

"Did you tell him? He might not know to wait."

"I told him. It's okay."

Her wrinkled face brightened. "You really think so?"

"I do." Susanna stepped aside to let Millie maneuver the transport device through the open doorway.

She glanced down the hallway in one direction then the other. "Which way did he go? Did you see which way he went?"

Susanna wanted to calm the woman, allay her fears if not her confusion. "Let's check this way."

"Yes, let's do. We have to find him. Will he be in my room? Is that where my room is?"

Truthfully, Susanna didn't have a clue. Somewhere behind these security doors. That much she did know. Falling into step next to Millie, they headed back the way Susanna had come.

Millie moved along at a surprisingly spry pace, which explained the need for a strolling walker. Likely not for support, but protection as Millie tooled through these halls at top speed, apparently in and out of strangers' rooms.

Arriving at the end of the hall, they were in sight of the empty nurses' station when Millie let out a soft cry.

"Oh, sweet Jesus, he left. He left me." She lifted her

panicked expression to Susanna's and burst into tears. "He's gone to see Jesus without me."

Millie sank onto the walker seat as if her legs had turned to rubber. Big tears squeezed from beneath tightly shut eyes. Her voice was a broken whisper as she chanted, "Sweet Jesus, have mercy on us, have mercy on us, have mercy on us."

Susanna sank to her knees and wrapped her hands around the knot of tightly held fingers. "Have mercy on us," she joined the prayer, their voices no more than a whisper.

Praying seemed to calm Millie, and Susanna watched the transformation until her knees ached. Millie finally took a shallow breath, then another. "He'll help me find him."

Susanna knew whom Millie meant. "He will."

Millie lifted teary eyes to Susanna, bringing to mind the memory of the time Brandon had pulled free of her grip and run off during a trip to Home Depot. He'd been mischievous and laughing as he tore off on his sturdy little legs for the chase. By the time Susanna had gotten to the end of the aisle, he'd vanished. Ten endless minutes and a dozen gray hairs later, she'd found her son cowering inside a garden shed display, a small boy who'd apparently suddenly realized he was alone.

"He will, Millie. No worries."

Kimberly caught sight of them as she pushed her cart around the corner. "Mrs. Carlson, what are you doing down here?"

Millie Carlson. Susanna pushed herself up on creaking knees. "We were looking for Mrs. Carlson's husband."

Kimberly nodded. "Well, you won't find him down here. Try room 112. Bed by the window. Unless you've changed your mind and want to go to the memory service,

Mrs. Carlson. You always like the balloons. Why don't you get out and get some fresh air."

"I love balloons." Mrs. Carlson perked up and a beaming smile broke through her tears like the sun from behind the clouds on a rainy day. "They go straight up to Jesus."

"That's right. They do," Kimberly agreed. "You want to go?"

"Oh, I do, honey. I do."

"I'm heading that way," Susanna offered.

Kimberly smiled. "I'll let Henry know where she is. Just hook her up with Cheyenne down there. She's got some of our crew there already. She'll be sure Mrs. Carlson makes it back."

"Thanks, Kimberly. Come on, Mrs. Carlson. This way."

Susanna motioned in the direction of the front lobby then had to hustle to keep up. She wondered if Jay had arrived by now or if they were waiting on her.

THE MEMORY SERVICE? Jay overheard the conversation and realized he had completely forgotten it. A quick glance at his watch confirmed he was late.

"Now what are you doing in those trees, Mr. C?" Kimberly fixed him with a quizzical gaze as he stepped from behind a bushy corn plant that would need to be repotted soon.

She glanced over her shoulder at Susanna and Mrs. Carlson making their way down the hall. "Oh. Spying. Got it."

"*Not* spying."

Kimberly pursed her mouth. "Guess you miss hiding in the bushes like you did when you were a kid. That it?"

"Something like that," he muttered beneath his breath as he sidestepped the med dispenser cart and started after Susanna.

"Be happy to fill you in with reports about your replacement, you know. Just say the word. We're all keeping our eyes on her, anyway."

"Not necessary." Jay wasn't embarrassed exactly, but not feeling the need to explain, either.

Wouldn't do any good. They all knew him too well. He'd come in through the employee door and was heading back to Walter's office when he'd heard Susanna's voice. That was all. He couldn't have walked past without interrupting them, and he hadn't wanted to do that. Not when Susanna had been doing such a bang-up job calming down Mrs. Carlson.

But Kimberly would think what Kimberly wanted to think then she'd share it with the rest of the caregivers in the break room.

Jay didn't bother with a reply but propelled himself into motion. Had he ever before forgotten a service? None that he could remember, which either testified to his turmoil about Susanna or proof he was exhibiting early-onset Alzheimer's symptoms. Not unheard-of at his age, unfortunately, and with a family history like his....

His head had been buzzing after his conversation with Gerald, which was the only reason Jay had almost bowled right into Mrs. Carlson, anyway. He hadn't even seen Susanna crouched beside the walker. Not at first. Not until he'd heard her voice, all brisk northern wind and hushed reverence, as steady and reassuring as Mrs. Carlson's had been fretful.

Mrs. Carlson was prone to panic spells, and Jay could easily imagine the scene Susanna had encountered. Mrs. Carlson was all about thanking Jesus for her every blessing and laughing with a childlike joy that had earned her resident of the month many times over during her years at The Arbors. But when the confusion set in, panic and fear were always right behind it.

Susanna's actions had been both unexpected and appropriate. She hadn't tried reasoning, which so many who were unfamiliar with Alzheimer's tried. Not usually staff, of course, because no one applied for a job without Alzheimer's qualifications.

Jay was quite explicit in his requirements on the website to the various job search agencies he worked with. But most families weren't blessed with medical history like Jay's family, which was why he and Kimberly conducted a series of mandatory basic management classes for the families of all new residents.

Understanding behaviors and good management skills were essential to successful handling of loved ones who suffered from Alzheimer's—for the resident and for the family members. Most of those skills involved correct understanding of the disease, common sense and caring.

Susanna had handled Mrs. Carlson with all three.

Inputting his passcode, Jay slipped through the doors before they'd barely opened and wound up hidden in the palm trees when he saw the large group of people congregated outside in the circle driveway.

The earth hadn't stopped revolving, and the service had gone on without him.

The scene was familiar but for the woman who stood beside the fountain addressing the group, sandwiched between Reverend Martin and Tessa. And Mrs. Carlson, whom Susanna seemed to have recruited as an assistant, judging by the scrapbooks Mrs. Carlson held stacked in her lap, which Jay knew contained memorabilia for the families who'd lost their loved ones.

For a moment all Jay could see was how natural Susanna looked there, an adornment that had been plunked down into the setting on purpose. Susanna's silky dark hair caught the sunlight, a smile lingering around her full mouth as she delivered the perfect words to make her audience smile, too.

She looked as *right* standing there as he felt *wrong* hiding in the potted plants instead of welcoming the families of residents he—not Susanna—had cared for. She didn't know who those folks had been before they'd died, before Alzheimer's had robbed them of every shred of personality that made them *them*.

As Jay watched Susanna turn the service over to the preacher, who would give a blessing, he could hear Gerald's voice. *"She needs The Arbors."*

Gerald had been right about one thing, as much as Jay hated to admit it. The best person to entrust administration of this place would be one who would invest herself with the most important asset of all.

The compassion to care.

Jay had just witnessed the caring firsthand.

SUSANNA STARED AT JAY. His chiseled features were unfamiliar in the glare of the floodlights surrounding the circle driveway, the only light besides the crescent moon.

Confrontation was coming.

She knew it with every fiber of her being. The only thing saving her right now was that the Olivanti family was still loading up in the car after a late-night facility visit, and Jay was too professional to air grievances in front of a potential resident's family.

In the days since he'd agreed to proceed with the transition if she agreed to be mentored, Susanna had learned to recognize when he was gearing up for battle. Of course she wanted to learn everything he had to share, but her agreement had subtly shifted the balance of power in their relationship.

Jay was a bit of a bully.

As far as he was concerned, he knew what was best for The Arbors in all circumstances and seemed determined to bring Northstar around to his way of thinking rather than work to come up with an effective compromise.

Susanna was growing concerned his attitude would undermine the entire process of a smooth transition and hoped this resistance was only a knee-jerk reaction to her inexperience. She was trying to ride out the storm, so to speak.

Unfortunately, she also had a niggling suspicion the real trouble was Jay. Her inexperience had only given him something tangible to latch onto because he wasn't at peace about leaving, which was why he'd been micro-managing from the start.

Things *would* have to change if the acquisition happened. Whether Northstar took over or another corporation. Whether she picked up the reins as property administrator or someone else did. The only way to maintain the status quo was for Jay to stay.

Or clone himself.

She wondered if he'd thought of that.

Exhaling heavily, she stood beside him, so aware of his tall presence in the cool night, the way the overhead lamps cast shadows that made him seem taller and bigger than he was. More masculine. Which he had in spades on a normal day.

Finally, the last of Mr. Olivanti's entourage drove away. The twinkle of red taillights hadn't yet faded into darkness before Jay asked, "Why did you have Mr. Llewellyn's recliner moved? Chester mentioned it this morning, but I forgot until we were in his room with Mr. Olivanti's son."

Here it was—the confrontation she'd known was coming.

"The chair was in the middle of the room, Jay, right between Mr. Llewellyn's bed and Mr. Shepherd's."

"And?"

"*And* it was blocking the room divider and obstructing the walkway."

Jay stared at her for a suspended moment, his eyes so dark in the shadows they might have belonged to a stranger. "Mr. Llewellyn's chair wasn't infringing on the easement. Lots of residents in the nursing center share their televisions, and Mr. Shepherd doesn't mind. Trust me on this. He has a macular problem. He can't even see the television."

"I understand you want to accommodate the residents. I want to accommodate them, too. But not by creating liability."

He gave a slight shake of his head, as if he wasn't sure he'd heard her correctly. "You're worried about liability?"

"Yes." He should be, too.

"This is memory care, Susanna. If we worried about every little thing that might go wrong, we wouldn't be able to provide any quality of life for our residents. We'd keep them locked in their rooms all day."

It was the smile playing at the corners of his mouth, his obvious condescension, which irked her so completely. "You're saying we shouldn't adhere to precautions for the residents' safety? Is that the lesson here?"

"No. No, that's not what I'm saying. I'm saying there are no hard-and-fast rules. You can't legislate common sense with corporate guidelines and legal worries."

Susanna may not have years as an administrator behind her, but she knew Northstar policy and procedure. That's where they needed to wind up—with an acceptable compromise. Toward that end, she'd welcomed Jay's instruction, had gracefully allowed their relationship to transform into one of mentor and protégé.

But to keep on equal footing, she had to educate him in the policies and procedures of corporate senior living. They both brought something to the table, but this man seemed determined to dig in his heels about the simplest things. She resisted the urge to ask him—again—why he was leaving The Arbors since he didn't want anything to change. Then at least she could stop obsessing and trying to figure out why he wanted to leave.

And help reassure him, if there was any way she could.

Maybe the tension only seemed magnified tonight because of the lateness. During the day, there'd have been a thousand other distractions to force them to deal with an issue and move on.

Right now there was just Susanna and Jay and Mr. Llewellyn's recliner.

The night was clear, the floodlights silvering the circle driveway and casting everything beyond into a black void. She and Jay were the only two specks in the light.

Maybe it was the hour, a time when normal people were in bed, asleep, wrapped around loved ones, legs twined together under the sheets, breaths hushed in the quiet.

For the lucky people who had loved ones, anyway.

She could barely remember. So much time had passed since she'd curled up with Skip, his arms her safe place in the world.

Taking a deep breath, she looked beyond Jay—a useful trick she'd been cultivating since that dream. If she looked hard into the spill of light from the floodlights, she could make out the vines reaching for the walls of the building in unexpected places, nature trying to take over.

Is that how Jay felt about her? That she was changing things that had worked before she'd gotten here, encroaching?

"A chair parked in the middle of a resident room doesn't make sense," she pointed out. "It's a bulky, solid piece of furniture that blocks the walkway between the beds even when it's not in a reclining position. It's not going to move out of anyone's way if someone accidentally bumps into it."

"No one could miss that chair. They walk around it."

"Even Mr. Shepherd with his macular problem?"

Jay narrowed his gaze.

Susanna went in for the kill. "Mr. Llewellyn has to circle the bed to get in the chair, and as you well know, he doesn't use his walker like he should. But if the recliner is back a few feet, he can slip right out of bed and into the seat. Chester left enough clearance with the wall, so the chair will still recline. A simple adjustment solves the problem."

"Except Mr. Llewellyn can't see the television from that distance."

"Then we'll need to move the television," she said simply, done with this conversation. "If Mr. Shepherd can't see it, anyway, then maybe we can rearrange things to accommodate Mr. Llewellyn and not create a potential hazard."

She wasn't backing down on this. Not with patient safety at risk. Not with liability what it was. A chair in the middle of the room was begging for trouble and the first question Northstar legal would ask was:

"Were there any obstructions in Mr. Llewellyn's room before he had the fall?"

Susanna might not have decades of memory-care experience, but she knew corporate liability like the back of her hand. Bracing herself, she lifted her face to meet his gaze.

Jay stared down at her, stubbornness all over him from

the way he braced his legs solidly apart to the way he leaned back on his heels, as if getting comfortable to wait her out.

Susanna wasn't sure what fired up inside her, but somewhere along the way this had turned into a gunfight between her and Jay. Mr. Llewellyn's chair was the weapon Jay used to take aim.

So much more was going on with this man than she understood. And she wanted to understand. So she wasn't dodging this bullet tonight. She was strapping on Kevlar.

He glared at her.

She folded her arms over her chest and glared right back.

The silence between them grew deafening.

His expression melted into exasperation a split second before he said, "We'll see if Chester can rig the television differently in the morning."

Not a concession but a compromise.

"Thank you." Her neatly professional tone came with effort because in her mind she said, *I was going to move it, anyway.*

This man was giving her whiplash with his mood swings.

"I was surprised all Mr. Olivanti's children came," she said genially to get them back on solid footing. "Six adults and two spouses. Quite an entourage for a two-in-the-morning visit."

Jay inputted his passcode with a nod. "I'm surprised we didn't wake up everyone in the place. They were actually quiet."

"Very respectful that everyone was asleep," Susanna agreed. A truce.

This had been her first impromptu facility tour, and Mr. Olivanti's family had witnessed firsthand that unlike many

ALFs running a skeletal staff on third shift—sometimes even leaving 100 residents under the frightening care of one LPN and one PCT—The Arbors staffed adequately at all hours.

One only had to walk those quiet halls as they had tonight to see several shift PCTs strolling in and out of resident rooms, a floor LPN making rounds, an R.N. overseeing the care staff as well as any unexpected med dispensing, the duty manager in the offices, the security personnel—one in the facility and another in the gatehouse—monitoring live video feed from all three floors and the immediate grounds.

Even the facility co-administrators had appeared on site within ten minutes of receiving the call that the Olivanti family had arrived for an unexpected visit. The Full Disclosure policy had a literal definition at The Arbors.

Susanna couldn't imagine what more a family could ask for from potential caregivers. But as she followed Jay into the front lobby, she realized this dedication to superb care came at a high personal cost for the man who held the yardstick.

CHAPTER TEN

JAY HADN'T BEEN HOME for ten minutes when his phone rang. No one called at 4:00 a.m. unless they needed something, but when he glanced at the display, Jay found the name of the one person in the world who might not need anything from him, after all.

"Drew. Hey, man, what's up?" Not even at this hour because for all Jay knew it was morning wherever in the world his brother was. Major Drew Canady, USMC, called when he got a chance. Period.

"Change of plans, little brother. Can't make leave on Thanksgiving."

Drew had never been big on small talk. Jay wasn't sure if the ability to zero straight in on the point was inherent in Drew's personality—it wasn't genetic—or a result of a dozen years in Special Forces.

"Sorry to hear that." He reached down and scrubbed Butters's head. It was the least he could do since the dog had made the effort to scramble off the couch where he'd been sleeping to greet Jay.

Gatsby only lifted his head, eyed Jay as if he'd been rude to make noise at this ungodly hour then promptly shut his eyes again. "Think you'll be able to make it back to the States before I sign the papers? Would hate to turn over your key without giving you a chance to say your goodbyes."

Not that his brother cared. Jay imposed his own sense

of nostalgia on a sibling who'd long ago proved he was all about looking ahead to the next challenge rather than behind him.

A trait that Jay admired—mostly. All that running had some downsides, too.

"You want me home to clean out my old room so you don't have to."

"You remembered. I'm shocked."

"You threatened to call Goodwill and have them pick up all my past history. Come on, Jay. Like I want my high school football and track trophies to wind up in someone else's trophy case." There was a laugh in there. The trophies in question were in a milk crate in the attic. No one but their mother had been interested in saving them, and she wasn't around anymore.

"You never took me seriously before," Jay said. "Didn't occur to me you'd start now."

The sharp silence on the line came as a surprise. Then Drew said, "Never thought I had to, but that was before Mom died and you started getting real about unloading our legacy."

Our legacy.

As Drew barely managed to make it home a few times a year. And then only if he wasn't currently involved with a woman in his various ports of call. Involved, he didn't come home. Single, he made an appearance.

Jay was glad someone was enjoying life.

But Drew never stayed for more than a week at a time. He seemed hardwired to spontaneously combust when he got too close to day seven of a visit.

No, the legacy was all Jay's. Drew's name just happened to be on the deed. A formality.

"Yeah, well. It's time. I offered you the once-in-a-lifetime chance to take my place. You weren't interested."

"No way, man. Not when you've been doing such a bang-up job around there."

A snort was the best Jay could come up with. Talking with Drew always brought mixed emotions. Appreciation for a living family member, which was a novelty in the Canady family. There was accompanying resentment because Drew never acted like more than a distant relation. He'd disconnected long ago, leaving Jay to deal with the family business as if he were an only child.

Why would Drew be interested in around-the-clock obligation when he was always knee-deep in some foreign conflict, his high-level security clearance making it impossible to discuss his work protecting the good old U.S. of A. from the bad guys?

Jay didn't think he'd be so eager to give up the challenges of a cloak-and-dagger life. Challenges. Travel. Noble causes. Sounded pretty good from where Jay stood. Of course, Jay's idea of excitement was sex on the beach, marriage and kids. All brothers weren't cut from the same cloth.

Climbing the stairs, Jay wondered if he'd be able to sleep, or if he should chalk up the night and get started on tomorrow. "If you've got something to say, Drew, now's the time. This place is half yours even though you're never here."

More silence, which was telling, but Drew finally said, "No, man. This is your call. You've done your time, and I haven't been a damn bit of help. Not with Mom, not with Gran, not with any of it. You've been holding down the fort, so I didn't have to feel guilty about not being around to deal with *our legacy*. If you want to move on, you go for it. I'd be the last person to hold you back."

Jay pulled the phone from his ear and stared down at the display, so surprised that he missed Butters make a play for the bed, nearly knocking Jay over in the process of scrambling up.

Jay frowned at the dog and motioned to the other side.

Sinking onto the edge of the bed, he said, "Where are you? It's got to be late at night because you're awfully self-reflective. That almost sounded like a thank-you."

"Not as late as where you are." He laughed. "Doesn't sound like I woke you up from your beauty sleep."

"Someone beat you to the punch."

"Not a woman. That much I know."

Toeing off his shoes, Jay sank back into the pillows and stretched out after a very long day. "You don't think?"

"Um…I suppose you could surprise me."

"Just goes to show you that you probably shouldn't think. It was five women, actually."

"Sheeeeeet." A snort of laughter. "Any of them *not* seniors? Or forgetting they have AARP cards."

"Yes. Two definitely. Maybe three." He couldn't be entirely sure about one of Mr. Olivanti's daughters. Maybe she'd been a few years behind her siblings or maybe she'd had good genes.

"Okay, so somebody either died tonight or you were giving the owl tour. Which was it?"

The fundamental truth of Jay's sorry existence. "Owl tour. With the new director."

"Like him?"

"Her."

"Her, hmm. Another senior?"

An image of Susanna popped into Jay's brain in all her feminine glory. Big blue eyes. Soft smile. Kissing lips. Unless that kissing mouth was pursed tight with a rebellious streak that was at odds with her feminine appearance.

Almost as if on cue, a light twinkled in his periphery. Jay glanced out his window to see another light blink out.

Susanna heading into the bedroom.

No, the new director definitely wasn't another senior. He turned his back, determined not to be distracted. "Your age. Little older, maybe."

By four years exactly. But Jay wasn't going to admit he was paying such close attention.

Not even to himself.

"She any good? Wait—" Drew chuckled. "Let me rephrase that. Is she good enough that you'll be able to leave the place without kicking yourself in the ass for the rest of your life?"

For a brother who hadn't been around much since Jay had been fourteen years old, Drew could read Jay better than anyone, which made no sense whatsoever.

"I think so. Yes," he said decidedly. "She'll be ready by the time I have to sign the final papers."

If he had to beat her into submission.

"I'll keep my fingers crossed. For your sake."

That's when it hit Jay—the uncustomary chattiness of a brother whose conversations always ran along the lines of mission briefings. Drew called often, but they were always touching-base kinds of calls.

Letting everyone know he was still alive. Checking up on what was happening on the homestead. Getting updates on who was currently losing their mind or in imminent danger of dying. Of course, now that everyone had lost their minds *and* died, there wasn't much to catch up on but the sale.

Drew had a life. Jay...not so much.

Of course, none of this explained why Drew was suddenly all sorts of chatty. So, one of two things was going on: either something was up with him or he had concerns about Jay.

"You good, Drew?" he asked.

"Never better, bro, and you can thank Northern Ireland for that. Do you know how long it's been since I've been anywhere but the Middle East?"

Jay supposed the cold north might be a refreshing change after a long stretch of desert sand and broiling sun. Of course, someone who'd never lived off the sixty acres where he'd been born wouldn't actually *know*...

"Bully for you. I was invited to Ireland to visit the cousins. Might actually make it when I get out of here. You need their addresses?"

"Working."

"Well, have fun with all that cold rain and ocean wind. So what's on your mind? You broke your record for phone conversations about ten minutes ago."

More laughter. "Can't call and shoot the breeze?"

"No."

"Just wanted to make sure you were good. That's all. Things have been changing since Mom."

Since Mom. Funny how a man in Special Forces, a First-to-Fight Marine, would deal in euphemism.

Since Mom *died*.

Guess in some ways he and Drew were more alike than he'd thought. They both dealt closely with death. Drew with war and terror and disaster. Jay with the inevitable slow grind of age and infirmity.

"Never better," Jay said. "Don't worry about me. I'm looking forward to getting the hell out of here." *Finally.*

"Got a plan for after you sign the papers?"

"Can you say Tahiti, no phones and beautiful women?"

"The beautiful women part sounds good. You have fun with the sand."

"I will, thank you."

"Guess Tahiti would sound good to someone who prunes arbors for fun."

"Do not start pissing in my cereal."

"Don't know how you've done it for all these years."

Jay had never figured out if Drew was squeezing in as much of life as possible before Alzheimer's robbed him of his faculties. Or was dangerous work his way of controlling fate? Going out with a bang was better than dying a slow death in a place like The Arbors with a healthy body and a rotting brain.

The one thing Jay did know was that Drew hadn't lost his mind yet. Or shared what was on it.

Drew himself confirmed that observation when he said, "I can make it for Christmas. That work for you?"

"As long as you clean out your room while you're here, so I don't have to."

Drew laughed. "You got it. I'll let you know my arrangements when I make them. We'll talk before then. Can't make leave for Thanksgiving, but I'll call."

"Stay safe."

"Will do. And, Jay."

"Yeah?"

"It was a thank-you."

CHAPTER ELEVEN

SUSANNA CLICKED ON THE software icon the instant it flashed a notice for a video call. Abandoning the budget she and Walter were *still* hammering into shape, she smiled in greeting as her daughter appeared on the computer monitor.

"I haven't heard from you since yesterday, Mother, so I figured I'd better call."

If the expression or the tone hadn't given Brooke away, her use of the title *Mother* would have.

"Hello, sweetie. What's up?"

"I haven't heard from you for one thing. A day, Mother. Not a call or a text or an email. No one's heard from you. Something could have happened to you, and no one would have had a clue."

Susanna had said those exact words a hundred times, so it took her a moment to decide if Brooke was being facetious.

There wasn't anything teasing about that *Mother*. Or the sour expression on her daughter's beautiful face, showcased on the monitor compliments of the webcam.

"Sorry about that. I meant to text you before bed last night, but I didn't get out of here until late. Sweet little lady named Mrs. Harper had to go to the hospital. I was a bit rattled. I hope I didn't worry you."

An impatient *humph* was Brooke's only reply.

Susanna grabbed the reins on this conversation fast.

She was up to her eyeballs with work and couldn't afford to end this telephone conversation with any less emotional energy than she had right now, which was precisely what would happen if she didn't have a successful conversation with Brooke.

She'd get off the phone running the emotional gauntlet about whatever was troubling her daughter and how she was unable to help because she was so far away. Then would come anxiety about whether or not she should have sold the house. After that would be guilt because a good mother would be able to figure out how to help her child, and if they lived closer, Susanna would be able to persist until she figured out how to help. Then the recriminations would start because a good mother would realize she couldn't control everything in her child's life nor should she want to.

And nowhere in that swirling soup of emotion would there be an ounce of room left for work, or dealing with the crazily demanding, utterly impossible and thoroughly irresistible mentor/co-administrator.

"So how'd your big exam go? Feeling good about it?"

"I got an A."

"Oh, that was fast. Congratulations. Can't say I'm surprised, though."

The compliment eased up Brooke's disapproval just a bit. When Susanna looked at Brooke, she saw Skip, knew when they'd stood side by side—now only in photos— there was no missing the familial relationship. But the same could be said—and was often—about mother and daughter.

Susanna recognized the fair skin, the delicate cheekbones and chin, but she also saw the startling blue of Skip's eyes, the charming smile that managed to animate her daughter's entire face. Brooke seemed to have taken the best of both parents and put them together to create her own unique and lovely self.

"Have you figured out what we're doing for Thanksgiving yet?" Brooke asked.

Thanksgiving? Still a good week away, and nowadays Susanna didn't deal with anything without a pop-up reminder on her computer calendar. Hmm. She might have hit the snooze on the first reminder now that she thought about it.

"Now's the perfect time. Let's decide."

Brooke scowled. "What's to decide? Brandon's got that special training camp, so he can't leave Columbia. I know because I already talked to him."

"So they're starting camp on Wednesday? Bummer. I was really hoping they waited until Friday and ran straight through the weekend."

"The only day he's not practicing is Thanksgiving."

"That does limit our options."

"We should still have a real Thanksgiving even if Brandon can't get home."

Home.

There it was. The problem.

"I'd feel bad if we excluded your brother from his first college holiday away from his family."

Brooke shrugged, twisted around to grab a bottle of vitamin water off the windowsill beside her computer desk. "He's the one with the scheduling problem."

"If we put our heads together, we can come up with something better. Remember, we're establishing new traditions."

But no one had yet seen the picturesque cottage that had replaced home. They didn't have a home base, and they were used to a mother who'd had the house decorated for Thanksgiving before they'd finished eating the Halloween candy.

"It's Thanksgiving, Mother. I took eighteen credit hours this semester. That's six classes and I have been working in the tutoring lab, too. I'd like to get off campus for a few days before I have to start killing myself again for finals." All that on one long breath.

"I understand completely." Oh, boy, did Susanna understand. She'd been dealing with Jay, going back and forth and back and forth on everything from Christmas bonus to coffee, which he said tasted horrible, anyway, so why shouldn't they try to save a bit of money there?

"Would you like to come here, Brooke? I can't wait for you to see the cottage. You're going to love it."

"But then it's only you and me. What kind of Thanksgiving is that?"

Brooke's complaint was the very thing that had the ability to drive a spear through Susanna's heart. Mom hadn't lived up to her daughter's expectations, hadn't provided the homey holiday that memories were made of. That was what good mothers were supposed to do.

But to Susanna's surprise, she was able to shake out the spear without too much effort. Change didn't come easily, after all, and establishing new routines would take some time.

"Christmas is our holiday, not Thanksgiving," Susanna reminded, shooting for some normalcy. Not everything had changed. "We always rotate, and this is Uncle Milton's year. Nana and Papa are driving up to Maine. We were invited, of course, but this wasn't a good time to make the trip. You helped me make that decision."

"But Grandma and Grandpa are going to be home alone."

Skip's parents. "They'd rather come to Charlotte for Christmas when you and Brandon have more time off."

"But they're going to be alone."

If we were home, they wouldn't have to choose.

Brooke didn't say it, but Susanna heard it loud and clear, evidenced by her daughter's sullen expression and the way she twisted the top of the vitamin water bottle, a vent for her agitation.

"They're old, Mother. We're their only family since Daddy died. They shouldn't have to pick and choose. We don't have Grandma and Grandpa or Aunt Karan or Brandon. We don't have anyone, so we can't have a holiday. I think I'm going to the Outer Banks. I have some friends who aren't heading home—"

Amazing how a little distance made it so easy to see past the attitude to the hurt fueling it. "Aunt Karan and Uncle Charles will invite Grandma and Grandpa, so they'll have a good time. You know the kind of parties Aunt Karan throws. And we always accommodate Brandon's training schedule in some way or another on the holidays, but if you want to go with your friends to the beach, Brooke, it's your holiday."

Brooke brought the bottle to her lips and took a long swig, silence her only reply as she reasoned through what to make of Susanna's acquiescence. Susanna knew she'd surprised her daughter. Truth be told, she'd surprised herself.

But this was Brooke's holiday. If she chose not to spend it with family then she'd live with that choice. Might turn out to be a good choice. Or not. Either way she'd grow and learn.

As much as Susanna wanted to be with her daughter on this all-important first Thanksgiving away from home, the urgency seemed to have faded. She wasn't sure why.

Maybe because they'd already distanced themselves from the long-standing holiday patterns. Or maybe suddenly the unknown future looked a little more exciting than scary. There was so much potential in creating new traditions.

Brooke gave a shrug. "Well, I'm not entirely sure I want to tackle an Atlantic beach in November."

"Definitely be cold." Susanna bit back a smile. "I have an idea. Why don't we meet in Raleigh? We'll spend the day before Thanksgiving shopping then drive down to South Carolina at night to surprise Brandon. We'll have Thanksgiving together then be there for his game on Friday. You and I can head back to Raleigh, hit the stores again on Saturday—after all that Black Friday nonsense— and come home on Sunday with enough time to rest before the week starts again. How does that sound?"

Some girl time sounded great to Susanna. So did a break from Jay Canady and his mood swings.

And her own unruly reactions to him.

Brooke took another swig to buy some time. Playing hard to get? Susanna couldn't be sure, but she held her breath, hoping this might signal a bit of growth for their relationship, too. Mom and daughter with some genuine friendship thrown in. Another transition. Susanna would like that.

"Shopping," Brooke said with a sudden smile. "Sounds like a plan."

The perfect plan from Susanna's perspective.

"ARE YOU SURE YOU DON'T want me to hang around, Jay?" Susanna asked. "I can rearrange my plans."

Jay met her gaze across the expanse of chairs in the hospital waiting room, where they'd come to touch base with Mrs. Harper's family and make arrangements for her homecoming.

News of Mrs. Harper's release had arrived early on a Saturday morning.

"No sense missing out on the holiday," he told her. "Go see your kids and have fun. You've been working nonstop since you came to Charlotte. I wasn't doing anything exciting, anyway."

"What will you do, then?"

"Walter and I usually get together to watch football."

"Sounds relaxing. No typical big family get-together?"

That simple question wasn't simple at all coming from this woman. This question was personal, which meant she was interested in knowing more about him. And while Jay knew her interest was only casual, it didn't feel casual. Not one bit.

"Not really. Not anymore. There's only my brother, and he's in the Marines. Can't make leave until Christmas."

She appeared to consider that, looked thoughtful. "You have so many people who care at The Arbors. Family-by-love."

A fanciful sentiment from a woman he hadn't realized was so fanciful. She cared. Gerald had been dead right about that. Jay didn't think too many people could find their way into her life and not be cared about. "Walter and I will see all of them on Thanksgiving, too. Liz throws her annual feast at the facility. She makes every one of her pies from scratch."

"Wow." Drawing her legs up, she tucked them around her on the bench seat, for once not wearing her customary business suit, but a long skirt made of some filmy stuff that flowed around her legs when she walked. "Who's the feast for? The residents and staff on duty?"

"Everyone, and I mean everyone. She's famous for her cooking, so residents' families show up, and staff families show up whether they're scheduled or not. Some of our local vendors show up, too."

"You're kidding?"

"Nope. The place is like a revolving door buffet until she closes up shop at three. For the record, she has permission to use our facilities to cook her family Thanksgiving meal. Her kids pack up everything to take home. That going to be a problem? She supplies her own food."

Give or take some seasonings and little items that were kept in the facility kitchen. Jay wouldn't muddy the waters with too much information.

Susanna's easy humor faded fast and she transformed into the practical administrator he knew so well. "She and her staff are doing all the cooking, right?"

He nodded.

"Then I don't think there'll be a problem."

"Good." He'd be sure to document the procedure and permission in the management manual he'd been working on for Susanna's reference in the event he actually got out of here as planned. He was glad he'd remembered to address the issue now. He'd been trying to cover every eventuality that might come up in his absence, but he hadn't considered Thanksgiving until this very moment. How many others had he missed?

"Sounds like I'll be missing a great time," Susanna said.

"There'll be photos up on the website. Tessa wanders around with that camera of hers then gets Amber to post everything on Facebook. You do know we have a Facebook page?"

"I do." She smiled again, and Jay decided he liked this chatty, easygoing woman. Off duty, Susanna was easy to be around. No wrestling back and forth about little things that made a world of difference at The Arbors. She could let all her caring come out without such black-and-white rules and regulations hemming her in on all sides.

"I liked our page," she admitted. "And I like the fact we'll have Mrs. Harper back. I hated thinking of her in the hospital over the holiday."

Jay definitely liked this Susanna with all the soft edges showing. He liked her a lot. "We should have an idea of her arrangements as soon as the doctor writes the orders. I didn't expect it to take so long. You're losing a lot of your day off."

"No problem here. I was reading commentary on North Carolina ALF certifications, and this is more important. You don't think the doctor will release Mrs. Harper to return to her apartment yet, do you?"

Jay leaned forward and clasped his hands over his knees, the small of his back beginning to ache after sitting so long in the plastic chair. "I think we're looking at a few weeks of physical and occupational therapy before she can pass the transfer tests to get back upstairs."

Unless Mrs. Harper was dramatically improved from his last visit, she was looking at a stint on the first floor until she could get in and out of the bathroom on her own, which was one of the criteria for assisted living.

"She was getting around so well. That's something that still surprises me about senior living, even after all these years."

"What?"

"How quickly things can change."

There was such wistfulness on her pretty face that Jay wondered who she'd lost. He didn't ask.

Susanna exhaled softly. "One day a resident looks like she's winding down then the next she's up scavenging bread and feeding the ducks."

"Hope that's the case with Mrs. Harper." But Jay also

knew what Susanna wasn't saying—that those changes worked in reverse. One day a resident was feeding the ducks then the next she was gone. "Keep in mind that Mrs. Harper is ninety-three. She's been getting around better and longer than most."

"True, true, but the ducks will miss her. Any chance of getting her a window bed that looks out on the lake?"

"That's a really good idea."

She smiled, clearly pleased she'd come up with an idea he approved. Hadn't been happening all too much of late, if he was honest with himself. Why? Because he was afraid she'd sacrifice all the important things when he was no longer around, all the things that made The Arbors The Arbors. And in the wake of her bright smile, Jay had to ask himself why he cared so much. If he wanted out so badly, shouldn't he be content to leave the future in the care of someone who obviously cared?

THANKSGIVING WAS A HEALING step for Susanna and the kids. A step that proved they were still a family no matter how much distance separated them. Being together was the best part of the holiday and *where* didn't seem to make any difference.

For Thanksgiving dinner they sat in a lovely restaurant next to Brandon's school that was a renovated post-World War I officers' club. An elegant place and a fine dining experience with a nineteenth-century bar and a balcony. They'd decided to splurge on their first nontraditional Thanksgiving meal.

Brandon barely glanced at the menu before setting it back on the table.

"You've decided?" Susanna hadn't yet selected a salad. A warm spinach salad or a house salad with cranberry merlot vinaigrette?

"Shrimp and grits."

Brooke eyed him over the menu. "Grits?"

"We live in the South." He replied with such deadpan delivery that Susanna chuckled.

Brandon had never been chatty like his sister. Reaching for his glass, he winked at Susanna, looking so much like his father in that moment she swallowed hard.

He could have been Skip at a similar age with the glossy black hair and lanky grace of a young man who hadn't yet grown into his body. The young man she'd fallen in love with. Oh, so charming with a sudden grin that reflected his love of mischief and making people laugh in as few words as possible.

He hadn't made a big deal of their surprise arrival last night, but he was thrilled with their visit. Susanna knew because she knew her son, understood that what he didn't say was actually more important than what he did. He hadn't waited for an invitation before packing a bag at his dorm and deciding to spend the nights in the hotel room Susanna had booked, a one-bedroom suite with plenty of room.

He might not call her as often as Brooke, but these first two semesters away from home had lent him a new appreciation for the women in his life. This newfound maturity was evidenced by the way he'd opened doors and ordered meals. The way he'd insisted on driving them around because he knew Columbia.

"Well, I'm looking into pasta of the day," Brooke informed them. "Mom, you?"

"Sweet tea pork just because it sounds so Southern." She closed the menu and set it aside. "Definitely a departure from eating stuffing out of Nana's turkey."

"Ugh, Mom! That's so gross." Brooke pulled a face.

"It's the highlight of my Thanksgiving, Ms. Vegetarian."

Always had been even as a little girl. Susanna's mom always made the turkey no matter who hosted Thanksgiving. She started thawing the turkey three days in advance then got up at three in the morning to start cooking her "bird" as she called it. Mom would hand Susanna a fork and she'd take the first piping hot taste of the stuffing to determine whether or not the bird was close to ready. A lifetime tradition.

"For the record." Brooke tossed her hair off her shoulders and set her menu down. "I'm not a vegetarian. Just selective."

"You could select the duck," Brandon suggested. "Looks like a turkey. Kind of."

"Um, you have fun with that."

Brandon shook his head. "I'm good with the grits, thanks. Not a fan of turkey."

"Really, Brandon. How come I did not know that?" Susanna had known Brooke didn't care for turkey. Everyone had known because Brooke had always made a performance out of piling her plate high with everything else that graced the Thanksgiving table. But Brandon... "Why do I always remember you eating turkey then coming back for seconds and thirds?"

"I was hungry."

Brooke rolled her gaze, but Susanna gasped.

"Brandon, I can't believe you never said anything. If I'd have known I would have baked a ham or something."

He shrugged, unfazed. Food was food, apparently. Then the waiter returned, and Brandon ordered for everyone, the way his father had once done when they'd dined out as a family. Brandon had only been thirteen when Skip had died, but clearly some things left a lasting impression.

"Come on, we've got to say grace." Brooke prompted when the appetizers arrived. She extended her hands to join the family in a circle. "Mom, you start."

Susanna began with thanks for the opportunity to be with her beautiful family. Brandon continued with gratitude to have his mom and sister within driving distance and their surprise visit. Brooke drew a deep breath, then said, "Lord, please bless our food, we ask with a shout. Save us all as we pig out. Some stranger cooked our meal and probably, uh, sweat. This food needs all the help it can get."

There was a beat of silence before they all dissolved into laughter, drawing notice from some other diners.

Skip had always been the one renowned for his theatrical performances of grace that would leave the entire table howling.

And in this moment, he was with them. He'd always be with them. Because they were his family. A unit. No matter how much distance separated them. No matter where they made home base. No matter who married and changed their name or added children, this family had always started with Dad, Mom, Brooke and Brandon at its center. Their family might grow up and grow, might move around near or far, might even physically have to say goodbye as they had to Skip, but they'd never lose each other because they were a part of each other, always.

There was a part of Susanna that settled down, finally at peace, so reassured that whatever changes life might throw their way, *they* were intact. And would be. They'd roll with the punches, make time for each other and savor each moment they spent together. For the first time in so long, she felt excited for the future. And she could see that there was a lifetime of possibilities ahead of them because the urgency and anxiety wasn't blinding her.

No, her gaze was filled with her beautiful children, so grown-up now, her ears filled with their laughter as they chatted over the meal, providing glimpses of life in Virginia, in Columbia, in Charlotte, and sharing plans and dreams.

Brooke wanted to go overseas for her graduate studies. As an art history major, she wouldn't be through with school until there was a Ph.D. behind her name and her minor in French translated into language fluency that would allow her to hold her own in international business.

Brandon surprised them all by revealing that while he intended to ride his scholarships as far as they'd take him, he wasn't interested in playing pro ball or sports management.

"Remember that ball camp I went to this summer?"

"The ball camp that dragged you away from home two days after high school graduation? That the one?" Susanna asked.

Brandon arched an eyebrow, clearly not missing the sarcasm. "A group of handicapped kids came to participate for a few weeks. It's a summer program the university conducts to provide opportunities for service hours that the undergrads involved with sports have trouble squeezing in during the normal semesters. You wouldn't believe the things these kids can do. Play ball. Race. Swim. You name it. They've got all kinds of equipment to help them work around their disabilities. It's amazing."

Susanna and Brooke sat in silence for a moment, too surprised to do more than blink at Brandon's unusual candor.

"So you're interested in working with handicapped kids?" Susanna asked.

"No, Mom. Orthopedic surgery. I talked to Uncle Charles before I went to see my advisor about classes for next semester. I don't waste time taking stuff I don't have to. Turns out Uncle Charles knows the chief of orthopedics at a hospital in Greensville. Dr. Spellman. He was great. Invited me in to tour their program. Just went a few weeks ago."

"Wow, honey. How wonderful" was all Susanna could think to say on the fly. This had completely come out of left field. She wondered if Karan knew, because she hadn't mentioned one word.

Brooke recovered faster. "How are you going to keep up with the coursework while you're playing ball?"

Brandon looked affronted she'd question his ability and glared back with a narrowed gaze.

"I think it's great you're so interested," Susanna said, stepping in before the interaction took a turn. Siblings. "I guess you've been playing ball so long I assumed you'd go into sports management or something like that."

He shrugged. "Ready for a change, I guess."

Reaching across the table, she patted his hand. "I'm excited for you."

Brandon grinned his father's grin, and then they were back to eating and chatting and being thankful for their enthusiasm about the future. Susanna shared stories about The Arbors and got excited about their visit in a few short weeks. They made plans for celebrating Christmas in their new home base. And by the time they were sipping coffee and sharing a dessert, Susanna couldn't help but think how proud Skip would have been of his kids.

That thought lingered, and he felt close as they wrapped up dinner and headed back to the car, which they'd parked on the street. It had been light when they'd entered the restaurant but dark now, so they didn't see a man emerge from the shadows until he startled them with a gravelly voiced greeting.

Brandon stepped around Susanna, keeping her and Brooke close as he herded them along, saying, "Have a good Thanksgiving, man."

Susanna saw him press something into the man's hand. Cash, she guessed.

"God bless you," the man replied with a shake of his grizzled head. No smile.

They continued on their way to the car without comment. Brandon had assumed control of the situation quickly, and kindly.

Skip would have been so proud of his son.

Of all his family.

CHAPTER TWELVE

SUSANNA RETURNED TO The Arbors more content than she'd felt in a long time. There was only one more situation that needed resolution…and Jay's departure at the end of the transition period would resolve that problem.

Her newfound peace manifested itself in a night of deep sleep, a refreshing change from the anxiety-riddled hours she'd endured since her arrival in Charlotte.

But as luck would have it, the ringing cell phone awoke her on the first night of her return. Bleary-eyed from deep slumber, Susanna attempted three times to answer the call before depressing the right button.

"Yes," she ground out.

"Sorry to wake you, Susanna," Walter said apologetically. "But I've got a situation here."

"What?" The word barely scratched past the gravel in her throat.

"Pipe break."

For a beat of silence, she stared into the darkness, wrapping her brain around what Walter had said.

Pipe break?

Sleep fell away fast. "Please tell me the first floor."

"Wish I could. Third."

"On my way."

Susanna reacted. She didn't bother with a bra but pulled on sweats and a pair of deck shoes before taking off at a run. She opted for a fast drive in her car to the facility.

Robbie from security waited in the main lobby and opened the main doors when he spotted her, saving her the effort.

"Walter put in a call to Mr. C. too," he said. "But he's not here yet."

"All right, so where are we?"

Robbie gave her the rundown as they made their way to the employee stairs. "Ryan heard the leak on a walk-through. By then it was coming through Mrs. Mason's second-floor bathroom."

"She's been evacuated?"

"Put her in the respite room."

Susanna nodded approvingly. "Have we figured out where the leak is coming from and has anyone turned off the water?"

Walter emerged from the employee stairwell, wet from head to toe, sodden shoes squeaking on the concrete with each careful step. Kimberly followed him with a stack of dry towels.

"Glad you could join us, Susanna." Walter shot her an ironic smile. "The leak is in Mrs. Harper's room."

"Thank God for small favors." Mrs. Harper was currently ensconced in her temporary room on the first floor.

Walter nodded, which sent wet white hair flopping heavily onto his forehead. Kimberly reached up with another towel to stem the flow into his eyes.

"It's a mess up there," she added.

"Tried to shut off the main for that wing, but I couldn't get the valve to budge," he explained. "Ryan got some tools, but we proceeded to snap the valve right off in the valve seat."

"Oh." Susanna dragged her gaze over wet Walter. Not good. "Is there a *main,* main for the facility?"

Robbie frowned, and Walter arched a bushy eyebrow.

She wasn't sure if their silence meant the facility couldn't be without water or if they'd have to call the water department to access the main valve. Either way, she'd clearly reached the limit of her plumbing experience. "Has anyone called Chester?"

"He told me to get into the plumbing cabinet in Mrs. Harper's room. Said there's some sort of shut-off valve in there. Ryan and I had a go. We weren't sure what we were supposed to be turning, and it was hard to see with all the water. Afraid we'd break something else and make matters worse."

"Okay, then. What are we doing to contain the water?"

"Ryan's sopping it up in Mrs. Harper's room, and Jane is in Mrs. Mason's room, keeping it from running down the wall—"

"Jay's here." Robbie headed back toward the door.

Jay strode through the doors wearing running pants and a scowl, and the rest of them stood there united in their relief at the mere sight of him.

Susanna included.

Jay would know what to do.

"Welcome home," he said before Walter launched into an explanation yet again and Jay sprang into action, reaching for the employee stair door and maneuvering around Walter with an impatient "We just need the angle stop. I got it."

The relief was tangible. Everyone had such faith in Jay. That was his gift and what made The Arbors so special.

Susanna chased after Jay. "Go dry off, Walter," she said before the door slammed shut behind her.

Taking the stairs two at a time, she finally caught up in the hallway outside Mrs. Harper's room.

He met her gaze, green eyes filled with resigned humor. "Have a good holiday?"

She laughed. "Lovely, thanks. You, too, I hope."

His eyes twinkled. "I did."

There was a laundry cart in the hall with stacks of dry, neatly folded towels, supplying Ryan, who was inside on his knees in the flood, damming the flow of water.

"Hey, Mr. C., Ms. Adams." He flashed a wet grin while layering another sodden towel onto the makeshift dam in the bathroom doorway.

"Toolbox?" Jay asked.

"In there, on the vanity. Hope you brought swim goggles."

Jay gave a snort of exasperation, or maybe laughter. Except that he didn't look all that amused. "Get out of here. Go dry off. Don't drip on the carpet."

"Yeah, right." Ryan pushed himself to his feet, scrubs soaked and molding every inch of his young body in thin cotton. "Chester's got a wet-vac."

"Thanks for your help, Ryan" was all Susanna said as she averted her gaze politely.

But she was pleased that his dam-building effort had been fairly successful because the carpet beneath her feet didn't feel squishy until she got close to the bathroom door.

"How may I help?" she asked while grabbing a few towels from the cart.

Jay stepped over the dam, bracing himself with a hand on the doorjamb. "Ugh, what a mess" was his only reply as he quickly surveyed the damage. "We'll have to gut this whole bathroom, and probably Mrs. Mason's downstairs too."

"What a blessing that Mrs. Harper has already been relocated. Who knew?" was all she could think to say.

"Yeah, well. You've got a point."

Then Jay was on his knees, giving her a prime shot of his backside as he leaned into the narrow space between the vanity and commode. Water sprayed out, not violently but steadily, and he tried to avert his face, which obstructed his ability to see inside. "I've just got to get down in here…."

If only this had been the first floor. The bathrooms in the nursing center were utilitarian, tiled with floor drains. But these were apartments in every sense of the word except for the lack of kitchens and any appliances that could be left plugged in, or on. The ALF floors, for all their monitoring and security, accommodated residents with limited-assistance needs.

Susanna continued to buttress the swollen dam. Her efforts were decidedly unhelpful at best, compared to Jay who was stretched out in that narrow space, getting rained on full in the face as he twisted around to work inside the cabinet.

And what a sight he made from this angle, providing a full shot of his backside. The running pants proved worse than Ryan's scrubs because once wet, they clung to Jay like a second skin. He moved one way and she could see the muscles in his thigh flex. Another way and she could see the muscles in his butt flex.

She made an honest effort to avert her gaze, but his sweatshirt rode up, treating her to skin and lots of it.

Was seven years really that big a deal?

The question popped into her brain unbidden, causing that embarrassed flush to start its aching crawl over her skin. But embarrassment didn't prove an effective deterrent, either. Every move he made brought her gaze riveting right back to the sight he made, squirming around in that spray, creating a wake every time he moved, long legs stretched, in all their shapely glory.

"Damn it," he finally exploded, creating a tidal wave as he shoved himself up, thrusting wet hair back from his forehead and swiping at his face. "This is ridiculous. There's plenty of room to get in there, if I could just see."

She held out a dry towel. He snatched it and swiped his face again.

"May I help?" Her voice, so small over the bubbling that echoed in the confines of the bathroom, got his attention.

"You're smaller than I am. Maybe you can avert the spray, so I can see."

"Of course. Just tell me what to do."

"Get wet."

"Please." She grimaced, resisting the urge to flinch while grabbing the doorjamb and stepping carefully into the flood.

"You get in first and hold this against the flow." He handed her back the towel she'd given him. "I just need two seconds to get a good grip and turn the valve."

Then Susanna was on her hands and knees in the water, which saturated the fabric of her sweats in a slow rise up her thighs. She imagined the sight she flashed Jay, then sputtered as the spray caught her full in the face.

"Oh." Wrangling the towel into the cabinet, she felt her way to the break by touch rather than sight.

Using the towel's bulk as lever, she blocked the stream enough so she wouldn't get sprayed in the face anymore.

"Good." Jay maneuvered behind her, around her, his big body close and closer, until she could feel every hard inch of him spooning against her.

There was no gentlemanly *excuse me*. There was no acknowledgment whatsoever of this ridiculously intimate position. There was nothing at all except the feel of their bodies pressed close for the first time.

"Try to aim the water that way," he growled against her ear, a rough-silk sound that filtered through every inch of her. "I can't get a grip."

Her unexpected reaction spurred her into motion, and she bunched up the sodden towel and tried to direct the flow away.

His chest heaved against her back as he stretched to position the wrench. His breathing came in fitful bursts. Her breaths were shallow, a direct result of their proximity rather than the barely cooperating spray she wrestled to contain.

Then two quick turns and the bubbling quieted, leaving them with only the awareness of how their bodies were touching.

Susanna knelt rooted to the spot, so grateful Jay couldn't see her face. Not with awareness surely written all over her expression. How was it even possible to hide her reaction with her cheeks blazing, every nerve impossibly alive?

With any luck he'd assume embarrassment, which wasn't a lie. She *was* embarrassed, to the very core of her soul.

For lusting after this man.

Regardless of every rational reason that she shouldn't feel this way.

Ever the gentleman, Jay slid away in a slow, controlled movement that did nothing but heighten the flexing of his muscles, the strength of his thighs supporting him as he reached for the vanity to brace himself as he pulled away from her.

He was entirely *male,* and the bulge of his crotch pressed into her backside for a split second until he managed to maneuver upright.

Susanna's eyes fluttered closed, doing nothing to block out the swooping response low in her belly, the way slumbering places deep inside awoke to the feel of his intimate parts.

Was six months over yet?

And shouldn't this frigid bath have cooled her off a little?

More splashing, then she felt his outstretched hand slip over her shoulder.

"Careful," he said in a throaty voice. "Let me help."

He guided her with light fingertips along her waist, helping her scoot back from the wall, presenting yet another show, until he could grab her hand and steady her while she sat back in the water with another splash that only emphasized the quiet.

Emphasized they were close, wet, alone.

He was still on his knees. She understood why. They'd have been foolish to try and stand in the wading pool that had once Mrs. Harper's neat bathroom.

Lifting her gaze, Susanna intended to thank him, to right their relationship again. Alternating companionable and combative professionalism was far more comfortable than this crazy intimacy.

A simple *thanks* would restore balance, distract her from the awareness making every nerve ending tingle, her breasts heavy as her nipples grazed the wet sweatshirt.

Why hadn't she thrown on a bra again?

Any answer was lost when she met Jay's gaze, saw his face. The awareness she saw in his expression mirrored hers, and it was torture.

For one wild moment, time stopped.

Not a breath passed between them.

Not a sound.

Only the awareness of the pent-up restraint they'd both held in check and the certainty that restraint was about to end.

Suddenly his grip tightened, fingers pressing into her arms as he dragged her full against him. Hard muscle met yielding skin in such an intimate joining. She tipped her face to his, unable to resist, and he growled low in his throat as his mouth slanted across hers with a need that proved however hard-won her restraint, he had fought even harder.

Susanna sighed as her mouth yielded beneath Jay's, his lips moist and chilly, such a striking contrast from the heat of their kiss. There was nothing tentative about the way his mouth moved over hers, nothing uncertain about the way he demanded a response, determined to take what he could. His kiss betrayed him as a man who wanted.

His strong arms slipped around her, and she melted against him, unable to resist, breasts pressing against him and eradicating the last of the boundaries.

One kiss invited her to touch, to yield to the attraction between them. Her body molded against his as if she'd waited forever for the simple privilege of touch.

It had felt like forever, anyway.

Her sigh broke against his lips in a warm burst. Their breaths mingled. Their tongues tangled as so many months of wanting welled up inside.

One kiss granted permission to stop resisting, to stop rationalizing all the reasons they shouldn't want each other.

Right now there was no work between them.

No age difference.

No disparity between all she'd done with her family and all he hoped to do with his life.

There wasn't even the inevitability of his departure, leaving her behind to run his family legacy.

There was only his kiss.

And the way he swept his tongue inside her mouth and the taste of his warm breaths, his need.

There was only the way he locked her against him with

one arm and brought the other to her face, fingers slipping around her jaw to tip her up and deepen their kiss, tangling his tongue with hers, exploring her mouth as if he'd waited forever, too.

There was only the way he leaned backward enough to force her whole body into the action. Muscular thighs braced her as he pressed the swell of his maleness into her belly, using his arm around her waist to pull her impossibly closer until all she could feel was *him,* everywhere.

The sheer masculinity of him was unfamiliar, but drew a response so enticingly familiar, long ago forgotten.

The purely physical awareness of *him.*

Her every breath dragged in the wet scent of his skin, the taste of his warm mouth, the sound of his ragged breathing. Heat surged to life deep inside her, made her body feel weighted and heavy with anticipation. There was no hesitation, only the ebb and flow of a rhythm that made her ache from the inside out.

There was only the needy way she touched him, her hands fluttering up, hesitating only a bare instant before instinct took over. Dragging her palms along his broad back, she traced the length of the sodden sweatshirt clinging to the hard strength of his muscles below, learning the feel of his shoulders, his ribs, his waist, the hard curve of his butt beneath those clingy running pants.

She couldn't stop touching him.

Didn't want to stop.

The radio crackled through the waterlogged quiet, shattered the unreality of the moment and jarred her from the trance.

"Chester here, Mr. C." came the announcement. "I'm on the property. You need me to get down to the street or did you get the leak stopped?"

That breathless kiss ended as suddenly as it had started.

The moment disconnected because their bodies still pressed provocatively together. Jay's gaze held hers, the intense green of his eyes hard, angry even, and she only stared at him, barely able to shake off her stupor.

Reason returned, but oh, so slowly, starting with the knowledge that they were wrapped around each other in Mrs. Harper's bathroom where anyone might walk in.

Knowledge reflected in Jay's scowl, the hard lines transforming his face. Why? Because he hadn't been able to resist kissing her? Because she'd responded to him? Or because they'd been interrupted?

If only she could read his mind, because she sensed his agitation, recognized it when his chest rose on a sharp breath.

But still he didn't let her go.

"This isn't smart on any level, Jay." Her voice echoed in the confines of the tiled bathroom like the sounds of their ragged breaths. Reason. One of them should.

"No," he agreed. "It's not."

There, that was all settled.

Now he just needed to let her go. With a slight shake of his head, he sent wet hair tumbling over his forehead. She resisted the urge to brush back the silky strands from his face, the droplets coursing down his temple onto his cheek.

His tension eased as he released the vise around her waist, allowed her to catch her breath as they parted.

She exhaled a deep sigh that was a little relief.

And a lot of regret.

"Come on," he ground out in a rough-edged tone as he braced a hand on the vanity and helped her stand. "Be careful."

Perfunctory touches that had only moments before been intimate. They dodged each other's gaze while drying off with towels as best they could, patted themselves down in the quiet hallway while residents slept and someone spoke in hushed tones in the admin office at the end of the hall.

Reality separated them again in a big way even before Susanna said unnecessarily, "We're going to leave a trail."

Jay followed her gaze to the long expanse of hallway that led to the employee stairs outside the security doors. "Take our shoes off?"

"Anything's got to help." Susanna slid off her deck shoes and carried them as she and Jay ran lightly, a vain attempt to keep wet cuffs from dragging on the carpet.

The scene would have been comical had it not been for the shattered lack of restraint that had changed everything.

They didn't bother stopping to put shoes back on, even though the employee stairs were concrete, until emerging in the stairwell on the first floor that had been transformed into a makeshift office.

Puddles slowly grew around their feet while they conferred with everyone on the action plan. Jay spoke with Chester, who already had the wet-vac in tow, while Susanna stood in the midst of her coworkers dripping wet *with no bra* as if she'd just participated in a wet T-shirt contest.

She assigned Kimberly as duty manager so Walter could go home to dry off.

Then Jay was beside her again, saying, "Come on, I'll give you a lift home."

"I drove my car."

He stared down at her with a gaze that softened while traveling the wet length of her. The hard edges of his expression faded, replaced by a bit of humor. The return of the man she knew. "Sure you don't mind soaking your front seat?"

Oh.

He grimaced rather animatedly, stroked his chin.

"Laundry has patient gowns. We can turn one backward and maybe get you out of here without—"

"I'll go with you, thank you." Even though the thought of being alone with Jay right now, to address what had passed between them made the heat crawl slowly to her cheeks.

God only knows why. She was an adult, not a ninth-grader. Owning responsibility for her actions came with the turf. Unfortunately.

Spurring everyone into action with a few words, Jay slipped his fingers over her elbow and guided her through the front lobby, where Robbie let them through the door.

"Thanks for coming, bosses," he said with a chuckle as the doors hissed shut again and the lock clicked.

The night air hit hard. Susanna should have been grateful for a chance to cool off. Suddenly she could feel every wet inch of her as if it were icing over.

"You going to be okay?" Jay asked, always perceptive, always thoughtful. "Robbie can bring a blanket—"

"No, thanks. I'll be fine."

He took her at her word and didn't look surprised.

Then they were maneuvering around the well-lit facility and onto the dark path. Jay drove the way easily, as if the light of the waxing moon wasn't necessary to keep him on the path. But that moon illuminated the still surface of the lake, cast the world in a glow as surreal as she felt, sitting beside this man, his strong fingers clasping the steering wheel, those fingers that had touched her so possessively, so demanding.

Neither of them said a word. The only sound to disturb the still night was the steady hum of the engine and the tires grinding over hard ground, breaking the occasional twig or crunching over a fallen bough of leaves.

The vinyl seats withstood their drenched selves, but she

clung to the windshield frame for balance so she wouldn't tumble off the slick seat as he whipped along at top speed.

Was he trying to get her home quickly? Surely he must be frozen, too. Or maybe he was only reacting to their earlier indiscretion. He must be wondering where they went from here, as well. Did they show up for work in the morning and pretend nothing had happened?

Susanna's inclination was to address the situation and negotiate a resolution, but that would mean discussing the kiss. She couldn't even think about his arms around her, about the needy way she'd responded. Not without her heartbeat speeding up dangerously.

Embarrassment?

She wished. The only safe thing to do right now was keep her mouth shut. She'd wake up fresh and able to think more clearly after a good night's sleep.

If she managed to close her eyes. She somehow doubted sleep would be part of the equation for the rest of this night.

And then he wheeled into her driveway. She'd had the foresight to leave the porch light on but didn't argue when he hopped out to escort her to her door.

This was Gentleman Jay, after all.

Gentleman Jay, who'd kissed her.

Dragging her cold, wet self onto the porch, she unlocked the front door. Then she turned to say goodbye… they might as well break the ice now, so tomorrow would be less awkward. If that was even possible.

Susanna was busy rallying every ounce of her resolve to present herself as nonchalant and unaffected, so she didn't notice that Jay had stepped in behind her. But he was so close she nearly landed back in his arms when she turned.

"Jay!" she said, surprised.

Planting a hand on the door above her head, he towered

over her, forcing Susanna to tip her head back to meet his gaze. And what she saw in his face made her heart slam a slow hard beat.

He was going to kiss her *again*.

No sooner had the thought popped into her head than he lowered his face to hers.

Every shred of reason rebelled. Not at the insanity of continuing what they'd started in Mrs. Harper's room, but at the thought of denying him, and herself, in this moment.

Though reason demanded she open her mouth and say one very simple word, "No!" she leaned up on her tiptoes to bridge the distance between them.

Then his mouth was on hers again.

And this was no kiss like the first, all loss of restraint and urgency. No, this was a premeditated kiss, a kiss designed to control the moment, a kiss meant to seduce an invitation.

He dragged his tongue across hers, a lingering stroke, savoring the taste of her before pressing his advantage. And the advantage was all his. He kissed her as though he never wanted to stop, so honest with his need that she had no choice but to be honest back, to lift her hands until she could touch his jaw, a featherlight touch just to make sure he was real, and this moment was real, and the sensation welling deep was real.

He blocked out the night with his body, trapped her with that hand braced over her head, as his free hand slid along her waist, beneath her sweatshirt. The feel of his hand on her bare skin made her gasp aloud, but he caught the sound with his mouth, dragged his palm up over her ribs.

Her breath hitched when he made contact with the sensitive curve of her breast, a bold stroke that made every nerve tingle until she could feel the heaviness of her breasts and the graze of wet fabric against the tight peaks, the cool air that slipped in against his warm hand that fondled her.

With the same perception that he displayed everywhere else in his life, he noticed her body's response.

And considered it an invitation to keep touching.

Thumbing the taut peak, he sent sensation spiraling through her, pooling in her most private places, making her breasts grow heavy with desire, making her yearn.

"Let me come inside, Susanna." He breathed the words against her mouth with warm breaths that become part of their kiss. "Let me make love to you."

Those bold words caused her own breath to catch in her throat, made her struggle to find a response as he gently tugged at her bottom lip with his teeth, thumbed her nipple until her knees felt liquid beneath her.

"We agreed this wasn't smart." She finally found the words, forced them out in a rush.

"Just because it isn't smart doesn't mean we can't do it."

Well, he had Susanna there.

And didn't let her go. He crowded out the night with his body, stole her reason with his kisses, promised her pleasure by the way he touched her, coaxing a response from deep, deep inside, a need that had been asleep so long.

The only thing left was to pull out of his arms, to tell him no, that she didn't want to kiss him.

And that would be a lie.

CHAPTER THIRTEEN

Jay waited. He stood there staring into Susanna's exquisite face, her delicate features cast in the golden warm glow of the porch light's single bulb. He tried to interpret the fleeting play of emotions over her expression. Surprise widened her eyes. Uncertainty played around her brow. Desire made her kiss-swollen mouth part around shallow breaths.

He thought she might be warring as hard as he was, but couldn't be sure.

And wanted to be.

Jay was done with wanting, and waiting. Giving in to their attraction made no sense. Not with him leaving and her staying. But this would be his only time to know this woman intimately, to discover how to coax those wispy sighs from her lips, to make her tremble with desire, for him.

They had no possible future, but they might have now.

This time. This day. This moment. That was all anyone had. Susanna had said that to him once.

He wanted this time with her.

So he waited with his breath lodged in his chest. Every muscle locked tight. Only the grainy wood beneath his palm grounded him, his only point of contact with reality.

The reality that she might deny him.

No matter how much she wanted him.

And she did.

She might be warring with herself about being practical—there was so much against him. But she wanted him.

He'd felt her want in his gut, in her response.

Would she deny him, herself, *them,* their moment to be together?

He didn't know. But Jay knew if he touched her again, he wouldn't be able to stop.

So he waited as indecision and desire battled across her expression, while he realized with each passing instant how much he wanted her to give them the gift of this moment.

The seconds passed, marked only by the heavy beats of his heart, the steady drip, drip, drip of their clothing on the porch. Then Susanna caught a hard breath, a determined gasp that filtered through the quiet, and him, because Jay knew in that instant she'd made her decision.

A tiny smile tipped the corners of her mouth as she raised her hands and speared her fingers into his hair, lifting up on tiptoe to meet him in a kiss.

Their mouths met, clinching the deal, and he savored the taste of her *yes.* She was suddenly all fire in his arms, determination to make the most of their moment. And that was his last rational thought because opportunity presented itself, the chance to coax soft sighs from Susanna's lips, to explore this chemistry they made together.

His body yielded to instinct, to his need for this woman, and with one deliberate move, he slipped his arms around her, brought her tightly against him.

Her body molded exactly as if she'd been designed to fit against him. The swell of her breasts crushed his chest. One slight tilting of her hips, and she cradled the heat of his growing arousal.

Grazing light fingers along his jaw, down his neck, she

left a simmering heat in the wake of her touch, warmth to heat the clammy cold of his skin.

He groaned aloud, startled by the sound coming from his own mouth, by how hard his need spiked now that she'd committed to the course and met his kiss with a demand of her own.

With a throaty laugh, she dragged her mouth from his, dropped light kisses along his jaw, down the length of his neck, trailing fire in the wake of her touch.

Apparently she would be a force to be reckoned with. Burying his face in her damp hair, he inhaled deeply, drinking in the fresh scent that had driven him crazy since they'd met.

Suddenly he wanted to feel her everywhere. And didn't temper the need. Sliding a hand along the curve of her waist, he moved beneath that chilly sweatshirt, sought the feel of her silken skin, dragged his open palm along her back, her spine, until she trembled against him.

He was impatient to explore, but to do that he needed to get her off this porch and inside. In the part of his brain still capable of reason, he acknowledged a perk to his home. There was no one around. This was their world right now to do with as they pleased.

Hooking his thumbs into her waistband, Jay tugged her sweatpants over her hips. Gravity obliged, and the wet mess fell to the porch with a muffled thump.

With a yelp, Susanna stepped out of the circle of fabric. Then she caught his gaze, and he recognized laughter in her beautiful face. He realized what she was going to do a split second before she broke away with a laugh. Spinning easily on her toes, she headed inside, bare bottom and long pale legs flexing sleekly with every light step.

He stood there like a total idiot, rooted to the spot by the sight of all that flashing skin, the strands of damp hair clinging to her shoulders. He might have pursued but before she cleared the living room, she raised her arms and dragged the sweatshirt over her head, revealing pale skin and trim curves in all her glorious nudity.

More laughter echoed from the confines of the house as she vanished from sight before Jay shook off his paralysis, ditched his own wet clothes in a pile right on the porch and headed after her. The door slammed behind him with more force than he'd intended, warning her of his approach.

He found her in the bedroom, exactly where he'd hoped she'd be, illuminated only by the moonlight through the windows and a small glow from the bathroom. With that cloud of dark hair tumbling over her profile and all that glowing fair skin, she presented a vision of such loveliness, she stole his breath. And again he found himself struck speechless, by the sight of her and the effect she had on him by just being there.

She'd turned down the comforter. She must have sensed his presence because she twisted around to face him, casual with her nudity but seemingly surprised by his.

"Oh." Her mouth pursed around the slight exclamation as her gaze trailed from his face down his body.

She inhaled a halting breath but couldn't seem to drag her gaze from the sight of him. And everything about her in that moment suggested she liked what she saw. Right then Jay knew he was in more trouble than he'd ever imagined because his body responded to her appreciation with an urgency that nearly brought him to his knees.

Out of necessity he closed the distance between them, guided her to the bed, where they were suddenly in each other's arms, and kissed the gasp from her lips. They stretched out together, legs twining eagerly, bodies curving close to savor the heat of each other and the silky warmth of the bedding a relief to waterlogged skin.

His hands trembled as he skimmed his fingers over her, barely daring to touch as anticipation built the excitement between them.

He could tell she liked these almost-touches because she shivered lightly, inviting him to greater boldness as he explored the smooth swell of her breasts, idly thumbed a nipple, until the rosy skin grew taut and she trembled again. Bracing on an elbow, he leaned forward to catch that tight peak with a gentle kiss, and she moaned, a yearning sound in the quiet dark.

His body pulsed with awareness as she arched upward into his erotic touch, her fingers lingering softly through his hair then down his back with whispery strokes.

Trailing kisses along the expanse of her chest, he worked his way up the slim column of her neck, tasting her eagerness, savoring the taste of her arousal. Then their mouths came together again, and their bodies sought each other, swayed gently, mimicking the rhythm that would bring them together.

Coaxing her legs apart, she was suddenly straddling his erection with those smooth thighs, cradling him. She tilted back erotically, all pale skin glowing in the moonlight. Then he pressed into her softness, causing her body to arch in liquid motion, all trembling curves and excitement.

Why now? He'd lived his entire life on these sixty acres, thirty-two years, and this woman finally shows up during his last metaphoric minutes. Jay sought his answers by driving deep inside her, by abandoning himself into yielding softness, by locking his fingers into her hips and hanging on for stroke after delicious stroke until he forgot the question completely.

Susanna should have passed out, but she lay there as the night deepened then faded beyond the windows. Jay had held her for a long time, but eventually did what she couldn't do—sleep.

She simply had too much racing through her mind, all beginning and ending with the man who lay wrapped around her, a beautiful, thoughtful, overly burdened man who, for these precious few hours, had allowed himself to just *be*.

Susanna had been working beside him for nearly three months, had trained with him, argued with him, shared companionable moments and lusted after him. But not until tonight had she realized how much he kept packed away deep inside his personable, capable demeanor.

Not until he'd lost all restraint in her arms.

He carried the weight of the world on his shoulders, this one did, and she had never realized it until this very second when he was naked inside her, the strength of his warm body all around her, just savoring the moment, the two of them without personality, without commitment or obligation or responsibility. Just the two of them, savoring the excitement of their first time together. The way their bodies fitted together. All her soft places molded the contours of his hard body as if she'd been made to fit perfectly against him.

Their legs twined beneath the sheets, hers smooth-shaven silk, his roughly muscled strength. The contrast made her aware of how very long it had been since her body had tingled with a desire that began deep inside and radiated outward, until every inch of her was heightened sensation.

And his strong arms held her. His big body surrounded her. There was only Jay, and her. The only place in the world she wanted to be, safe in his arms in the dark.

He was a man who cared about so many.

And as she listened to the even sounds of his breathing, she asked herself how could she *not* have known how much he kept locked away inside his oh, so capable self?

She glimpsed his urgency to put The Arbors and everything associated with it behind him.

Including her.

Because without her, he couldn't leave.

Sleeping with him had been such a mistake. But what else could Susanna have done? Lied to him. She *had* wanted to kiss him, even knowing where those kisses would eventually lead.

Susanna didn't believe in lying. Lies of omission, maybe. To spare someone's feelings. To avoid a situation she would only complicate with her opinions. To allow her children to find their own ways, make their own decisions, learn to trust their instincts and gain confidence. To not fuel the fires with Karan back in the days whenever her BFF restlessly manufactured drama to keep life interesting.

To Skip when it became clear he was losing his battle with cancer, yet worried about how she was holding up…

"I'm hanging in there, hon. As long as you're with me."

Definitely not a lie.

Why was she even thinking about Skip right now, staring into the darkness wrapped around another man? She supposed it was natural. Skip had been her one and only. Until now.

But there was tomorrow to contend with, the aftermath of this pleasurable night. Susanna didn't have a clue if there'd be awkwardness or more arguments or even if she'd undermined the acquisition. But in this drowsy contentment, the wake of a satisfaction she'd almost forgotten, she thought about the last time she and Skip had made love as normal lovers, without illness between them, without the realization that each time they made love might be their last, sex without the burden of life and death.

She couldn't remember the last time.

Because the night before Skip had gone to the doctor for a prescription of antibiotics to deal with the bug he couldn't shake, he'd rolled over and kissed her. He'd wanted to make love, but she'd been too tired, too worried about his health, too wrapped up in the things that comprised their lives—kids, illness, work, lunches, homework, dinner and on and on. If she had expressed an interest in sex, they'd have made love.

But she'd only kissed him, uninterested in anything more than the lingering taste of his mouth, the warm strength of his arms cradling her close as she'd fallen asleep.

Susanna remembered that.

She'd sacrificed their last time as normal lovers. It had never once occurred to her their time together would be limited. They were planning to grow old together, to chase their children wherever life led them, to dote on grandchildren as active grandparents. She'd taken their time together for granted.

And missed their last time completely.

In that moment, Susanna knew. No matter what tomorrow would bring with Jay—the potential awkwardness, the problems, the age difference, the inevitable parting....

She was still glad they'd had tonight.

JAY STARED AT A SLEEPING Susanna, soft waves partially hiding her face, the sky paling to dawn beyond the windows. He could feel every warm inch of her pressed against him, her body so perfectly aligned with his.

How was it she felt familiar in his arms, this woman he

hadn't known but for an instant against the backdrop of a lifetime? Jay didn't know, but he could lie here forever wrapped around her, his cheek resting on the top of her head, inhaling the cool scent of her hair with every breath.

The feeling was so comfortable, so recognizable, an almost-overwhelming sense of need—the same way he'd felt last night when he hadn't been able to keep his hands off her. Not when it would have meant letting this feeling slip away.

The familiarity had nothing to do with the cottage. He never slept here. Why would he when he had a house to himself?

But as he held Susanna and watched the fading night chase the shadows from the bedroom, he realized this familiarity wasn't so much Susanna but the very act of *feeling.*

He hadn't in such a long time.

When had he died? It had happened so slowly, so subtly, he couldn't even remember, just one morning, possibly a morning like this one, he simply didn't wake up. Life at The Arbors had finally sucked him dry. Or maybe loss had done the deed. Losing everyone, one at a time— even losing his brother to the Marines—until he was the only man standing.

But not alive. He knew the difference, could feel the difference, knew he'd died a slow death that mirrored Alzheimer's, seconds ticking away until eventually awareness simply wasn't there anymore.

He hadn't known.

Not until this morning when he'd awakened in Susanna's arms after a night of coming back to life.

Jay had no idea how long he lay there, realizing, *feeling,* but by the time Susanna stirred against him, the sun was bright beyond the windows.

He sensed the moment she became aware. One moment she was molded against him, a smooth-skinned extension of him, and the next she was simply lying close, still touching but separate. As if awareness had come invisibly between them.

She didn't open her eyes although he knew she was awake. Maybe, like him, she wasn't eager to give up this feeling, didn't want reality to intrude on this warm contentment.

Her lashes finally fluttered, and she opened her eyes. Their gazes met, but there was no room for words in the quiet, at least not any words he wanted to hear. He could see reality in those deep blue eyes, wasn't surprised when she finally whispered, "This wasn't smart, Jay. There's no place for us to go."

"I know."

He pulled her closer, as if he could physically bridge the distance reality had created between them, bring back that feeling of oneness.

She exhaled a soft sigh, and her eyes fluttered shut again, her expression dreamy and still soft from sleep.

And contentment.

He saw that in her expression, too.

And guessed it had been a long time since she'd felt this way, as well. Since her husband died?

"We're just going to make a big mess."

"I know."

But he lowered his mouth and caught hers gently, tasting the morning on her lips, discovering that the arousal of the previous night had been as potent as he remembered, and he didn't care about anything except not losing this feeling again.

CHAPTER FOURTEEN

JAY FINISHED CHOPPING garlic then pressed the knife blade on the fragrant chunks to release the flavor. He sensed Susanna's gaze on him.

He turned to find her watching him. "What?"

"You are a man of many talents, Jay." Dropping a freshly washed spoon into the drain board, she smiled then leaned down to rub Butters's head.

Gatsby wanted in on the action and they wound up with both dogs crowding the limited space in the kitchen.

Jay shooed them out again. "Go, beasts. Settle down."

Then when Susanna slipped her hands into the sink again to wash away the dog fur, he said, "I'm trying to impress you. Sounds like it's working."

"Definitely. Cooking is unexpected, I must admit. I can't think of anything you're not good at."

After drying her hands, she came up behind him and slipped her arms around his waist, pressing close. "Running The Arbors. Taking care of everyone around you. Fixing broken pipes. Cooking delicious meals."

"Sex. You forgot sex."

Pressing a kiss to his shoulder, she exhaled a breath penetrating the flannel shirt in a burst of warmth against his skin and sent the blood skittering to his crotch.

"No. You're not good at sex," she whispered. "You excel at sex. Different list." She tightened her grip around his waist and rubbed her cheek against him to emphasize the point.

Leaning into her, Jay savored the familiar feel of her against him. "That was the right answer, so you can eat."

"Good, because I'm starving."

"Good, because we're making enough food here to feed half the nursing center. Think we should pack some up and bring it to third-shift staff?" He brushed the garlic off the cutting board into the skillet and left it to brown in simmering olive oil.

"Good idea. They don't ever get the goodies Liz puts out during the day. Not fresh at least." Susanna released him, leaving a cool emptiness where she'd been, and went to the vegetable basket hanging beside the baker's rack.

"Speaking of feeding the multitudes." She handled a few peppers and onions and then chose one of each. A woman who knew her vegetables and understood that appearances could be deceiving. Jay liked that about her.

"I should shop for an air mattress this weekend," she said. "Where's a good place to find one?"

"Hmm. Let me think." Jay considered the choices, liked how she'd consulted him, and wondered if he could invite himself along on her shopping trip.

Each day they traversed new terrain in this turn their relationship had taken. *Playing house,* Susanna called it, and *enjoying the moment.*

This *moment* had been going on two weeks.

Jay had definitely enjoyed every second. Susanna was easy to play house with. As long as he didn't get sidetracked thinking about what would happen when the clock stopped ticking and their time together ran out.

"Got a couple of bedding warehouses that might have a good selection and decent prices. Then there's always Walmart."

"Good idea. I should probably check online so I don't wind up running around for something I don't want. Brandon won't mind sleeping on the couch, but he'll be here for nearly two weeks. I want him to be comfortable."

She was being a good mom. A nurturer, Gerald had called her. Jay liked that about her, too.

"Where's this air mattress going? The office?"

"Where else? Brooke can sleep with me."

She sounded so matter-of-fact Jay knew she must have been debating the decision for a while. He was getting the hang of Susanna, the more intimately he got to know her. The more uncertain she was, the more no-nonsense she got. He hadn't realized that about her before.

"Will your daughter keep my spot warm?"

"I suppose." The response was noncommittal but the mention of their sleeping arrangements sent color into her cheeks.

For as no-nonsense as Susanna could be, she blushed so easily. Jay found all it took was a well-placed word about their relationship to get a response.

In the darkness of her bed, where they'd done most of their getting to know each other, she'd shared a lot about her life. She'd married young and hadn't done much actual dating before her husband. So the sum total of her experience with men wasn't a whole lot.

Funny, how he was the one who hadn't left his family home, but he had a lot more experience dating than this caring woman who'd experienced so many of the things in life he wanted to.

"So who all's coming for Christmas?" he asked, then looked at his dogs. "Besides these two greedy beggars, I mean."

Butters and Gatsby were a given at every meal.

But Jay did wonder what her kids would be like in person. He'd seen their photos in her office and in the cottage. Good-looking kids who looked way too grown up to belong to Susanna. He wondered how she'd introduce him. As her co-administrator? He supposed that worked under the circumstances.

He didn't like the thought of being her little secret. He also didn't relish the idea of sacrificing two weeks when they were on a time limit.

Of course, he'd never begrudge her a visit with her kids, not when she was so starved to be with the people she loved. And she was. He'd come to recognize the symptoms in the way she panicked whenever her cell phone wasn't within easy reach, the way she dropped everything to take a call or respond to a text.

Connections to her life.

What was it about The Arbors that disconnected everyone from reality? When he and Drew were younger, they'd speculated that The Arbors resided in an atmospheric bubble that sealed them off from the real world, protected them from natural disasters and nuclear attacks and even alien invasions.

Jay had thought those scenarios were the product of two imaginative brothers going through the science fiction phase of boyhood, but there's been some truth, after all.

No, Jay didn't have any right at all to demand to be introduced to her kids as anything other than a co-administrator. Not when he had nothing more to offer than a few months of playing house.

SUSANNA QUICKLY DISCOVERED that decking out The Arbors for Christmas was a weeklong event that involved everyone. Tessa worked so hard decorating for Thanksgiving that unlike retail stores where Christmas displays went up for Black Friday, they were into December before the remnants of Thanksgiving vanished.

"I don't see the point in rushing," Tessa told Susanna while covering the activity room windows with sheets of white paper, creating the backdrop to a winter scene that would dominate the entrance to the first-floor lockdown. "I can keep Christmas until Epiphany, which is well into the new year. That's why I do a combo holiday theme. Then I can start taking down Christmas a little at a time while we're still glittery for the New Year."

Her process made sense. No question about how labor intensive decorating could be. Every lobby of every wing got a separate winter scene. Then there were archways strung with lights, plus foil snowflakes hanging from ceiling grids every three feet on every wing of every floor. There must have been a thousand of them, all hung with painstaking care, all creating a sparkling ambience with the facility's lighting.

And Tessa made sure there was a display for every religion of the residents' demographic. Beautiful Nativity scenes showcased the Holy Family, as well as a collection of stars of Bethlehem, ranging from artistic cut glass to strobe lights. A festival of lights celebrated Hanukkah. Kinara centerpieces decorated the dining room tables for Kwanzaa. Wreaths, garland, holly and mistletoe abounded wherever one turned.

Then there were the trees.

Every corner and cubby had one. Each decorated with an individual theme. Chester with his toolbox and ladder seemed to be everywhere Susanna turned. And she did her part to share in the excitement, recruiting her own team of decorating assistants to help with the trees on the ALF floors.

"What a marvelous idea," Tessa told Susanna. "I never

thought to involve the residents, but there's no reason not to. Not up on the ALF, anyway."

"They always helped decorate in New York," Susanna explained. "Kicked off the excitement. Dining would provide coffee and cookies and we'd make a party of it."

Of course, that had been in the ALF and the massive twelve-hundred unit independent living facility, where residents didn't require too much supervision. Susanna kept that part to herself. Everyone around The Arbors knew the ins and outs of protecting their charges. That was the job and they were well trained.

Tessa also liked the party idea, and it wasn't long before Liz showed up with Christmas-flavored coffee and baked goods.

The only person noticeably absent from the decorating was Jay. Somehow whenever anything needed to be hung, draped or wrapped, the man was nowhere to be found. Then one day he vanished completely.

Susanna asked Tessa if Jay was typically missing in action while they were outside in the cold, stringing the lights around a life-size crèche that Tessa said had been handcrafted by Jay's father, specifically to decorate the facility entrance.

"Do not even talk to me about Mr. C." Tessa waved a dismissive hand. "He is on my list of people to kill. Number one, in fact."

Her response didn't invite questions, but Susanna would have asked Jay if she could have tracked him down. No one seemed to have seen him, and when she text-messaged him, she received no response. She tried him on the radio, and all she got was a cryptic message, telling her he was in the middle of something and would get back to her soon.

Soon didn't happen by any reasonable person's definition of the word. But the day wore on without him, keeping her busy with the nonstop pace of a shift change, three types of therapy and two transfers. Transfer literally meant a resident transferring from the bed to a chair and from the chair to a walker and using the walker to visit the bathroom without assistance. There were a series of progressive behavioral tests, but this final test made the determination if the resident could be released from the first-floor nursing center and returned to the ALF. As a result, it was a bit of an emotional roller coaster for the residents.

One passed. One didn't.

"Yet," she said, explaining to Mr. Minahan why he couldn't rejoin his wife of sixty-five years in their third-floor apartment. "We can try again in another few days when you're feeling stronger after a few more therapy sessions. In the meantime, you're still free to go upstairs and spend the day visiting—"

"I'm not an infant, young lady," Mr. Minahan, normally an easygoing man, informed her in a dull roar. "I pay a fortune to live in this establishment. I'll decide where I can and can't spend the night without your help, thank you very much."

The exchange degenerated from there, despite Susanna's best efforts to assuage his disappointment. Mr. Minahan did finally settle down, but only when his wife and the occupational therapist took him upstairs for his daily visit.

Jay must have heard about the incident because when he finally showed up, he insisted they leave even though they normally waited until the place settled down after dinner.

"You don't have anything left to do that can't wait until tomorrow, do you?"

He was being strange. Susanna couldn't put her finger on why, but said, "No, we can leave if you want."

His smile flashed wide then he was unplugging her laptop and hurrying her to pack her belongings.

Susanna didn't bother asking, just shrugged on her coat. Then he led her through the back employee door and to his golf cart parked at the maintenance and engineering building.

To her surprise, though, Jay steered away from the family path by the lake and onto the hard road.

"Okay, you're flipping me out." She couldn't keep silent any longer. "What's going on?"

He slanted a laughing glance her way, green eyes sparkling. "Trust me."

He might be spiking her curiosity right now, but Susanna did indeed trust him. Whatever he had going on was exciting him in a way she'd never seen before. Flashing a smile as the chill wind bit her cheeks, she said, "I do."

The hard road veered to the right, and when he wheeled off the road toward the cottage, she saw instantly why he'd insisted they'd leave the facility early.

She would have missed his surprise once darkness fell.

"Oh, is this what you were doing today?" She breathed the words on the edge of a breath.

"It is." The golf cart ground to a stop, and Jay turned to her, propping his arm over the seat to watch her reaction.

The front of the cottage had been touched by Christmas. Wreathes with bright red bows perched in the center of each window and on the door. Lush evergreen garland twined around the column and swagged along the eaves and down the banister. Mistletoe hung from the arch leading up the steps.

He'd even covered the caned chairs with red-and-green runners, and strung lights in the bushes, transforming her charming cottage with welcoming Christmas cheer.

"I wanted your first Christmas in your new home to be special."

Oh. The breath caught in her throat, making it impossible to respond until that feeling of humility filtered through her, eased up its grip to know how much he cared.

On what a big, big mess they were making together.

"It's special." She dragged her gaze from the sight, pressed a kiss on his cheek. "And you're special."

Simple words she meant from the bottom of her heart, her heart that was melting around the edges at the sight of his grimace. This man had trouble accepting compliments.

"I only decorated outside. I didn't want to go in without you."

Keeping those boundaries firmly in place. She understood. "You could have, you know."

"I know. But if my plan works, I won't have to."

"What plan?"

"You'll see. Done admiring my handiwork yet?" He swept a hand toward the newly decorated cottage.

She nodded.

He threw the golf cart into gear so fast that she grabbed onto the frame and hung on for dear life. Wheeling around the cottage, he drove onto the path leading back to the facility. His excitement was contagious, and she was melting inside because of his thoughtfulness. They didn't go far, and he surprised her when he slowed to make the turn into his backyard.

"Jay, what are—"

"Just wait." He wheeled onto the flagstone path. "I want you to close your eyes. I'd cover them just to make sure you don't peek, but I obviously can't do that and drive."

She laughed. "Okay, no peeking."

Somehow sitting beside him with her eyes closed heightened her awareness of his excitement. She could practically feel his anticipation, although she couldn't explain why. But it was there between them, had been since the first, a connection that made being with this man so easy.

The golf cart slowed then jerked to a stop. Followed by the barking. A welcome. A furry body brushed against her and she kept her eyes squeezed tightly shut and petted someone. Butters? Gatsby? She couldn't be sure.

"Come on, you two," Jay said. "Calm down."

The golf cart rocked wildly off balance as he hopped out. His footsteps ground over the gravel before he pressed an open hand over her eyes for good measure.

"Don't look. Not yet. I'll tell you when." With his free hand, he helped her step from the golf cart then circled her around, shooing the dogs out of her way. "Chill out, guys."

Then he said, "Ready?" but didn't wait for a reply before moving his hand away. "Open your eyes."

Susanna did, and gasped aloud.

Jay's decorations on her cottage had only been a preview of what he'd done to his home. The same evergreen swags and twining garland. The same wreaths with bright red bows.

On a grand scale.

Multicolored lights twinkled all over the formal landscaping. There was another crèche on the lawn, smaller than the one at the facility, but designed with the same attention to detail in the woodworking that would make Susanna bet money Jay's dad had built this one, too.

Rows of solar-powered lights in red and green lined the driveway along the oak alley leading to the hard road. Each stately oak tree had been wound with red-and-white lights so they looked like peppermint sticks standing guard on both sides.

"Oh. My. Gosh." There were no words to describe the

sight as she turned slowly, taking in the merry sight, the dusk giving an inkling of the festive effect of all those lights.

"I wanted our Christmas together to be perfect."

Their one and only Christmas.

She brutally squelched that thought. She was grateful for this glorious time with this special man and wasn't wasting one single millisecond on regrets.

He grabbed her hand and led her up the grand stairs to his house. She was breathless with laughter as he shoved open the doors, urging her ahead of him.

"Ladies first."

Then she stepped inside the grand foyer of his home to find the place transformed into a cheery Christmas celebration straight from another century.

Pine boughs draped the banister up the curving staircase. Big gold bells hung between each baluster. Swags dripped from the archways and lights twinkled from the foliage. Angels holding trumpets greeted her from a shelf beside a coatrack, and a smiling fat Santa shouted, "Ho, ho, ho!" activated by the motion of the opening door.

The effort to create this Christmas wonderland had been no less than enormous, and Susanna understood why he'd been MIA so much. His generosity of spirit simply stole her breath.

"Jay, this is possibly the most thoughtful gift anyone has ever given me. It couldn't be more perfect."

He glanced down at her, his expression melting into amusement. "This isn't the gift. Well, only a part of it."

"Oh."

Slipping his hands over her shoulders, he nudged her around to face him. "I want you to cancel those rooms at the Hilton and have Christmas here with your family."

Oh. *"Oh."* She stared into his face, that oh, so handsome face so eager for her to accept his gift, and she was swept away by his tenderness, so completely touched by his thoughtfulness that tears stung her eyes.

"I wanted your first Christmas in your new home to be special."

Her impulse was to wrap her arms around him and not let go. She wanted to hold him close and make him feel how much his kindness meant. How much *he* meant.

He cared. She couldn't possibly miss how much in his kindness, in his eagerness to please her.

But Susanna wouldn't repay his generosity by becoming a quivering heap in his arms, refused to give in to the emotion taking over. "Is this why you talked me out of buying the air mattress? You don't have one packed away in storage, do you?"

He shook his head.

"You are so, so sweet. But are you absolutely sure?"

"Susanna, there are eight bedrooms and ten bathrooms in this place. There are plenty of other rooms we can convert into bedrooms if we need them."

She exhaled. "Jay, I don't even know what to say. We're talking a bunch of people. We'll run roughshod all over Christmas with your brother."

"A party sounds exactly like what this big old house needs, don't you think? Haven't had one in a long time, since before my mother got sick. But we still have to get a tree. I figured we could do that together. Sound good?"

Susanna couldn't say anything. She had no words even if she could have gotten them past the tears welling up in her throat. So she launched up on her tiptoes and tossed her arms around his neck to hug him close, and she held him, savoring his laughter that burst warmly against her ear, the way he felt warm and strong and perfect against her.

And promising herself that she would absolutely, positively *not* let longing for the future interfere with the now.
    Her gift to both of them.

CHAPTER FIFTEEN

CHRISTMAS SEASON IN Susanna's life had always involved festive celebrations—some recital or another, Nativity plays, classroom parties filled with cookies, laughter and excitement.

Preparations at home involved many cups of hot cocoa with marshmallows as Skip climbed on the roof to string lights, then he and the kids would lay tracks for his trains throughout the house. Susanna set up railway stations in tiny villages on puffy white fabric to resemble snow.

Christmas tree wars invariably ensued as the family marched around the tree farm, debating which tree should lose its life for a few shining weeks of glory and honor displayed in the Adams' living room.

Baking started early so decorative tins of cookies could be given as gifts. Susanna, Brooke and both grandmothers would search for recipes, each year introducing a few new cookies with the tried and true.

But this Christmas…Susanna's old and new lives collided in a bittersweet way that had less to do with mourning her old life than fearing the new.

The clock was ticking. She tried to rein in her feelings about Jay, but she'd created a mess. She'd arrived in Charlotte to convince Jay to leave so she could stay. Now she didn't want him to go, which meant she'd have to leave.

But she didn't want to leave, either.

This was never more apparent than when she and the kids arrived at Jay's house for their holiday visit.

"Oh. My. God. I don't even believe this place." Brooke hung out the window snapping photos as Susanna drove down the oak alley leading to the main house standing majestically ahead.

As an art history major, Brooke appreciated architecture and atmosphere. The Arbors had both.

She grilled Susanna for details, who could only say, "I'll introduce you to the owner. He's lived here his whole life, so I'm sure he'll be able to answer your questions."

Susanna knew Brooke would love everything about The Arbors. Brandon was more reserved, not so much unimpressed by the surroundings as uninterested. Give him a bed and a fridge and he was good. She could easily see him snatching a few precious minutes of sleep on a cot in some hospital back room during the all-important internships. Her son the future doctor.

That thought made her smile.

"Want me to get the bags, Mom?" Brandon asked as they got out of the car.

"Smile," Brooke directed, still snapping photos.

Susanna struck a pose with Brandon then said, "Thanks, but don't bother. We can come down and get them later."

Then the main door swung wide and Jay appeared, looking so handsome with his broad shoulders and low-slung jeans that Susanna had to consciously keep her expression neutral. Both dogs bolted through the door behind Jay, bounding down the stairs toward her.

Suddenly Brandon was interested.

"Hey, you guys." He crouched down to let the dogs sniff him before petting them. A hand for each. "You live here?"

"All their lives," Jay said. "Butters and Gatsby. Butters is the one trying to knock you down."

Brandon smiled, welcoming the attention. "Hey guys."

"This is Jay Canady, owner and property administrator of The Arbors." Susanna leaned down to ruffle Gatsby's head when he came to visit. "Jay, my son, Brandon, and my daughter, Brooke."

Brooke let the camera dangle around her neck and went to the stairs with her hand outstretched. "So you're the boss. Nice to meet you. Great house."

"Great dogs." Brandon stood wiping his now-dog-covered hands on his jeans before he headed toward Jay.

"Pleased to meet you both. Welcome to The Arbors." Jay flashed that easy smile, the epitome of charming host. "Glad you could come."

For one surreal moment Susanna simply stood there, absorbing the sight of her kids and Jay together on those front steps. The perfect Christmas gift. Could Jay possibly have known? Even beyond the festive decorations and warm invitation was seeing her beautiful children and this charming man together, all people she cared for so much.

And she did care. For her children with her heart and soul and everything she was. And for Jay, even though she shouldn't. Not this much. Such a bittersweet admission for the way she felt right now. Blessed with so much love.

Jay suggested a tour to give everyone the lay of the land and to see their rooms. With the dogs on their heels, they headed inside to the living museum that was his house.

Through room after room, he graciously answered Brooke's many questions, and Susanna learned much about the history of this man, who'd come to mean a great deal to her.

Enjoy the moment, she cautioned herself. *Only the moment.*

She was already in too deep.

"I'll just show you the important places now," Jay explained. "You feel free to explore whenever you want."

She'd seen Jay tour people through the facility a number of times. He turned on that Southern charm, and her kids warmed right up to him. They chatted, mostly Brooke asking about the house until Jay sounded like a tour guide. But he made an effort to include Brandon in the conversation, too, and both her kids were smiling and gracious as Jay showed them their rooms and explained the arrangements.

"Is everybody's stuff at the cottage or in the car?" Jay asked, stepping aside to allow everyone to pass him and head downstairs.

"In the car," Susanna said, pausing before she followed the kids, glancing at Jay.

Their gazes met, and for that one instant, there was nothing but the two of them on the second-floor landing. Yearning, so potent, swept over her as his gaze caressed her face, a kiss in his expression. They drank in the sight of each other, the boundaries firmly in place for the holiday ahead, and a feeling of such longing, such loss filled her when she couldn't reach up to brush the hair from his temple, the easy familiarity they'd shared now something that must be hidden.

She wasn't sure who broke first. Him, she guessed because he sidestepped her and headed down the stairs, saying, "Come on, Brandon. Let's get the bags, and please tell me the ladies didn't pack for a month."

Susanna hung back on the stairs, watching the two of them head cross the foyer in companionable silence, her handsome young son and her handsome young lover. One dark, one light, both tall, one lanky in youth, the other solidly masculine.

And she reminded herself to savor the moment because that's all this was and would ever be.

One moment in time.

JAY GRABBED THE EMPTY snifter from the table and asked Walter, "Refill?"

Walter deliberated as he slanted a narrowed gaze between the snifter and Jay then back again. "You know, I think I will. It's Christmas Eve. You'll put me up tonight?"

"Plenty of room." More likely Jay would drop off Walter at his house on the way to midnight mass if he got plowed on the pricey port Jay kept around specifically for him.

Walter didn't know it yet but there was another bottle under the tree wrapped with a bow and a tag with his name on it.

Merry Christmas.

Jay slipped from the family room where everyone had congregated to relax after the meal and get their second wind before midnight mass. Butters was hard on his heels, probably thinking he could finagle a few more table scraps, but Gatsby stuck close to Susanna, who remained seated, greedy for attention rather than food.

He found Drew at the counter, contemplating a dark beer with the bottle opener in his hand.

"Too much life out there for you?" Jay asked.

Drew must have been deep in thought because his head snapped up at Jay's question. But whatever was on his mind vanished beneath an easy smile.

"Hey, Jay. No. Not too much. It's good to see Walter."

Jay held up the snifter. "Round three. I think he's having a good time."

"Must be. Maybe that's what I'll go for. Don't really want this beer."

"Good. Help Walter polish off the bottle so we can keep

him off the streets." Jay headed to the hutch to retrieve another snifter while Drew replaced the beer in the fridge.

"Man, do you even remember the last time the house was this packed? It's like the old days when we were kids." Drew leaned back against the counter and folded his arms over his chest. "Unless you're partying it up when I'm not around."

Which was most of the time. Jay gave a snort of laughter. "There's so much life in here tonight, I can barely breathe. And I think the last time the house was this packed would have to have been Gran's funeral."

"That long ago?"

Jay held the port poised over Walter's empty glass. "Yeah, I don't think we've actually had a party since Mom went to the facility. I wouldn't call Mom's or Dad's funeral a party."

Drew flinched at mention of their parents, and Jay was sorry he'd brought up the subject. He poured both glasses and slid a snifter Drew's way.

Drew inhaled the aroma then took a hefty mouthful. "What the hell is it with this family, anyway?"

He didn't need to elaborate. Jay knew what he meant. Everyone died young or lived to be really old and not in possession of their faculties.

Then again... "Gran lived a good long time and kept her wits. Granddad, too."

"Not Dad and Mom. Or Great-Grandmom."

"No, not them." Dad died too young. Mom, too, but one might argue that Dad died because Mom had lost her mind. Then Mom had died because Dad had died.

Did it really matter?

Jay looked at his brother, really looked hard. He didn't get the opportunity all that often. But Drew looked like he always looked. Except for the gray hairs sprouting around the temples. Barely noticeable with the buzz cut. Definite family resemblance. Drew was older, and all sharp edges and razor creases. Muscular and lean. The Terminator version of Jay. And the brother who drank the most, Jay realized as Drew tossed back the remainder of the port.

As he hadn't even replaced the stopper in the bottle, he held it out. Drew nodded. Jay poured.

"You good?" Jay asked.

"Yeah, good to be home. Not looking forward to packing up that room, though. What are you doing with everything? Didn't sound like you knew where you'd be settling yet."

"No clue. As far as the stuff goes, I figured I'd give you a shot to take whatever you want. I'll store what I want then have an estate sale for the rest."

"Northstar doesn't want anything?"

Jay shrugged. "They don't even know what they'll be doing with this place yet. That's one of the things Susanna's doing—making recommendations about how to best utilize this property."

"Shit, Jay." Drew took another healthy swallow.

Silence fell. A hard silence filled with all the things neither of them was saying.

"You got something to say, now's the time."

Drew frowned, looked undecided. He swallowed another sip. "I have no right to weigh in. Let's get that straight up front."

Jay set the bottle back on the counter and braced himself. A big part of him wanted to shut up Drew before he got started. Instead, he said, "Shoot."

"Are you sure selling this place is the right thing to do?"

"No."

Drew shook his head as if he didn't hear correctly.

"Didn't see that coming. What do you mean *no?* That's all you talk about."

"The *only* thing to do. Not necessarily the *right* thing."

"Got it." Drew pushed the snifter Jay's way, motioned him to drink.

Jay obliged by taking a hearty swig that seared a smooth path all the way down his throat. Walter liked this stuff why?

"Any way I can help?" Drew asked.

"You volunteering to run this place?"

Drew snorted. "That'd be some learning curve. I steered clear of the place even when I was home."

"Cut to the chase, Drew. I have guests." And he wasn't inclined to ease Drew through any guilt he might be feeling for jumping ship when he had.

Drew narrowed his gaze, and alcohol hadn't seemed to dilute the hard look in his eyes. "I know you, Jay. You devoted your life to deal with this place and everyone in it. I don't want you to give up everything and live to regret it."

A few months ago Jay would have told his brother not to worry. A few months ago he'd been sure going through with the acquisition was the right thing to do. But now... now that he'd come back to life and realized what some of the problem was, he also realized that he didn't have much of a plan about what came next. Live. That covered a lot of things.

Marriage. Family. New home. New line of work.

"I'm sketchy about what comes after I leave." Island sex with some random woman beneath tiki torches no longer interested him and hadn't since he and Susanna had become lovers. "I've been working on this deal for a long time, Drew. It's not like I'm running away."

"You sure about that?"

Turned out Drew hadn't earned the right to question

Jay. He'd been smart enough to know even if Jay hadn't realized it until now. "You don't have a clue what you're talking about."

"Dude, I ran away. I freaking missed the only time I could have had with everyone. Mom, Dad, Gran, Granddad even. I screwed up. Don't make the same mistake."

"How in hell am I going to make the same mistake? Everyone's dead already."

"You got something here now. Don't throw it away because you've got your head wrapped around leaving."

"What are you talking about?"

"Susanna."

That stopped him cold. "What about her?"

Drew fixed Jay with a gaze that made him feel dense without a word. "Whatever's going on with you two."

Jay's turn to drink. And not a random sip, either. Heading back to the hutch, he grabbed another snifter. "No comment."

And he didn't have one.

The only part of this holiday gathering he didn't like involved Susanna and the way he had to keep his hands to himself for appearance' sake. He didn't have the same obligations as she had to her kids, but there was the staff to consider.

Walter and The Arbors staff didn't need to know he and Susanna were involved. Not when he'd pretty well decided to sign the papers and leave them in her care. Jay didn't want to undermine her relationship with the staff in any way.

And that wasn't even touching the issue of honorable intentions. He wasn't entirely comfortable with the way he would come off if everyone knew he'd gotten involved with Susanna, intending to leave town. That categorized their relationship in a way that didn't really describe what was happening between them. Even island sex with name-less women left the potential for an honest relationship to develop. His relationship with Susanna had a foregone conclusion.

So what in hell was he doing with her?

Enjoying the moment?

That's exactly what she'd say. Leave it to him to find the perfect woman when he was leaving…. But he couldn't leave unless Susanna stayed, and how could she be the woman when she had already been living the life that he wanted?

He stared at Drew, not having a clue what to say.

"You're going to leave me to guess?" Drew finally asked.

"Nothing to guess about."

"Yeah, right." Drew raised the snifter as a toast. "Here's to screwing your head on straight. Merry Christmas."

SUSANNA SETTLED HER parents in their room. Early birds, they declined the late-night Christmas tradition of mid-night mass that most of their guests would participate in.

"We'll catch mass after we open gifts in the morning, dear," her mom said. "There are several times to choose from. Dad already checked. You go have fun tonight and leave the old folks here to rest."

"Who's old?" Susanna kissed her mom's smooth cheek. "I've never been able to keep up with you. Still can't."

Mom beamed. "I don't know. Looks like you're giving me a run for my money around here."

Dad gave Susanna a quick squeeze. "Your new arrange-ment suits. I haven't seen you look this happy in too long. And I'm glad, Susanna. It's been a long time."

All true. She was happy.

For the moment.

"Oh, Daddy." She moved in for another hug, rested her cheek on his shoulder, a safe place always. "I'm so glad you're here."

He stroked the back of her hair with a big hand, as he had when she'd been little, when he'd been praising her after some accomplishment or comforting her during some disappointment. The gesture was one and the same, meant he was always there to deal with life's ups and downs, creating the sort of family life that Susanna had dreamed of recreating with her own husband and kids.

"Now that Dad's retiring, we're thinking of investing in an RV," her mom said. "Then we could make road trips."

"Looks like you've got plenty of room to park around here," Dad added.

Susanna shifted her gaze between them, smiled, reassured her parents would continue to be an active part of her life no matter where she wound up. "I like that idea. A lot."

Then she was kissing them good-night and heading back out, debating whether or not she had enough time before midnight mass to make one last check on the gifts. The last thing she wanted to do was trek back to the cottage in the wee hours after mass because she'd forgotten something.

The tradition was the kids woke up to their presents under the tree. That tradition would continue no matter where they were. They might have grown past the days when Skip would clamber around on the roof and track reindeer hoofprints all over the yard, but the kids had long ago picked up the torch. Brooke would sneak her gifts for everyone under the tree at night to surprise everyone upon awakening. Brandon would make an appearance to eat the cookies Susanna always left on Santa's plate, leaving crumbs the way Skip had.

Susanna knew the Santa plate had made the trip but

gave herself a mental note to put the cookies out when she put the gifts under the tree. On the table beside the tree in the family room, she thought, so Brandon wouldn't have to look too hard to find them.

Just as she reached the door to her own bedroom, Karan appeared at the end of the hallway.

"Exactly who I was looking for," she said.

Karan looked as lovely as usual, and the sight of her approaching, dressed elegantly, as always, in a festive gold skirt-and-blouse ensemble that complemented her fair hair and creamy skin, made Susanna realize how much she'd missed her best friend. Phone calls weren't the same, no matter how often they talked and texted.

"I've got your gift," Karan said. "And I wanted to give it to you when we were alone."

"Come on in and I'll grab mine so we can exchange—"

"No, not necessary. I still have your official gift for under the tree. This one's special. Just for us."

Translated, this meant Karan's special gift was likely so over-the-top that she didn't want to draw attention to it. That was also typical Karan, so Susanna motioned her friend into the bedroom, bracing herself.

She'd barely shut the door when Karan demanded, "First, I want to know why you don't listen to me. *Ever.* Why don't you ever listen to me?"

Susanna stood at the door, staring into the lovely bedroom Jay had assigned her with the four-poster bed and the hand-carved mantel from a cypress home on the Georgia coast. "What are you talking about?"

"I told you not to mate for life."

Oh. Susanna feigned confusion. "Who, me?"

Karan's expression revealed utter disbelief. "You know exactly what I'm talking about so don't even go there with me or you will not get your Christmas present. I swear,

Susanna." She gave a huff for good measure. "I can't even believe you'd try to play stupid."

Susanna sank to the edge of the bed and spread her hands helplessly, unable to admit the truth. As if admitting she'd been playing house with Jay, had been *enjoying the moment* would make the reality of his inevitable departure real.

The Arbors made it easy to keep reality at bay.

"I know you're involved with Jay," Karan said. "I knew it the instant you introduced him."

"That's not—"

"Please," Karan scoffed. "You blush every time you look at him. I told you not to go from zero to sixty. What is wrong with you? Are you really incapable of *dating?*"

Susanna rocked forward and covered her face with her hands. "Ugh. I'm trying. I'm totally trying."

"Obviously not hard enough."

"Is it really that obvious?"

"Oh, please. I know Brooke suspects because she told me. And your mom. Skip's mom, too. And Drew's been giving Jay such a hard time, I'd bet money he suspects. Charles agrees, so don't be surprised if he starts picking Jay's brain to make sure his intentions are honorable. You know how he is."

"Shoot. Me. Now," Susanna ground out between splayed fingers. "Take back whatever you bought me because all I want for Christmas is for you to stop making me feel stupid."

Karan sank down to the bed next to her, wrapped an arm around Susanna's shoulders. "Suze, Suze, Suze. We've been best friends since middle school. Aren't any of my manhandling skills ever going to rub off on you?"

"I'm hopeless."

"A hopeless romantic. For as pragmatic as you can be

sometimes…well, most of the time, you still believe in happily ever afters."

"You should, too, since you're living yours with Charles."

Karan relented with a sigh. "You're right. I should be appreciative because life couldn't be more perfect."

Something in her voice brought Susanna to attention. There was a look on Karan's beautiful face Susanna hadn't seen before, a peaceful contentment that was simply alien to a woman who'd never ever been peaceful or content.

Whatever had put that expression on her face was *big*.

"Dish," Susanna said. "Now."

That smile played around Karan's mouth another moment before she said, "That's your special Christmas gift. You're going to be an aunt."

That announcement filtered through Susanna in degrees.

An aunt?

Arching a delicate eyebrow, Karan admitted, "I've been trying to tell you since I first suspected."

The crack-of-dawn phone calls suddenly made sense.

"Oh, Karan. I can't believe I've been so wrapped up in my own angst that I didn't give you the chance."

"You earned that right, trust me." Karan patted Susanna's hand reassuringly. "But since I can't take my gift back, I'll have to give you another." She smiled, the picture of contentment. "Everyone likes Jay a lot. Merry Christmas."

JAY SHOULD HAVE BEEN tired. They'd been running nonstop since the first of the guests had arrived. There were large meals in the formal dining room where Great-Grandmom's china made an appearance after nearly a decade of sitting on a shelf.

Late nights chatting around the fire in the family room. Afternoons spent playing ball with Brandon on the lawn by the lake. Excursions to the mall. Christmas preparations.

In addition to all the partying, there'd been work…but Jay felt *alive* as he toted two big bags of wrapped gifts down the stairs in the heavy quiet of late night.

Susanna led the way, running ahead to peer around every corner and insure the coast was clear. Only the glow of the Christmas lights marked their way, their muffled footsteps betrayed by the odd creak of the floorboards.

Jay was reminded of long-ago Christmases when he and Drew would hide in the shadows of this old house, trying to catch a glimpse of Santa coming down the chimney through one of the real fireplaces. Mom had always made a big production of leaving cocoa with extra marshmallows for Santa on the sideboard before tucking Jay and Drew into bed. But there had always been three cups when Drew dragged Jay out of bed to see if they could catch Santa. And the cocoa was always warm.

He smiled at the memory, imagined his parents, grandparents, too, probably, watching mischievous young boys tiptoe down the stairs…. The thought made him smile. There'd been life in this house once.

He remembered because of Susanna.

She darted across the foyer and peered into the family room then motioned him to follow her.

"Coast's clear."

Hauling the two flannel bags that weren't so much heavy as bulky and awkward, he set them in front of the tree. Susanna dove in. He rolled his gaze when she reached into one of the bags and whipped out a ceramic tray that read *Cookies for Santa* on top of her kids' small handprints immortalized in red-and-green paint. Then she pulled out an unopened bag of Oreos.

"Brandon's favorite," she whispered.

"I shouldn't be surprised by how organized you are," he whispered back, dropping beside her to start unpacking gifts. "But I unloaded your luggage and would swear you didn't bring enough clothes for six months let alone Christmas decorations."

"Priorities."

That made him smile, made him think about how much she cared. The loving mom, who saw to all the details, who made it her business to make sure those she loved felt loved. His mom had been the same way.

And she was exactly the kind of woman he wanted to make new memories with, the kind he wanted a life with. A woman who would scoot along the floor on her knees, half-hidden by fir branches and twinkling lights, giving him a prime shot of her curvy bottom as she placed gifts under the tree.

This woman.

The woman who stole a kiss beneath the mistletoe after they finished playing Santa, wrapping her arms around him while whispering "Merry Christmas" against his mouth.

The woman who slipped inside a guest bedroom after a final kiss good-night. The woman who left him wishing he was crawling into bed with her as the door shut with a squeak that reminded him to oil the hinges.

Those thoughts turned over and over in Jay's head and kept him from stealing even a few precious hours of sleep.

Or maybe he couldn't sleep because Susanna wasn't here. He'd gotten so used to the feel of her beside him.

Or maybe Jay was finally facing reality, the inevitable

truth that what he wanted conflicted so dramatically with what he'd found with Susanna.

Watching her sneak around playing mom tonight, watching her interact with her kids the past few days… he wanted what she had. Close, loving relationships with great kids. Sure, life had dealt her family a rough blow, but they were still a family, still living their lives together.

Jay admired that. Envied it, too.

By the time the sun rose and he heard Susanna's parents, the earliest risers, moving around in the kitchen, he had no answers for any of the questions that had robbed him of sleep.

He only knew how he felt.

He felt eager to get out of this room when he finally abandoned futile attempts at sleep and took a shower.

He felt welcomed when arriving in the kitchen to find both older couples working together side by side to provide a feast for the people they loved. Susanna's mother shoved a mug of hot coffee into his hands and steered him to the family room to relax beside the fire Susanna's father had brought back to life.

He'd felt surprised there were so many presents for him under the tree, and not just from Drew and Walter. Brooke declared herself the gift distributor and sat in her warm robe with her hair pulled up in a lopsided ponytail, an organizer like her mom. She kept track of who hadn't yet opened a gift.

"No, no, Grandpa, hang on to that for a second. Uncle Charles hasn't opened the one from Mom yet."

She read each tag aloud. "This one's for Jay from Aunt Karan and Uncle Charles."

He glanced at the blond couple sitting close together on the divan. "Appreciated, but not necessary."

"Of course it was." Karan waved a dismissive hand.

"You've opened your home to us, Jay. We're having a lovely time."

"I chose that gift, though, so you're safe." Charles pulled his wife close to him and pressed a kiss to the top of her head. "She wanted me to pick you up a surgical sanitizing wand from one of my hospital suppliers."

"I didn't. I swear." Karan laughed. "But it would be handy for traveling."

Smiling and aware that everyone watched him, Jay unwrapped a wheeled leather travel bag that must have cost a small fortune. Designed to carry essentials that met airline requirements, it was large enough to hold items a traveler wouldn't want to check, like a laptop.

"Now that is a handy gift." Drew inspected the finely tooled leather bag with approval. "Flying commercial nowadays with all that security."

"Appreciate it." Jay meant it. "I'll put it to good use."

There were gifts from Susanna's parents and her in-laws: a practical travel pet-care kit and a necktie carrier. He liked the closeness of this family, the generations that were all an active part of one another's lives.

When he watched the way everyone interacted with Charles and Karan, he knew that Susanna understood the concept of family-by-love, as she called it, the only family he had nowadays except for Drew.

But the running theme through all these gifts told him Susanna had been the one to suggest them. All were useful for a man getting ready to cut ties with everything he'd known. And she knew what that would entail firsthand.

She obviously cared so much.

"Here's Jay's stocking stuffer," Brooke announced. "From Mom, Brandan and me."

"Now when did you all find time to shop for me?" Jay asked. "You haven't stopped running since you got here."

Brendan shook his head. "No clue, dude."

Jay laughed.

Brooke scowled at her brother. "Come on, Jay. Open it."

The box contained a travel coffee cup and a hefty supply of VIA in several varieties.

"The coffee's from Brandon." Brooke scowled at her brother, who shrugged.

"Caffeine no matter where I am. Thanks," Jay said.

"So what was your contribution?" Brandon asked his sister. "You tied the bow?"

"I took the photo, thank you very much."

"Photo?" Jay inspected the travel cup and encased securely behind hard plastic was indeed a photo that had been sized to fit around the entire cup. A photo of tiny smiling faces.

The Arbors' staff.

Walter came up beside him. "I'm there behind Tessa."

Jay turned the cup and identified the faces of every one of his staff. Administrators. R.N.s. LPNs. PCTs. Dietary. Aides. Housekeepers. Laundry. The guys in maintenance and engineering huddled around Chester.

He was silent so long that when he did finally glance up, that blush was back in Susanna's cheeks, and she jumped to fill the quiet. "I know it's not as amazing as hosting my first Christmas in Charlotte in your antebellum plantation. But I wanted you to take away something that will remind you everything's fine where you left it."

God, how did he even respond to such caring?

"When did you get everyone together—" He stopped. "*How* did you manage to get everyone together?"

"We helped," Drew said.

Charles nodded. "Each of us grabbed a radio and manned a nurses' station to hold down the fort. Staff on shift was gone maybe ten minutes tops. You should have seen the stampede getting everyone back inside."

As a doctor, Charles understood better than most what pulling staff off the floor involved, but Jay had also been referring to the fact that everyone off shift would have had to come in on their days off, before or after their shifts, all to crowd together and smile for a ten-minute photo.

For him.

Humbled didn't even begin to describe how he felt. He met Susanna's gaze, noticed the color high in her cheeks, wasn't concerned who saw how much he cared.

"Thank you."

For caring enough to reassure him.

For giving him a Christmas filled with laughter.

For bringing him back to life.

CHAPTER SIXTEEN

AFTER SPENDING THE better part of two weeks living in Jay's house for the holidays, Susanna was ready to head back to her cottage. Not because she didn't love his house. Living there had come too easily, if anything, as though once she'd cut ties with her life in New York, she instinctively needed to set roots down elsewhere. Jay's house had been easy to fill with happy family memories. But the holidays were over and everyone had gone home.

Jay would be leaving, too.

Northstar had been pushing to get the acquisition date on the calendar, so they had a date in writing only eight weeks away. Gerald and VIPs from the partners would be flying in to sign the final papers.

So, in self-defense, she sent her kids back to school, packed her bags and told Jay it was time to go home.

He hadn't asked her to stay.

Something had changed between them during the holidays, something that had her clinging to whatever distance she could keep between them, which wasn't much. Not when they returned to doing everything together—working, eating, making love, sleeping then awakening to start the cycle all over again.

That *something* had the opposite effect on Jay. He possessed their every second together as if afraid to miss even one.

After work, anyway.

At work, he'd become even more of a handful.

Such as the day during the second week of the quarantine to contain an airborne virus making the rounds through all three floors and turning an active facility into a ghost town.

Jay encountered Nancy, a PCT scheduled in the north wing, maneuvering Mr. Parrish from bed to wheelchair in the Hoyer lift. He showed up in Susanna's office, as handsome as always with his crisp shirt and tie at odds with his scowl.

"Kimberly told me you sent Ryan home," he said.

"I did."

"He was scheduled seven to three today."

She nodded. "He wanted to take his motorcycle to the dealer."

"That's what days off the schedule are for."

Susanna leaned back in her chair and steepled her hands before her, racking her brain for the most diplomatic way to phrase an admission Jay wouldn't want to hear. She settled on, "The numbers were off on the profit-and-loss report. Ryan was willing to work less than eight hours which helped me shave a bit off the payroll variance."

Jay stared, long and hard enough to give Susanna ample opportunity to brace herself for the coming argument. And the way he bristled in his neat sports jacket broadcasted loud and clear that an argument was coming.

"Let me get this straight," he said. "I don't have a PCT on first shift to help move Mr. Parrish so we can balance the profit-and-loss report?"

"Cost overrun."

"That's only because we had extra expenditures with Christmas and Mrs. Harper's new wheelchair."

Susanna spread her hands in entreaty. "I understand,

but the numbers were off. I have to rein them in the way I see best, otherwise Northstar will dictate what to cut."

"Christmas is over and Mrs. Harper won't need another wheelchair. The numbers will be on again this report."

Susanna wished the resolution were so simple. Jay took a liberal perspective on profit and loss. What didn't balance one quarter would balance the next. Northstar tended toward a more controlled perspective because they reported to many partners.

"All three floors are quarantined with the virus. Ryan appreciated the time, Jay. I made sure I wasn't depriving him of hours. Apparently the dealer isn't open for service on Saturdays, and he has classes at night so it's almost impossible for him to get in for service after a shift."

"We schedule a man specifically to insure we have help with the Hoyer lift."

"Women can work it."

"But the bigger men like Mr. Parrish and Mr. Wells don't feel comfortable with a woman. They don't understand how the transfer equipment works. All they see is the floor underneath them. They don't want to break anything. You understand that."

"Of course I do." No arguing Jay's perspective with his focus on individual residents. "But that's what we're here for—to help them understand and reassure them. As I'm sure you did."

His expression set in granite, which told her he had indeed explained and reassured but didn't want to admit it. He wasn't backing down. "What happens when I'm not here?"

Her heart would break all over again. That's what would happen, and Susanna had no one but herself to blame. Because she couldn't enjoy a fling like a normal person.

She'd given in to her attraction to this younger man,

knowing he was going off to sow his oats, and her one wild and crazy attempt to savor the moment setting her up for heartbreak.

And failure. Because at the rate they were going, the final acquisition may never happen. And if the acquisition didn't happen, this man she cared so deeply for would be miserable.

"Jay." Susanna injected every shred of patience she possessed into her voice. "I understand your concern. Ryan would have been best-case scenario. But we have the proper equipment, the properly trained staff. When you're not here, I will be."

But judging by his reaction, as if the top of his head might blow off, he didn't need the reminder. She kept her mouth shut and waited for him to make the next move, for him to back down or to explode or to work through whatever his issue was.

God, Susanna hated this. She'd been killing herself to control the budget variance. Even Walter had complimented her in front of Jay for her ingenuity in controlling the internal supplies variance. She gotten a local church's shawl club to contribute colored lap robes to match the flowers Mrs. Selmon wore in her hair.

And the coffee…Jay himself admitted even the best blend tasted terrible brewed in bulk, so coffee was a great place to trim more excess so the effect wasn't as noticeable.

Nothing she did was good enough. Not because of her efforts but because Jay didn't know what he wanted.

He half sat on her desk, folded his arms over his chest and glanced down at her, clearly managing to rein in his reaction. "You saw an opportunity to cut the numbers and took it. You weren't invasive, so I should be reassured, right?"

He was asking her? Crazy man. "Yes, you should."

"All right. I should trust that you're looking after the best interests of this place and let you do your job."

There was another question in there, a problem, too, but Susanna wouldn't point out what Jay was missing.

No, she tipped her face to his and stole a kiss before he headed to therapy to insure everyone was making good use of the downtime during the quarantine. The man was a complete control freak.

Therein lay the problem.

Jay was The Arbors. Susanna worked for Northstar. There would always be a disconnect, a potential conflict, much in the way there was conflict now.

Professionally, she needed to transform The Arbors into a Northstar property.

Personally, she wanted to live up to Jay's vision of the personalized care for his residents.

Sometimes the two came hand in hand. Sometimes not.

Swinging her chair around with a sigh, she stared out into the crisp wintry morning, so many winter branches bare, such a marked difference from the explosion of autumn colors that had surrounded the lake when she'd arrived.

She wished they could go back to that companionable working relationship they'd had in the beginning. Jay had been so pleased with the skill set she displayed before discovering her lack of memory-care experience. Before they'd complicated everything by breaching professionalism and becoming involved.

But Susanna also knew she hadn't been implementing changes back then. She'd been conducting performance evaluations of the staff and monitoring variance information. Jay would have to know that she'd get to budget justification. Walter had.

Yes, their relationship may have complicated the issues, but their closeness had also given Susanna insight. The conflict originated with the changes no matter how minute they were.

So why was Jay selling this property again?

There was much more to the answer than Jay had shared. So much more than he knew, she suspected. But she hated watching him struggle this hard. What he said about the sale and the way he behaved weren't related. She didn't know why and would never get the chance to help.

Tearing her gaze from the window, she took action to tackle her anxiety and keep his imminent departure a reality. The time had come to file her official recommendation for his house.

The quarantine provided the perfect opportunity. The therapy schedule and activities calendar had come to an abrupt stop as residents were confined to their rooms to keep those who didn't already have the virus from contracting it.

Tessa and Shirley seized the opportunity to remove the last of the holiday decorations. Maintenance and engineering were painting and rewiring the dining rooms that normally couldn't be out of commission for more than a few hours between common meals. Susanna would complete this report without all the usual distractions.

After staying in the house, she was recommending providing another level of service of limited support for couples where one spouse was demonstrating the beginning stages of Alzheimer's. Northstar could staff the house minimally and provide access to the ALF when the residents needed step-up care. Of course, that option would mean significant renovations to bring the house up to code, combining charming bedrooms with their whimsical mantels into suites and eliminating the glorious winding staircase to provide elevator access.

And that would be such a loss.

But that was only personal reluctance from the woman who'd brought her family into Jay's home to share a wonderful holiday.

The professional businesswoman couldn't be concerned with antique mantels or staircases from another era. Not when there would be underutilized square footage on the property.

Her problem was a division of loyalties.

She would do everything in her power to uphold Jay's ideal, but when push came to shove, her loyalties must be to the company that paid her salary and provided healthcare coverage for herself and her kids.

Not to the man who held her during the night.

WHEN MRS. HARPER'S family asked Jay to arrange for a local priest to visit, he wasn't surprised. Mrs. Harper hadn't gotten out of bed for the past few days. She wasn't sick, just winding down, as his grandmother used to say. Another of those euphemisms to sugarcoat reality.

The active woman who'd been acquainted with every duck on the property looked so tiny in her bed. Jay went to kneel beside her, gently awakened her to announce her visitor.

"Father's here to visit," Jay said, not knowing if Mrs. Harper would comprehend. She was weak and her memory was hit or miss on a good day. The progression of Alzheimer's hadn't outpaced her declining health. She'd been lucky in that regard.

She opened her eyes with effort and when her lips moved dryly, he reached for the moistener on the side table.

But Susanna was already there, tearing open the packaging, extracting the swab to moisten Mrs. Harper's lips.

Jay had to lean close when she asked, "My rosary beads."

A good day.

He reached for the top drawer of the nightstand, where he knew she kept the case, but again Susanna was there, handing him the strand of blue glass beads.

Pressing them into Mrs. Harper's fragile hands, Jay gave a reassuring squeeze then stood and stepped aside.

The priest took things from there, providing the Sacrament of the Sick then praying with Mrs. Harper while Jay and Susanna stood behind him, joining in the prayers they knew, sharing in the "Amen" when they didn't.

Mrs. Harper clung to the priest's hands and seemed strengthened when she whispered loud enough for them to hear, "Thank you, Father. God has been so good to me."

A miracle that she remembered God. Susanna apparently thought so, too, because Jay glanced down to find her expression cast in marble, her blue eyes glinting suspiciously as she fought back tears.

He wanted to slip his arm around her, to comfort her from this rare display of emotion. But he had no right to touch her in the one place they spent more time than any other.

Theirs was not a public relationship, but a private one, and as such he had to curb his need and allow the priest to be the one to gently touch Susanna's shoulder and say, "She'll be in good hands. I promise."

SUSANNA AWOKE IN THE dark of late night and instinctively bolted across the bedroom before sleep cleared and her brain finally caught up.

Nausea. Big-time.

She made it to the bathroom, and by the time she was curled up in a fetal ball on the bathroom rug, she knew she'd rather die than have to drag herself up and be sick one more time.

She lay there shivering, too weak to reach up and grab a towel to cover her, would rather freeze than move. Some vague place in her memory remembered what it felt like to be alone and miserable. She'd had a life before Skip had gotten sick, before every minute of every day had become urgent, a lesson in not letting a precious moment pass unlived while surviving on one income, with one car, with one parent trying to be in three places at once with two children who needed two parents.

Even through her sick haze, she knew life hadn't always been that way. She hadn't always been alone. Once upon a time she'd been part of a happy family, when the kids had been little and their days full of caring for each other, enjoying each other, living and loving and *living...*

Susanna didn't know what had driven her from sleep. One moment she'd been curled up around Skip in bed. The next moment she was on her knees, heaving up her guts in the commode.

When she finally sank down onto the bathroom rug, a puddle of weakness, grateful she'd thrown in that last load of laundry the other night because the rug still smelled fresh.

She must have dozed, because she startled awake, every inch of her aching, her stomach rebelling again... Just when she thought there couldn't possibly be anything left, she was forced to drag herself up again.

She was burning up, pressing her cheek to the cold tile.

She was shivering so hard her rattling teeth echoed in the quiet. And it was so quiet. Not a creature was stirring....

Funny how every minute of her every day was filled with family life. Meeting everyone's needs. Organizing play groups and cooking and reading stories and laundry and Christmas shopping and cleaning and listening to Skip deliver a blow-by-blow about contracting a huge firm and Karan's meltdown about her unraveling marriage, all while squeezing in a full-time career around what was really important—her loved ones.

She'd spent thirty minutes tracking down Lambie tonight after dinner because Brooke couldn't possibly sleep without him. While Skip regaled them with his success story and they both took turns helping Brandon with his vocabulary sheet....

Yet here she was, alone, while her family slept peacefully. Not even Skip to care for her in this hour of need.

He'd be here if she woke him. But she didn't have the strength to call out or the heart to interrupt his sleep when he had an important meeting with the vice president of sales and their newest, and now biggest, client tomorrow.

So she just lay there trying to draw warmth from the woolly bath rug, teeth chattering, until forced to reach for the toilet seat and drag herself up yet again.

Only this time when she sank back to the bathroom rug, she sensed a presence in the doorway. Even turning her head took a monumental effort. Two glinting eyes surveyed her from a furry golden face.

Hershel.

He didn't take long to assess the situation before maneuvering the tight passage into the bathroom, tail thumping the wooden hamper as he did. He flopped down beside her with his big warm body, solid and safe, a gesture that said louder than any words that she wasn't alone anymore.

Warmth finally chased away the cold. Not the feverish

sort of burning up, but a gentle warmth that finally lulled her from sleep. A blanket.

Jay, not Hershel.

It took a moment to make sense of him, sitting with his back against the bathroom wall, his arm hooked over his knee.

"I'm dying." That hoarse voice wasn't hers, was it?

"You're not dying." Jay's chuckle was an assault on her weakened senses, an offense to her misery. "You probably just picked up the virus everyone else had. Remember?"

No, she didn't. She was dying.

"I won't let you die," he said softly. "I promise."

And he seemed determined to make good. When she was forced to drag herself up, he was there to support her, pull her hair back with gentle fingers. He pressed a cool washcloth to her face and neck.

He didn't rebel at the sheer grossness of the situation—not that she cared, she was *that* sick. But she would care. If she ever felt better, she'd die of embarrassment. But right now he took the situation in stride and cared for her.

And she wasn't alone.

Not yet, anyway.

LIKE EVERY RESIDENT WHO'D been felled by the horrible virus, Susanna took days to shake off the effects. In the meantime she lay curled up in a pathetic ball under a mountain of blankets—on the couch during the day and in bed at night. She sipped warm broth and nibbled saltines and slept.

Jay ran the facility, returning to the cottage to check on her every few hours. Liz sent soup. Jay updated Brooke and Brandon on Susanna's condition via text messages, took her mom's and Karan's calls every night.

The only time he left for any stretch was when Mrs. Harper passed away as the sun rose one morning.

"To start her first day in heaven," Mrs. Harper's son had said while he held her hand.

Jay relayed the peace of the passing, reassured Susanna she wouldn't have been able to do anything more to help had she not been sick. But Mrs. Harper's death inspired Susanna to drag her sorry self into the shower for the first time in days. She fully intended to attend the memorial service at the end of the week without worries of infecting the guests.

The best part of her illness was that she was so entrenched in her misery that she didn't have any time to angst about Jay because if she'd been well, his thoughtful care of her during this illness from hell would have pitched her over the edge.

As it was, it took a call from Gerald to do that. He caught her one afternoon as she slept.

"Hello, Susanna." His sober tone helped her shake off sleep. "Glad I caught you. Got a minute to talk?"

"Of course." She didn't confess to lying around her living room and hoped she didn't sound half-dead. "What's up?"

"We got some news this week I need to share with you. I haven't called until now because we wanted to come up with an action plan before the news broke. But the news is getting ready to go public, and I wanted you to hear it from me."

Adrenaline surged. Closing her eyes, she fought a wave of nausea and ground out, "Doesn't sound good."

"Not a crisis. Just a bit of a setback." He went on to explain that one of the partners in the senior living venture, University, was going into Chapter Eleven reorganization and the news was about to break publicly with considerable fallout.

"Please tell me you're kidding."

"Wish I was, trust me. We've been in meetings all week, reviewing the details. We've decided to ride out their window until they have to file the reorganization plan. Unfortunately, your transition period will be up before University files that plan with the court."

"So what are you saying, Gerald? We're pulling the plug on the acquisition?"

"No, no. Nothing like that. The rest of the partners want to hang in, but you know as well, if not better, than I do the situation down there. We're talking tightening our belts to ride out this setback, and Jay hasn't been all that open to tightening anything."

Gerald didn't know the half of it. "Have you considered bringing in a new partner?"

"Of course. We want to see how much we can recover because we're taking a hit. But if the creditors' committee can come up with a viable plan of reorganization, something the court and creditors can live with, we'll minimize damage considerably."

There was silence on the other end of the line, Gerald giving Susanna a chance to think of the questions that needed asking, to figure out where she fit into the picture.

The bottom line was always about the money.

Money, money, money. Making her life miserable again.

When the silence stretched for too long, Gerald said, "You know that even if the deal falls through, you'll still have a job. Don't stress about that. We'll come up with another situation that will work for you. Maybe not quite as optimum as The Arbors, but something you can live with."

"I appreciate knowing that," she ground out between clenched teeth.

"I wanted to get to you before you pulled up the internet or heard about this on the six-o'clock news."

Not that Susanna would have seen the news on the computer or the television. Her head pounded so hard that even the thought of listening to the drone of the TV made her head ache.

"You want to break the news to Jay or shall I?" Gerald asked. "Your call. Either way, I'm going to send you the draft of our report. You and Jay will be able to see how the numbers play out. We still have time before the end of the transition period forces a decision. Maybe you can smooth things over with him. We're not going to let the standard of service suffer at any of our properties. We just need to ride things out until University gets on their feet or we get someone else on board."

Jay wouldn't care. He took every single decision personally. He wanted to argue about every change she made from the software they used to the coffee. From Jay's perspective this news would constitute a crisis.

And that's exactly how the news felt to her.

She didn't like cutting corners on things that impacted quality of life for people. Sometimes they were little things that made all the difference between a frown and a smile.

Susanna hadn't genuinely understood the difference until The Arbors, until watching Jay make a leap of faith that the profit-and-loss report would balance next month so Mrs. Harper could have a specialized wheelchair to keep her mobile.

Northstar's margins didn't really have room for leaps of faith. Sure, she could find places to shave down numbers, but at what cost?

"I'll tell Jay what's going on." That's all she could promise.

"Good girl. Tell him to call me with his questions."

She dropped the phone and stumbled to the bathroom. But the nausea appeared to be a false alarm this time, which must mean she was on the mend. She didn't trust it, so she curled up on the rug with a towel beneath her head and tried to think.

She couldn't. Adrenaline made her thoughts race, her head pound and her stomach ache.

God, what was wrong with her? Was she cracking under the pressure, coming completely unglued? She hadn't eaten solid food in days, hadn't slept well in months. Unless Jay was with her. Then she'd slept the exhausted sleep of a woman with her lover. A woman in love.

Her head ached. She felt conflicted, out of sorts about everything The Arbors was and Northstar wasn't. A dangerous conflict that would lead to nowhere but her own discontent since she owed her allegiance to the company that signed her paycheck.

Why didn't anything feel normal anymore? Not her life. Not her mood. Not her schedule. Not her periods. She couldn't even remember the last time she'd had one.

That stopped her.

Eyes opening, Susanna lay there staring at the bathroom wall, where the mitered corners of the baseboards met in precision angles, so still, she didn't think her heart beat.

Her periods?

Her mind went blank. Why couldn't she remember having a period? She'd been intimate with Jay for the better part of two months and hadn't once had to face the awkwardness of addressing why they couldn't be intimate.

When was the last time she'd had a period?

Suddenly the most important thing in Susanna's world was getting to her calendar.

She was meticulous about noting her cycles, always had been out of habit because she hated wasting even one brain cell on such a mundane detail but equally hated getting to her ob/gyn and not having a clue when they asked. They always asked.

Maneuvering through the display on her phone, she pulled up her calendar, scrolled through the previous weeks…the previous *month*…*two* months.

Impossible.

She and Jay were meticulous about birth control. Except for that first night when passion had caught them off guard.

"Oh, God." The words were out of her mouth on a hard breath. "No, that's not possible."

Reason rebelled. Her brain simply couldn't wrap around the impossible thought.

Not so impossible really.

Then in the recesses of her stunned brain, she could hear a voice saying, *Mother, you should practice what you preach.*

And she laid her head on the sofa cushion, and shut her eyes, trying to breathe through the panic.

JAY ARRIVED AT THE COTTAGE to find Susanna on the couch hunched over a laptop. Butters and Gatsby raced toward her. With a sharp command, Jay stopped them before they jumped up.

"Hey, babies," she said, her voice rough, as if she'd been crying. Cradling the laptop close, she petted the dogs, cooing to keep them satisfied, while Jay took in her pallor and the dark circles beneath her eyes.

"You okay?"

"Fine." But she didn't meet his gaze. She just sat there, holding tight to the laptop with one hand, petting the dogs in turns with the other.

Taking the bottle of sports water, he headed into the

kitchen to grab a fresh one from the fridge. He cracked the lid, set it on the table beside her. "You're overdoing it."

That's when she finally looked his way, and the distance he saw in the deep blue depths of her eyes surprised him.

"We need to talk." Her tone warned he wasn't going to like what he heard.

He didn't really want to hear about the problems they faced because he didn't have any answers. Not an answer for how he was supposed to leave her now that he'd found her. Or how he could ask her to quit her job and stay with him if he couldn't leave.

The fact that she already had a family and he'd wanted one…well, turned out that part was negotiable. He wanted to be with Susanna. She had a great family already, and when he really got down to it, did he want to pass along the death sentence of Alzheimer's to his kids?

He shooed the dogs away and sat down on the couch by her feet, Butters at his feet. Gatsby opting for his own space on the ottoman. "Okay. Let's talk."

"Gerald called." Then she explained what he needed to know and Jay's day turned end over end.

"I've been going over the report, Jay. And I'm worried you're not going to be happy with the numbers. You okay?"

Not okay. He was having visions of The Arbors filling beds on the government's dime. Not that he had a thing against the government providing for patients who needed care. He didn't. He supported that assistance through his taxes and was grateful people who needed care could get some.

But The Arbors wasn't about spreading around the minimum level of care. The Arbors was about utilizing cutting-edge advancements and supporting the research that broke ground with Alzheimer's. Risking that status would undermine The Arbors' fundamental goal. The first step onto a slippery slope that would only lead one way—down.

He couldn't answer Susanna's question, so he asked one of his own. "Anything else?"

Their gazes met across the length of her lovely body stretched between them, an intimate connection. He hadn't expected Susanna in his life.

She shook her head. "No."

CHAPTER SEVENTEEN

"THEN SHUT DOWN THAT laptop and forget all about Gerald and that report right now," Jay told Susanna. "Neither of us can do anything. And no worrying about the staff, either. I'd be surprised if any of them has a clue who the partners are. We'll handle the situation the same way Northstar did. Once we decide what to do, we'll tell them."

But Jay didn't have a clue what that might be. Leaving The Arbors to Northstar's care in these circumstances was simply unacceptable. This entire transition period had been an exercise in relinquishing control. Jay hadn't. Not much, anyway. He'd been stubbornly resisting one change after another. That much was evident in the face of a really big change, one that would impact The Arbors much more than the kind of coffee they served.

The only thing he could do was take a deep breath and clear his head, so he could look at all the angles.

He had way too much emotion right now. His whole life felt as if it hung in the balance of this acquisition, as if he might implode if he couldn't get out of here.

But he didn't want to leave Susanna and what he'd found with her.

And he'd promised everyone at The Arbors not to leave them on unstable ground.

"I still have things to do at the facility before I'm done for the day, but I won't go back unless you promise you won't sit here and stress out for the rest of the afternoon."

He would stress enough for the both of them.

"I promise." She forced a smile.

The fact that she had to work so hard for that smile told him he shouldn't believe her.

But Jay had to leave to get a grip. He needed a new plan because the one he had was coming apart.

Butters and Gatsby accompanied him from the cottage, and he didn't bother taking the golf cart. The walk would help him work off the edginess, calm the frustration. With any luck. And as far as he could tell, his luck had taken another unexpected turn.

He was not going to allow medication to be dispensed by folks with sixteen hours of training. He was not going to allow patient assistants earning minimum wage to be responsible for more residents than they could reasonably care for.

He didn't give a hoot about the regulatory bureau, which did nothing but put deterrents in place to avoid catastrophes.

The Compassion to Care.

He had trusted Northstar to provide that level of service…no, he had *hoped* Northstar would hold to the same standard, but he hadn't trusted them. If he had, there would have been no need for any transition period.

That truth suddenly seemed so simple.

His trying to cover all the bases…and Susanna in the middle. He hadn't understood the position she'd been in until right now. She wasn't happy with what was going on, but she needed her job to provide for her family. All along she'd been trying to appease both Northstar and Jay, jumping through hoops to find some common ground.

And he'd fought her every step of the way. Over coffee, for Christ's sake.

Butters let out a bark and chased after something scampering in the underbrush. Jay dragged himself from his thoughts and realized he hadn't walked to the facility, but to his granddad's old farmhouse. He hadn't been here in a while.

Leaning against the fence, he waited for Butters to return, noticing the rotted slats his great-granddad had insisted be replaced every spring. He'd corral Jay and Drew, have Gran pack a picnic then herd them down here for a day of hard work....

"Why do we have to work?" Drew asked, tossing the knife so hard that the blade sliced into the hard-packed dirt halfway to the hilt. "We're only kids."

Great-Granddad didn't answer right away, kept rolling that toothpick around his lips until Drew withdrew the knife and gave Great-Granddad his attention.

"You're part of this family, Drew. You have to do your share whether you feel like it or not."

Drew didn't say anything, but Jay could tell he didn't like that answer one bit.

"Is that why Gran takes care of Great-Grandmom?" Jay wanted to know.

Great-Granddad nodded slowly. He did everything slowly because he was real old. Walking and talking and milking the cows. And he didn't fix the fence at all because he couldn't get up when he knelt down anymore. So he handed Drew and Jay the tools and gave orders.

"That's exactly right, Jay-boy," Great-Granddad said. "Makes your Gran feel better. She's taking good care of her mama and the more she learns about the Alzheimer's disease, the more she feels in control. She's putting things in place in case she winds up like your great-grandmom."

"Will she? Wind up that way, I mean?" The thought of his strong, laughing Gran sitting in a wheelchair, staring out the windows with the same smile on her face during

*every Sunday dinner, every birthday party, every time
the wisteria bloomed then the peonies then the gardenias
then the azaleas.*

*Even Drew wanted to know. He was back to playing
with the knife again, but he was listening real closely. Jay
could tell because they both knew that Great-Granddad
only told the truth. He didn't care how old they were. He
treated them like men.*

*"There's no way of telling, Jay-boy. We just got to
hope."*

Jay wasn't sure why he remembered that long-ago conversation now, several lifetimes after the fact. Now when
the fence was rotting and there was no one left to run this
place but him. And Susanna.

But it turned out his grandmother hadn't come down
with the disease. His mother had. It had started with her
lists. If she didn't write it down, she wouldn't remember.
She'd laugh and blame menopause, which she swore would
kill her. It hadn't, but the need for lists never went away
even after the hot flashes did. Lists in her purse. Lists in
her pockets. Post-it notes all over the house. Even on her
rearview mirror in the car.

Then one day they'd found her trimming the arbors in
the midsummer when everything was in full bloom.

Things had gone downhill from there.

She hadn't lingered like her own grandmother. Maybe
she'd decided she wouldn't live unless she could live as
herself.

As educated as Jay was about the disease, he still
couldn't shake that idea. That somehow she had the will
to know she didn't want to linger that way.

One day, she just started winding down.

Doctors couldn't find a thing wrong with her. Dad had
said to stop looking, to let her be. Then Dad had died sud-

denly. Mom went right behind him. And somewhere along the way, Jay had stopped caring about this fence and the abandoned farmhouse now aging into disrepair.

When he finally pushed away from that rotting old fence, there was one question standing out from all the others he had no answers for. One question that felt more urgent than the rest put together.

Had he lost his hope somewhere along the way, too?

SUSANNA NEVER THOUGHT she'd appreciate catching a virus, but that virus was the only thing saving her from a complete meltdown. She simply didn't have the strength.

"Are you sure you're feeling up to this?" Jay asked again. "I don't want you to get wiped out and not be able to attend Mrs. Harper's memorial service tomorrow."

Susanna smiled to reassure him, heart melting, as always, by his concern for her. All his careful plans for the final sale had exploded. He was trying to salvage something from the wreckage of his hopes to leave The Arbors. And now she had an even bigger bomb to drop.

She hadn't had the heart to tell him of her suspicions. Not until she knew for sure, anyway. And that wouldn't happen until she took a pregnancy test. Of course, her ob/gyn was in New York, which meant she was considered a new patient with the practice Charles had suggested. The first available appointment was over a month away. She'd go the home pregnancy kit route. But another day or two of denial wouldn't hurt.

"Jay, I've been cooped up in that cottage for four days. I'm happy to get outside. The vitamin D is good for me." She wouldn't give up one minute of the time they could spend together. Not now.

He eyed her thoughtfully then gave a decided shake of

his head. "All right, then. You sit right in that chair and start absorbing vitamin D. And don't get up, got it?"

"I thought I was supposed to hand you the tools, so you could show me what to do?" Knowledge she probably would never need now. The chances of this deal happening were looking less promising by the day.

Which left her wondering where Northstar would send her. And how she could possibly leave...especially now. The future loomed before her more uncertain than ever before. How could she possibly work these sorts of hours as a nearly forty-year-old single mother? Just the thought made her head pound. But there was positive thought in there somewhere. Karan was pregnant, too. Maybe Susanna should consider returning to New York, so they could rear their kids together.

Jay eyed her with a frown. "Are you sure you're—"

"I'm fine."

He didn't believe her. So she motioned him to get going. Then she sat back and watched him climb the ladder with a wicked curved-blade trimmer. He wore only jeans and a flannel shirt. He didn't seem to mind the wind that had her bundled up in a layered sweater and jacket. And he looked great with the breeze ruffling his hair, his movements all bristling with contained energy, entirely male.

"This is important, Susanna. Chester knows how to trim back the arbors, but he doesn't have men to spare."

"That's why you do it yourself?"

"Pretty much. But I work at it nonstop for every day after work and on weekends. Takes me the better part of two weeks, and that's really the only window. If you don't catch things at the right time, you'll undermine growth for the entire season. They won't withstand the cold and will be susceptible to diseases."

"Sounds like taking care of kids."

Don't freak out. Don't freak out. Don't freak out.

"Really old kids maybe. My great-grandmother planted most of these when she first came to live here after marrying my great-grandfather. Place was a farm back then."

"And your family has kept them up ever since?"

"Hard not to. My great-grandmother loved them even when she couldn't remember she was the one who'd planted them. My grandparents would wheel her out here and let her sit in the shade while they worked on pruning everything. My grandmother took care of them the longest, but my mother was definitely more into them. She added a lot of new vines around the lake. Different strands more climate resistant. They're the ones you can see from your office. She planted them as a gift for my grandmother on Mother's Day one year."

"Your grandmother didn't get out of that office all that often, I'm guessing."

Jay shook his head.

"What a thoughtful gift, then." Like mother like son, apparently. "Walter said they'd be beautiful in spring."

"They will."

There was wistfulness in that admission, Susanna was sure. She couldn't understand Jay. By his own admission he wanted love in his life. He wanted everything she'd been so blessed with—beautiful kids, great family, supportive friends. She'd seen yearning in the way he'd handled everyone over Christmas, the charming, skilled host who never met a stranger.

But he lived such an isolated life.

Why had his world narrowed until it only encompassed work, and her? She wanted to know more than anything and wondered if he even knew.

"I gave Chester the name of the arborist I use." Jay trimmed back dry twigs skillfully, letting them drop to the path below. "Don't need him all that often, but when something comes up, it's best to call right away. He can handle anything if we catch it quickly enough. In fact, if everything does work out, it might be best to pay him to visit regularly. He's got a service. The money for up-keep has always come from the household budget, but that might have to change if Northstar does takes over. Guess I should put all this in the manual. I hadn't factored in the logistics of upkeep."

That was a significant admission for a man who'd tried to cover every base. This whole situation boiled down to Jay and what he was willing to live with. Would he be able to walk away and trust her, *anyone,* with his legacy?

The Arbors. The residents. The staff. The arbors that his great-grandmother had planted. He knew everything about these flowers, his green thumb passed down genetically.

A gift she hoped he would pass along.

She took notes as he showed her where to cut back on each variety of vine, how the wisteria differed from the peonies from the lilacs. He explained why it was so im-portant to slant each cut to minimize the risk of disease. He brought the care of these flowers to life until she could almost see this knowledge being handed down generation to generation.

So she listened and jotted notes as Jay spoke in that deep-silk voice until the futility of her notes finally got the better of her.

"Do you think you'll need to finish the manual, Jay?"

He was a long time in answering. "I'm having a hard time thinking clearly about everything."

"Oh."

To her surprise, he hung the clippers on the ladder and climbed down. Grabbing the bottled water from beside the toolbox of garden supplies, he took a deep swig. Then he sat down on the top of the box and faced her.

"I wasn't going to bring this up until you were feeling a little better, but I'm thinking of taking off for a while if you'd be willing to cover for me here."

She forced herself not to feel, not to automatically jump to conclusions. Instead, she let his words filter through her. She could make sense of them later when she had time. And she'd have plenty.

He wanted to leave.

Not forever.

"You'll trust me to cover for you?'

Something about that appeared to soften the hard lines around his mouth. Reaching for her hands, he cradled them both within his, as if he knew about the chill that was freezing her from the inside out. "Yeah, I trust you to cover for me. That's one of the things that's making it a little hard to think straight. I trust you with the place completely."

"But I work for Northstar."

"But you work for Northstar. If I were leaving the place in your care, I'd feel okay about leaving." He met her gaze with those big green eyes that let her see inside. "If I were leaving the place to you then I don't really want to leave. That's one of the other things that's making it hard to think straight."

"Oh." She was surprised by his honesty. Not necessarily by his words. He may not have come out and admitted he cared about her, but it was there in this thoughtfulness. Care in his surprises. Care in his kisses. Care in his every action.

He cared. She didn't question that.

"You want me to hold down the fort while you're gone?"

He gave her hands a squeeze. "Would you mind if I

go? I've got some decisions to make, and the clock is still ticking. I technically don't have to give Northstar an answer until the end of the transition period, but I don't want to hold them up if I know I'm not going to be comfortable with what they've got to offer. But there are so many things to consider, and everything feels contingent on everything else. I really need to think things through, and I can't seem to do that here."

He lifted her hands and pressed a kiss to her knuckles, let his eyes flutter shut for a moment. "I'm afraid you've complicated everything."

"I know."

And she did. Because he'd done the same for her. In more ways than he knew if her suspicions were right. The signs were all there. The weepiness. The exhaustion. The mood swings. Even her body felt more alive, but she'd attributed that to having a younger lover who'd made her feel like a woman again.

She hadn't had the heart to include him in her suspicions on top of everything else. Now she was glad. He'd been so invested in leaving. She still wasn't sure why, but she did know whatever decision he made, he needed to be at peace with it. Not influenced by more obligation. This time to her and a child.

In addition to the residents, the staff, the arbors...

"Any idea where you'll go?" she asked.

He looked relieved. "Not really. Just away. It's been so long since I've left for more than a few days. Not since before—" He squeezed her hands again. "Thank you. I won't leave until you're feeling better. I should probably finish up the trimming before I go, too."

Which he'd already said would take the better part of two weeks. "I'd like you to ask for my opinion."

That made him grin. "What do you think, Susanna?"

"I think you should take me to Mrs. Harper's memorial service tomorrow then spend the rest of the day wrapping up whatever you need to wrap up. I think you should call that arborist you were telling me about and get a crew in here to do this job. Chester and I can oversee the work if that'll put you at ease. Then I think you should pack your bags and go."

"I won't leave until you feel—"

"I'll be back at work Monday whether you're here or not." Now it was her turn to press her mouth to his knuckles, rest her cheek against his strong hand. "Go."

This kind, thoughtful man had been operating on obligation for too long from what Susanna could see. She would never keep his child from him, if they had made one together, but she could give him the gift of some time to figure out what he wanted.

SUSANNA SET THE DECORATIVE plaque on top of her computer monitor, where she'd be sure to see it every time she sat down at this desk.

You can't change the past, but you can ruin the present by worrying over the future.

Karan excelled at finding perfect gifts because to Karan shopping was an art form. And she knew Susanna would have too much time to "catastrophize" with Jay gone, and being forced to deal with the dot on the pregnancy test.

When Susanna came right down to it, she didn't care how many states currently separated them. She simply hadn't been able to face that little dot without her best friend by her side—or over the cell phone in this case.

The dot turned pink.

Karan had been kind. She'd blown off some hospital function with Charles to help Susanna process this life-altering confirmation. For hours, killing one cell phone battery and forcing Susanna to plug into an outlet, she and Karan had hashed through the stages of denial, anger, bargaining and depression before Susanna arrived at grudging acceptance. All the while Karan had pointed out the positives of the situation.

No more empty nest.

They'd be pregnant together, and who would have ever thought that would happen?

Susanna had already practiced her parenting skills, so rearing this child should be a piece of cake.

The enormity of the situation overwhelmed Susanna. Not during the days when work distracted her, but at night, alone in the cottage, without Jay. But she had Butters and Gatsby, her temporary roommates and constant companions through the long, quiet nights as she worked around the cottage or read.

Even now, as she spun her chair around and glanced at the lake, she could see them loping along beside Chester as he trekked toward the arbors to check on the trimming crew.

Butters and Gatsby were as out of sorts as she was. Jay's absence impacted everything. This place seemed quieter without his larger-than-life presence to fill the halls. His laughter. His camaraderie with his staff. His concern for the residents.

He was so determined to sell this place and leave. He'd explained some very rational reasons for wanting to go, even. Expansion of the facility. For a chance to live his own life instead of overseeing the lives of everyone around him.

Susanna saw firsthand how insular life could become on these sixty acres and understood why Jay might feel as if leaving was the only way to break free.

But she didn't understand why he couldn't live his own

life here, when he was clearly conflicted about selling The Arbors. How hard could it possibly be to live when his whole life had set exactly that example?

To get away the way he'd left now?

Or go out to dinner in town with friends or invite the guys over to watch a game?

Or fall in love, get married and raise a family in this amazing place that was his family home?

Didn't seem that difficult from where Susanna stood.

Yes, The Arbors could be consuming, but only if she let it be. She had a learning curve and an empty nest. The immersion method of work suited her situation right now. She'd needed the distraction, hoping that when she finally came up for air, she'd know what came next.

Now she knew. At least some of what to expect.

She'd be a mom again.

During the time of her life when she'd expected to become a grandparent—not too soon, of course. But once the kids got through school and started their own lives. But now she'd be starting from scratch with her own new little one.

The very thought made her catch her breath.

Yes, overwhelmed, but excited, too.

She couldn't begin to imagine how Jay would feel with his life and his expectations up in the air, already feeling so obligated to everyone. But she also couldn't help but wonder why a man who'd lived his entire life on this property couldn't balance life and work a little better.

She was missing something. That much she knew.

So she stared into the morning, watched Chester and the dogs vanish into the arbors that Jay's mother had planted as a thoughtful gift for the woman who'd once occupied this office. And a question occurred to her. Spinning toward the desk, she glanced at her decorative plaque and smiled. Then she accessed the archived residents' database and typed in a name.

Canady.

An entry popped up: Felicia Hayes Canady. Susanna scanned the biographical information.

Jay's mother.

Suddenly a piece of the puzzle of this man she'd fallen in love with, the man she'd reproduced with, fell into place. She hadn't made this connection before.

Pulling up a web search engine, she inputted the name and discovered links leading to stories, anthology collections, even a biography on a publishing house website. She clicked on the link and found a promotional shot of a lovely blonde woman with laughter in her big green eyes.

Without giving herself time to think better of this impulsive course of action, Susanna hopped up from her chair and headed straight to Walter's office.

He was behind his desk hard at work, a cup of coffee—he didn't complain about the new blend—at his elbow, reading glasses poised at the end of his nose.

He glanced up and smiled absently. "Good morning, Susanna. What may I do for you?"

She went to him and half sat on the edge of his desk, drawing his surprised glance. "I have a question. If you're not comfortable answering, please just say so. I don't know who else to ask. I know how much you care and I trust this conversation will stay between us."

"This is about Jay." Not a question.

Susanna explained her impressions about Jay's conflict and summed up her thoughts with one diplomatic statement. "He wants to leave but seems to be having a hard time letting go."

To her surprise, Walter chuckled. "That's one way to phrase it. That boy was always hardheaded."

Susanna smiled. She'd seen that part of Jay herself.

"Jay's not letting go because he doesn't want to leave."

Okay, she was *finally* going to ask the question. "Then why is he selling The Arbors?"

"Because he doesn't want things to stay the way they are and he doesn't know how to change them. I've told him. He doesn't listen."

She'd seen that part of Jay, too. "Does losing his mother have something to do with his wanting to leave?"

"I think so. If you look at the big picture, it's not hard to see why he wound up where he is. He went from having a big family to being the only one left here. When he was a little kid, he had parents, grandparents, great-grandparents. Everyone was involved. Or needed caring for. Then one by one they were gone. Jay's mom took ill with Alzheimer's and wound up here. His dad died not long afterward. Now that was a tragedy. Perfectly healthy man until one day he collapses at the grocery store. Massive heart attack."

"Oh, how sad." Susanna wrapped her arms around her middle, as if she could ward off the wave of hurt. For as much as Skip had suffered with his illness, he'd been so grateful to have the chance to make the most of his last minutes with his family, to say his goodbyes. Susanna had been, too.

"When Jay should have been filling up the house with his own family, he was too busy helping his old Gran run this place and taking care of his mom."

"And Drew hasn't been around to help."

Walter shook his head. "Don't get me started on that boy."

"And you really don't think Jay wants to leave?"

"Does he act like someone who wants to leave?" Walter scowled. "Ask him what he wants to do with his life, and he doesn't have a clue. He just knows he doesn't want to keep doing what he's doing. Selling this place isn't his answer. He'll live to regret it, you mark my words."

"Maybe this time away will help him think things through."

"Maybe, but I wouldn't hold your breath. Susanna, you have to understand Jay looks at me and sees himself."

"How is that bad?"

Walter leaned back in his chair and toyed with a pen between long fingers, contemplating. "Well, it's not really about me. That's the problem. Jay looks at me and sees a life gone by. Just biding time and still here at The Arbors. He doesn't usually factor in that I did a lot of living before I even got here. Or that I did a lot of living while I was here. He doesn't feel as if he has."

"But I don't understand why. His grandmother may have been older, but from what I've heard, she was always on the move."

"She was that." His expression reflected fond memories.

"What's holding Jay back?"

Walter shrugged. "Only Jay can answer that question."

She frowned. "But you must have an idea."

"I do."

That was all he said. She wouldn't pressure him no matter how much she wanted to ask. But then Walter smiled. And right then Susanna knew for all the business decisions between them, for any disapproval or conflict of concern that Walter might have had about Northstar taking over, he'd already seen what she hadn't shared—that she genuinely cared about Jay.

"Susanna, suffice to say Alzheimer's has had a big impact on Jay's life from the get-go. You couple that with the fact he's so capable and caring, and you wind up with a young man who never felt it was right to leave and who never figured out how to create his own life here."

Susanna could totally see it. Jay caring for everyone around him, putting out every single fire that flared, the man to depend on, all the while brushing aside his own desires.

Caring for everyone's needs but his own.

Year after year, decade after decade, until he was ready to run screaming.

To Tahiti with tiki torches flickering in the beach breeze.

"He is such a good man," she said softly.

Walter met her gaze with those fading eyes that saw so much. "He is. One of the very best."

CHAPTER EIGHTEEN

OKAY, PUERTO VALLARTA wasn't Tahiti, but the coastline was different from the Atlantic beach trips Jay had been making all his life. He wanted to experience *luxury redefined* where *relaxation and adventure were at his fingertips.*

He'd genuinely considered Tahiti but couldn't rationalize the expense with what he'd paid the arborist and his crew to trim the arbors. Not without sitting pretty on his portion of the sale at any rate. And at the rate things were going, he wouldn't be sitting pretty anytime soon.

Not and still be able to look himself in the mirror.

So he made the best of the time he had because he didn't feel right leaving Susanna for too long. He boarded a plane and forced everything out of his head. He needed to clean the slate, to take a deep breath, to unwind, so he could think.

He relaxed at a world-class spa and found adventure fishing on a deep-sea excursion. He stayed up late walking along the beach. He slept late, unworried about people who might need him. He let the constant crash of the Pacific surf lull him.

He ate in five-star restaurants when he was hungry and slept through dinner when he wasn't. He drank intensely alcoholic drinks with little umbrellas in the middle of the day.

He didn't even text Susanna for the first five days.

She had his number and had promised to call if the roof caved in.

And he was okay with that. Because day by day he thought less about what was going on in North Carolina and more about what was happening in Puerto Vallarta. Until one day, the day he'd taken his first scuba diving lesson; in fact, he made it back to his room after dark, sat down with a beer completely sunburned and exhausted from the day, and realized he hadn't thought about home once all day. It was as if North Carolina and everyone in it had fallen off the planet.

Except for Susanna.

Thoughts of her managed to creep in as he sat in bed watching episode after episode of *Special Victims Unit.* He remembered the way she curled around him as they lay together in bed at night, her cheek pressed to his chest, her breaths soft against his skin.

How she hopped out of bed in the morning, asleep one minute then fully awake the next, going from room to room, opening the plantation shutters, flooding the cottage with sunlight.

The way she propped up against pillows, reading before bed, her lashes fluttering shut and chin dropping to her chest as she dozed with the book still in her hands. When he'd go to take the book, she'd awake instantly and whisper in that drowsy voice, "I'm not asleep. Just resting my eyes."

He wondered what she'd look like in a bikini with all those delicate curves, her beautiful body such a tempting combination of womanly softness and neatly maintained strength.

Did she even like the beach? If so, did she prefer splashing around in the surf or tanning on the shore?

There was so much about Susanna he didn't know.

And wanted to.

Something happened then because the next morning as he walked the beach, deciding how he wanted to spend the hours until sunset, he noticed two boys fishing in the distance.

The smaller of the two cast then stood visibly bristling with impatience as the line drifted back toward shore. The other one cast then leaned over with some suggestion or advice. Probably telling the fidgety kid to chill out. Then their lines tangled and they started bickering.

Jay thought of himself and Drew, remembered long-ago fishing trips with their dad and grandfather, remembered dragging the skiff out into the middle of the lake themselves when they could sneak away for a few hours during summer afternoons before someone gave them something else to do—like repair rotting slats on the fence around the barn, repainting the gallery railing at the house, pruning the arbors or the thousand other things that needed doing around home.

He also remembered Drew asking, *"What's with this family?"*

Alzheimer's was what was with this family. That much didn't need saying. Drew had run from the reality of their genetics and regretted handling things that way. He was worried that Jay was doing the same. Is that what Jay was doing?

He smiled and wished those young boys a good catch as he passed and continued his walk in the surf, amazed by how clear everything suddenly seemed in his uncluttered brain, as clear and sharp as the sun sparkling on that Pacific surf.

Finally.

SUSANNA STROLLED THROUGH the arbors with Walter, Chester and the arborist, inspecting the work. The annual pruning had been completed in a week, but the crew had discovered rotting wood on the trellises that supported the climbing roses. She'd learned then that the climbing roses weren't actually true vines. They relied upon the trellises for support, so after conferring with Chester, she had Walter authorize the funds to have the work done. Replacing the wood without disturbing the climbers was a delicate job but after they were resecured to the new portions of trellis, they appeared to have never even been touched. The arborist proudly displayed his work by giving the new wood a sturdy shake.

"These old beauties are good to go. Unless a hurricane blows through, and I happen to know they've weathered a few of those already."

"Mr. C.'s going to be real happy with the job you did," Chester said.

Butters and Gatsby arrived then, tails wagging as they barreled right into midst of the group looking for attention.

"Hi, guys." Susanna knelt, petting the dogs to keep them from knocking down Walter in their excitement.

"Come with me and I'll write you the check." Walter glanced at Susanna. "You heading back?"

"You go ahead." She smiled at the arborist. "Please don't forget to leave that information about the monthly service contract with Walter, okay?"

"You got it, Ms. Adams," the arborist replied before following Walter and Chester to the golf cart, leaving Susanna and the dogs alone in the bright noon sun.

"Come on over here, guys." She plopped down and tucked her feet up on the bench. "That's better. I'm tired today."

Not such a surprise as she'd pulled an all-nighter when

a family had arrived on the property to tour the facility at midnight. Susanna had thrown on clothes and arrived quickly, but as they'd traveled in from Delaware, they hadn't been in a hurry to leave. Susanna had invited them into her office, where she'd served steaming mugs of VIA, and chatted for two hours about The Arbors and the care they could expect for their mother.

Idly stroking the dogs' heads, she savored the warmth of a sunbeam and hoped Chester was right and Jay would be pleased. She hadn't mentioned the job to him.

In fact, they hadn't spoken all that much in the nearly five weeks he'd been away. He texted the occasional cell phone photo of a particularly beautiful sunset or plumeria blossom. He called every few days, and began the conversation by asking, "Anything I need to know?"

She'd been fortunate enough to be able to honestly answer, "Not a thing."

Then the conversations were strictly about them. How Susanna was holding up with her and the dogs at night. How the dogs were behaving. What was going on with Brooke and Brandon. How Jay was enjoying his downtime. What his latest adventure involved. Scuba diving. Snorkeling. Deep-sea fishing. The latest political thriller in a beach chair while getting plowed on local rum.

She was happy he was having a good time but yearned to be with him. She missed him terribly but was glad she could provide peace of mind so he could actually leave. She felt relieved she didn't have anything eventful to share and protective of his need for privacy when anyone asked where he was.

And, always, she felt the stress of knowing this situation mirrored the reality of their lives.

In order for Jay to leave, she'd need to stay.

If Jay stayed, she'd need to leave.

Then there was the biggest life-changer of all, a life-changer responsible for her erratic emotions, a life-changer yet to be addressed.

Susanna must have dozed in that glorious sunbeam because the next thing she knew the dogs' barking awakened her.

Yawning widely, she opened her eyes and found Jay, as though kneeling in the walkway beneath the neatly trimmed arbors was exactly where he should be.

His beautiful green eyes raked over her, a melting expression. "Sorry to disturb you. You looked so peaceful."

Something inside her sighed in relief at the sound of his voice—he wasn't a dream. "You're home."

"Straight from the airport."

Pushing into a sitting position, she resisted the impulse to go to him. Suddenly the most important thing in her world was feeling his arms around her. But the dogs were busy trying to lick his face. All was right in their world again.

Susanna said the only thing she could think to say. "You look well."

"Enjoyed myself immensely. I'm not going to lie. Need to take vacations more often."

"That's a good idea."

"Only one thing would have made the trip better."

"What's that?"

"If you'd have gone with me."

That worried place inside eased up a bit more. Susanna understood that what had been happening inside Jay had started long before she'd entered the picture.

"I'm glad you're home." She'd fallen in love against all practical arguments, was relieved to see him again, so healthy and alive and incredibly handsome with his deeply tanned skin and sun-bleached hair.

She hadn't realized until this very moment that she'd never seen him at peace. What came next didn't matter so much, not when she knew he'd found whatever he'd gone in search of.

"I missed you," he said softly, and she saw her own longing mirrored in his gaze, which suddenly looked so much greener against his burnished skin.

"Me, too." Such simple words that weren't simple at all.

"You okay?" he asked.

"Fine. I didn't sleep last night. The Coltranes came in from Delaware for a midnight visit. By the time they left, I figured I'd play catch-up tonight."

He didn't ask how the visit went.

"I didn't think you'd be back until sometime next week." Before he had to give Northstar a firm decision.

The sudden intensity of his expression warned that there was nothing casual about his mood. "There wasn't any need to stay away. I know what I need to do."

Was it possible time stopped? That the breeze no longer rustled the dry leaves overhead? That the birds scrambling in the nearby brush silenced their chirping twitters? That the sun stopped baking the midday air with its heat, a drowsy effect that was contagious?

Even Butters and Gatsby seemed unnaturally still, as if sensing their future rested on Jay's next words.

"I won't be signing the papers, Susanna."

His admission filtered through her slowly. He would stay, which meant she would go. Hopefully not to Seattle.

"You'll be at peace with that decision, Jay?" That was all that mattered.

"Once I got away, I started thinking with a bit of clarity, and I knew what I wanted. Not all that hard to figure out once I realized what my problem was." He chuckled, a bit sheepishly, as if he still couldn't quite believe the answer had been there when he'd looked for it.

"Oh." She waited.

Pushing to his feet, he sat beside her on the bench, stretching his legs before him. He reached for her hand and threaded his fingers through hers, the casual touch of a man with the right to touch. "What I want isn't out there. It's here with the people I care about. You helped me figure that out. I need to start living again. That's been my problem all along. I can't run from that."

Susanna had no words, nothing profound to say. All she could do was squeeze his hand to acknowledge the enormity of this admission, manage her own heartbeat, which was suddenly racing.

"I'm the only one holding me back from living my life. And now I know what I want, I need to get out of my own way. I know what I want."

Their gazes met for a suspended instant and she knew right then what he was going to do. Leaning forward, he pressed his mouth to her forehead, such a tender touch.

"I want you, Susanna." Then he rested his forehead against hers and they were nose to nose, breath to breath.

"What about the family you want?" she whispered.

"You've got one. I'm thinking there's a place for me in it. Brooke and Brandon are great. I liked them, and they liked me. One day they'll have kids of their own, who'll need a granddad. I can be that. I can't think of anything I want more."

She shut her eyes to resist the tears suddenly tickling behind her eyes.

"I came up with a great plan for The Arbors, too."

"Another one?" She sounded almost normal. As long as she kept her eyes closed.

He chuckled, a burst of warm breath against her mouth, almost a kiss. "It requires a leap of faith on your part."

"Really?" As if she hadn't been making *those* left and right since deciding to leave New York.

"I want you to quit Northstar and run this place with me." Squeezing her hands tightly in his, he said, "You won't get this kind of job security anywhere else."

"I've got good benefits and a great retirement package."

"But if you marry me, you'll have my retirement, too. And the house is paid off. Both of them, actually."

A relief so profound washed through her, robbed her ability to reply. She just held on to him, her anchor in the whirling emotions. The future suddenly didn't feel so uncertain, lonely.

But then a thought occurred to her. "How am I going to benefit from your retirement when I'm so much older than you?"

His head came up, and she met his gaze, a curious gaze. "You're worried about that?"

She nodded.

He caressed her hand with an idle thumb, considering. "Did I mention Alzheimer's runs in my family?"

"No, but I figured it out."

"Neither of us can predict the future, Susanna. We only get right now. I say we stop worrying and enjoy what we have together. You game?"

All those feelings swirling inside started to calm. There was only one answer. "I'm game."

"Then put all thoughts of age out of your pretty head because you're in luck. It so happens I have a knack for dealing with old folks."

She gave a watery laugh. "And you're sure you'll be content with becoming a part of my family?"

"That's the only thing I want."

That's when her tears finally broke free, relieved tears and happy tears, in a moment filled with such promise.

Guiding his hands to her stomach, she held them there, where a little person who wasn't much more than a tiny heartbeat was waiting to be loved. "Think you could find a little room in your heart for one more?"

He simply sat there, his expression transforming as he visibly reasoned *that* through. He shook his head slightly. He finally said, "Are you saying what I think you're saying?"

She nodded, the tears flowing.

He gathered her close as if he'd waited forever to hold her, whispering, "I love you, Susanna." And she melted against him, the only place in the world she wanted to be in *right now*.

EPILOGUE

JAY BROKE THROUGH the last of the surf and sank onto the sugary white sand. The sunset built to what was sure to be a grand finale tonight, already layering the sky in streaks of blues and hazy purples, casting the water in gold. Colors were more vibrant in this part of the world, and Polynesian beaches were everything Jay had heard they'd be.

Most beautiful of all was the mermaid who emerged from the surf at a slightly slower pace, the very reason Jay had rushed ahead, so he could enjoy the enticing view she made.

His wife.

Her soft curves were molten in the setting sun. Water sluiced over her, leaving her hair slicked back from her face, her skin glossy, perfect to caress every bare inch of her.

Jay knew exactly what her wet skin would feel like to the touch, because he'd already made love to her on this pristine beach, had realized yet another dream in a life that was suddenly filled with living out his dreams.

And none were as amazing as the one who grew inside his beautiful wife, the roundness of her belly so natural against her slim curves, so bold in her white bikini that only showcased the lush terrain of her body.

She knew he watched her. He could see her heightened awareness in the way she stepped lightly on the sand, knew that had the sun not begun to set, there'd be color riding high in her cheeks. She still didn't quite believe he found her so incredibly gorgeous, and Jay relished the opportunity of every minute of every day to prove it.

Sinking beside him, all fluid grace, she leaned into him and he wrapped his arm around her. He could see the smile play at the corners of her mouth when he pressed a kiss to her wet hair. They sat in silence as the sunset swelled in the sky, the light growing sharper in those surreal moments before the sun vanished below the horizon.

The tiki torches had been lit, presumably by some of the invisible staff at this island paradise resort. The flames dotted the path to their overwater bungalow, their luxury accommodations for the duration of their honeymoon, the perfect place to kick off the start of their lives as husband and wife.

Jay rested a hand on her warm belly, loved to touch the tightness of her skin, a miracle in the making. Their lives had been filled with everyday miracles since his return from Mexico. So many more than they could have possibly imagined, or maybe they were just determined to appreciate each and every one.

Every single thing seemed to fall into place from Northstar's mutual agreement to shelve the deal in an effort to streamline investments during their financial challenges to Drew's leave in time to serve as best man in the wedding.

A lavish affair that welcomed family and friends from all over, including the staff of The Arbors and their guests.

They'd brought in temp help from an agency, and invited the residents' families to accompany the residents to the wedding if they were able, and many of them were. There'd been weddings before at his house, but never so lavish.

Susanna was determined that Jay live every one of his dreams. Seeing her emerge from the house on her father's arm to meet him beneath the arbors in full bloom was a moment that would live in his wildest dreams.

He prayed he'd never forget the sight of her.

But he wouldn't waste one second worrying about the future. Not when it would cause him to miss one second of now.

Not when they were surrounded by so much love.

Brooke had stood as maid of honor beside Karan, Susanna's mom and mother-in-law. Jay's groomsmen had been Drew, Walter, Pete and Brandon. There'd been professional photos and video footage, and all the traditional wedding events. They danced their first dance as husband and wife. They cut cake and tossed bouquets and garters.

Brooke and Brandon had delighted them with a toast welcoming Jay to the family that humbled him by their graciousness and had Susanna in tears.

Susanna's parents had surprised them by announcing they'd purchased an RV large enough to invite the in-laws to make trips from New York.

Karan and Charles had nearly killed them with shock. Their wedding gift turned out to be the gift of themselves. Now that they were starting their own family, Charles wanted to be closer to his family in Tampa. Karan leaped at the opportunity to be nearer Susanna, so they could raise their babies together.

Charles had connections. All he'd had to do was mention relocating and the prestigious Carolinas Medical Research Center offered him a position as chief of his specialty. He and Karan were working with a real estate agent to find a house.

Chester had surprised them by decking out a golf cart complete with tin cans and streamers that read Just Married. He had another gift, too, but that one wouldn't be ready until their return. At Jay's request Chester had downsized the old desk in the administrator's office so there would comfortably be room for two desks. Jay would stop hiding in Walter's office, and he and Susanna would share that magnificent view of the arbors around the lake while they ran the facility together.

When they weren't taking family vacations.

Or making family memories with all their children.

Or simply savoring their every moment together.

* * * * *

#1824 THE OTHER SIDE OF US
by Sarah Mayberry

After a few less-than-impressive meetings, Mackenzie Williams and Oliver Garrett have concluded that good fences make good neighbors. The less they see of each other, the better. Too bad their wayward dogs have other ideas, however, and won't stay apart. The canine antics bring Mackenzie and Oliver into contact so much that those poor first impressions turn into a spark of attraction...and that could lead to some *very* friendly relations!

#1825 A HOMETOWN BOY
by Janice Kay Johnson

Acadia Henderson once had a secret crush on David Owen. Then they went their separate ways. Now they're both back in their hometown trying to make sense of a tragic turn of events. Given what's happened, they shouldn't have anything to say to each other. Yet despite the odds, something powerful—something mutual—is pulling them together. Maybe it's the situation. Or maybe they're finally getting their chance at happiness.

#1826 SOMETHING TO BELIEVE IN
Family in Paradise • by Kimberly Van Meter

Lilah has always been the quiet, meek Bell sister, the one to follow what everyone expects from her. Then she meets Justin Cales. The playboy turns her head and she allows herself to indulge in a very uncharacteristic and passionate affair. But when that leads to an unexpected pregnancy, Lilah discovers she has an inner strength she has never recognized

#1827 THAT WEEKEND...
by Jennifer McKenzie

A weekend covering a film festival is what TV host Ava Christensen has been waiting for—her dream assignment. But not if it means being alone with her boss! Jake Durham recently denied her a big promotion, so Ava wants as little to do with him as possible. That's virtually impossible at the festival. Somehow, though, with all that time together, everything starts to look different. Must be the influence of the stars...

#1828 BACK TO THE GOOD FORTUNE DINER
by Vicki Essex

Tiffany Cheung has tasted big-city success—and she's hungry for more. So when she ends up at home, working in her parents' restaurant, all she wants is to leave again. Nothing will change her mind. Not even the distraction of Chris Jamieson, her old crush. Yes, the adult version of him is even more tempting—especially because he seems equally attracted. But her dreams are taking her somewhere else, and Chris's life is deeply rooted here. There's no future...unless they can compromise.

#1829 THE TRUTH ABOUT COMFORT COVE
It Happened in Comfort Cove • by Tara Taylor Quinn

The twenty-five-year-old abduction that cold-case detectives Lucy Hayes and Ramsey Miller are working together is taking its toll—especially with their attempt to ignore the intense attraction between them. The effort has been worth it, because they're close to solving this one. And once they do, then maybe they can explore their feelings. But as they get closer to the truth, they aren't prepared for what they discover!

REQUEST YOUR FREE BOOKS!
2 FREE NOVELS PLUS 2 FREE GIFTS!

Harlequin Super Romance®

Exciting, emotional, unexpected!

YES! Please send me 2 FREE Harlequin® Superromance® novels and my 2 FREE gifts (gifts are worth about $10). After receiving them, if I don't wish to receive any more books, I can return the shipping statement marked "cancel." If I don't cancel, I will receive 6 brand-new novels every month and be billed just $4.69 per book in the U.S. or $5.24 per book in Canada. That's a saving of at least 15% off the cover price! It's quite a bargain! Shipping and handling is just 50¢ per book in the U.S. and 75¢ per book in Canada.* I understand that accepting the 2 free books and gifts places me under no obligation to buy anything. I can always return a shipment and cancel at any time. Even if I never buy another book, the two free books and gifts are mine to keep forever.

135/336 HDN FC6T

Name	(PLEASE PRINT)	

Address		Apt. #

City	State/Prov.	Zip/Postal Code

Signature (if under 18, a parent or guardian must sign)

Mail to the **Reader Service:**
IN U.S.A.: P.O. Box 1867, Buffalo, NY 14240-1867
IN CANADA: P.O. Box 609, Fort Erie, Ontario L2A 5X3

Not valid for current subscribers to Harlequin Superromance books.
**Are you a current subscriber to Harlequin Superromance books
and want to receive the larger-print edition?
Call 1-800-873-8635 or visit www.ReaderService.com.**

* Terms and prices subject to change without notice. Prices do not include applicable taxes. Sales tax applicable in N.Y. Canadian residents will be charged applicable taxes. Offer not valid in Quebec. This offer is limited to one order per household. All orders subject to credit approval. Credit or debit balances in a customer's account(s) may be offset by any other outstanding balance owed by or to the customer. Please allow 4 to 6 weeks for delivery. Offer available while quantities last.